BARCELONA NOIR

BARCELONA NOIR

EDITED BY
ADRIANA V. LÓPEZ & CARMEN OSPINA

Translated by Achy Obejas

Published by Akashic Books
©2011 Akashic Books

Series concept by Tim McLoughlin and Johnny Temple
Barcelona map by Aaron Petrovich

ISBN-13: 978-1-936070-95-4
Library of Congress Control Number: 2010939099
All rights reserved

First printing

Akashic Books
PO Box 1456
New York, NY 10009
info@akashicbooks.com
www.akashicbooks.com

TABLE OF CONTENTS

11   *Introduction*

PART I: FOLLOW ME IF YOU CAN

19   **ANDREU MARTÍN**   Villa Olímpica
     The Law of Escape

34   **ANTONIA CORTIJOS**   El Born
     Brawner's Shadows

48   **SANTIAGO RONCAGLIOLO**   Barri Gòtic
     The Predator

63   **ISABEL FRANC**   Poble Nou
     The Enigma of Her Voice

79   **LOLITA BOSCH**   Sant Gervasi
     In This World, and at the Time Mercedes Died

PART II: SHELTERED LIVES, SECRET CRIMES

101 **DAVID BARBA**   El Carmel
     Sweet Croquette

120 **TERESA SOLANA**   Sant Antoni
     The Offering
     (Translated from Catalan by PETER BUSH)

138 **JORDI SIERRA I FABRA**   Turó Parc
     A High-End Neighborhood

156 **IMMA MONSÓ**   L'Eixample
     The Customer Is Always Right
     (Translated from Catalan by VALERIE MILES)

PART III: DAYS OF WINE (WHITE LINES) AND ROSES

171   ERIC TAYLOR-ARAGÓN   Barceloneta
Epiphany

185   CRISTINA FALLARÁS   Nou Barris
The Story of a Scar

199   VALERIE MILES   Gràcia
Bringing Down the Moon

216   RAÚL ARGEMÍ   Montjuic
The Slender Charm of Chinese Women

239   FRANCISCO GONZÁLEZ LEDESMA   El Raval
The Police Inspector Who Loved Books

242   **About the Contributors**

INTRODUCTION

I ts physical beauty alone, surrounded by mountains with a view of the sea, was cause enough for architect Antoni Gaudí to raise his version of Candy Land upon its soil; a daily impetus for the city's mimes and living statues to claim a spot along Las Ramblas and transform it into their stage.

But don't be fooled: Barcelona, with all its illustrious color and exterior fineness, hasn't always been able to curb the darker yearnings of its Hyde to its Jekyll. Blame it on a bubbling, repressive concoction made with a pinch of Church, a touch of Crown, and a large dose of General Francisco Franco to stir up the insides of its very independent and anarchic Catalonian spirit. One that has allowed it to conserve its own language and modus operandi from the rest of Spain, and that has always attracted the vanguard to create under the sereneness of its palm trees and Mediterranean light.

It may be hard to imagine, but Barcelona, presumably named after the Carthaginian general Hamilcar Barca in third century B.C., was once trapped behind the shadows of Roman walls, hidden within the largest concentrated labyrinth of Gothic architecture in all of Europe. Hundreds of years later, the thriving port city would open itself up to commerce, its industrial age, and with it came immigrants, workers, revolution, and vice. Then the city would endure the bloodshed of the Spanish Civil War (1936–1939), thirty-five years of Franco's iron fist, and, when that was finally over, its cobblestoned streets became breeding grounds of resentment.

If noir is the genre most apt to expressing unease and malice within a society, it took awhile for Barcelona to feel safe to do so. In fact, Spain didn't produce its first *novela negra*, with a police character and crimes of passion, until 1853, with the publication of Pedro Antonio de Alarcón's *El Clavo* (*The Nail*). But bear in mind that Spain, in general, was not the easiest of places to be an author. Those brave or crazy enough to question the orthodoxy through their writing faced torture, imprisonment, or worse: death. Just remember Federico García Lorca's tragic fate at the hands of the Nationalists in 1936.

Over time, more crime fiction was published, though it still faced heavy censorship. Francisco García Pavón's *novelas policíacas* featuring the police chief Manuel González, a.k.a. Plinio, garnered a following in the 1950s and were eventually adapted into a popular television series. This Plinio character—who could be described as a man of few words, with his right hip attached to his gun and a cigarette appended to the side of his mouth—was without a doubt a pioneer of his time. But a true noir fan would rate the series tepid in comparison to the brutality of Franco's very real hit men; the violence portrayed, well, a mere stroll in the park.

It wasn't until Franco's death in 1975 that grittier tales began pounding themselves out upon typewriter keys soiled with absinthe and cigarette ash. The bans had been lifted and a new era had emerged. But instead of your classic whodunit style of noir that was popular in the U.K., Spain's take on the genre stung with social criticism. Thanks to memorable protagonists created by Catalan novelists such as Francisco "Paco" González Ledesma, with his jaded inspector Ricardo

Méndez (featured in this collection), as well as the great and late Manuel Vázquez Montalbán, with his bon vivant detective Pepe Carvalho, Barcelona began to be depicted as it actually was: a city riddled with violence, endemic corruption, and lack of social mobility.

While some of the stories in *Barcelona Noir* still capture a certain air of this former era, a strange if more sadistic mood lurks through this small postindustrial city of today. Smeared with the pleasure-seeking sheen of its rampant tourist industry, combined with a constant stream of immigration from Africa, Latin America, and Asia, and with the ever-growing tensions of Catalonian nationalism, the city has spawned a fresh new batch of resentments and culture clashes. Enter the underground world of Raúl Argemí's "The Slender Charm of Chinese Women," where drugs, xenophobia, and people trafficking manage to remain hidden in the city's darkest corners. In Eric Taylor-Aragón's "Epiphany," two heartbroken outsiders meet at a bar and make a horrid attempt to escape their existential pain together, while in Jordi Sierra i Fabra's "A High-End Neighborhood," the city's rich outright torture the foreign help.

There are portraits here of Catalans struggling with their own sense of identity, feeling suffocated in a conservative society, as depicted in Imma Monsó's mind-bending retail story "The Customer Is Always Right"; in Teresa Solana's "The Offering," where a respectable clinic becomes the setting for surgical terror; and in tiny clues scattered throughout Lolita Bosch's scandalous tale of crosscontinental hate crimes. This repression is also expressed in Santiago Roncagliolo's "The Predator," where a group of officemates partake in Carnival night's fun by putting on masks so they can take their real-life ones off; and in Valerie Miles's "Bringing Down the Moon," when the magic surrounding Saint John's festival becomes the perfect excuse to commit murder.

In the meantime, plots take us back in time in search of ghosts of the Second World War, such as in "Brawner's Shadows" by Antonia Cortijos. And even further back, to the era of the gangster anarchists running scared through the Ciutat Vella, in Andreu Martín's "The Law of Escape." Today, the detectives and the pursuers aren't necessarily men anymore either; they can be lesbian and pregnant, and penned by respected writers in the genre such as Isabel Franc and Cristina Fallarás.

In fact, noir is so entrenched in Barcelona's pop culture and street lore that a tourist can easily partake in it browsing the shelves of the Negra y Criminal bookstore in the Barceloneta, at its yearly BCNegra literary festival, or visiting the plaza between Sant Rafael Street and the Rambla del Raval dedicated to the memory of Vázquez Montalbán—the aforementioned creator of beloved character Pepe Carvalho, an ex-Communist detective and food connoisseur who, accompanied by his prostitute girlfriend, baptized the Raval district's watering holes and best restaurants. There are fine-dining tour-guide musts, such as the Boquería Market's Pinotxo bar or Casa Leopoldo, where if you tell your waiter, "Pepe Carvalho recommended I come, so serve me whatever you wish," you're bound for a killer meal you'll never forget. If you are seeking a hard-to-swallow serving of Catalonia's culinary snobbism, we recommend your next course be David Barba's "Sweet Croquette," a fascinating journey into one man's obsession with the star chef Ferran Adrià.

Repression, vice, immigration . . . the fourteen stories within will divert your eyes from Barcelona's lively Ramblas and Gaudí spires, opening them onto the city's tainted side.

One that will never appear in any recommended walking tour.

Adriana V. López & Carmen Ospina
Barcelona, Spain
January 2011

PART I

FOLLOW ME IF YOU CAN

THE LAW OF ESCAPE

BY Andreu Martín

Villa Olímpica

*At the end of the nineteenth century and beginning of the twen-
tieth, Barcelona was known as "The City of Bombs." It was
considered the world capital of anarchy. More than seven hundred political assassinations were carried out between January
1919 and December 1923. This tale is based on a true story
that took place on September 1, 1922; a review of the case
appeared in León-Ignacio's book,* Los años del pistolerismo
(The Years of Gangsterism).

Tino Orté's father was pinched by the cops while
painting *No God, No Master, No King* on the walls
of the Poble Nou cemetery. He had the brush in his
hand, ready to dip it into the bucket with the shiny black tar
that Gerardo was holding, while Fabregat encouraged them
and, supposedly, looked out to make sure they weren't caught.

But Fabregat was paying much more attention to the actual painting, to the text, to his two friends' fears, and to hur-
rying them along, than to the movements in the fog around
them. Fabregat was the one who'd recruited the other two
to fill the neighborhood of Poble Nou with anarchist slogans:
"C'mon, damnit, come with me right now and we'll make sure
that by the time everyone wakes up tomorrow, they'll be con-
verted to anarchism." Nobody said no to Fabregat, who always

carried a pistol, was part of the union leadership, and boasted of having gotten rid of two bosses the previous month. If anybody said no, he took them for scabs and killed them right then and there.

The police didn't come with horns and sirens, nor was it a coincidence the three men were caught. They had been looking for Fabregat, because they'd gotten a tip that he'd be there. They approached him stealthily, hidden within the shadows, and then they shouted: "Stop! Police! Hands up!" The bucket of tar spilled on the ground and over the anarchists' feet as they raised their hands, offering no resistance.

Five uniformed police with rifles and two undercover cops wearing derbies and carrying pistols shoved them against the wall, frisked them, and asked, "Are you the one called Fabregat?" And to the other two they said: "Who are you?"

Tino's father should have said, *Constantino Orté, at God's and your service*, because the priests had taught him humility and life had taught him that the police were Catholic and would never kill another Catholic.

"So, *No God, No Master, No King*, eh?" an undercover cop said. "You can stop being such a fool and just go."

Tino's father and Gerardo thought they'd gotten a pass and smiled gratefully at the benevolence of those officers of the law and went ahead and turned their backs. Fabregat, however, knew what was really up.

"You can go now."

They'd all heard talk about the Law of Escape, but Gerardo and Tino's father probably thought it was an urban legend, or that it didn't apply to them because they'd never been in trouble and that those felled by the bosses' bullets were probably "up to something." But Fabregat knew it wasn't like that. Fabregat knew that twenty-three comrades had already fallen, all shot in the back, since the Law of Escape had been instituted on December 5, 1920.

The police officer repeated, "You can go now," and Fabregat let out an anguished cry: "The Law of Escape!" And they took off running, their six espadrille-covered feet leaving a trail of black tar footprints on the sidewalks, and then there was galloping, and the sounds of guns cocking, and an endless volley of bullets that shook the neighbors who'd been hiding in the dark on their balconies and looking out at the cemetery.

Tino found out what happened from one of those neighbors who heard, and more precisely saw, everything from one of the balconies. She told him about it at the Poble Nou cemetery, the oldest in Barcelona, on the other side of the wall where his father had been painting, just as the city workers were putting his father's coffin in the crypt where it would rest forever.

"You're his son?" the woman asked, full of hate. "I saw what happened." And then she told him how they were painting *No God, No Master, No King* and how the police shouted and the tar footprints on the sidewalk detailed the last steps of the three men before the shooting, the red blood spilling over the black tar like a symbol. The anarchists' flag was black and red.

"Ma'am, please," was all Tino could manage to say.

He hugged his wife Elena and stepped away from the crypt's high walls, from the modest bouquet of flowers, from the crowd of indignant workers, from the cemetery, from the wall his father had been painting.

He didn't want any trouble.

Tino wanted to tear off the worker's skin that had covered him his whole life. He'd been born in Poble Nou—an area so proud of being proletariat, so poor and dirty, a cauldron of conspiracies and hate—but he'd managed to save up and buy a flashy white car from a member of the bourgeoisie who was afraid to drive, and he'd fled from Poble Nou and taken up residence in Gràcia, also a worker's neighborhood, but cleaner, more bourgeois. When you went out on the streets, you could greet tidy middle-class people. Neither the bosses' bullets, which pursued workers in Ciudad Antigua and in their barracks, nor the proletariat's hunt for impresarios in rich neighborhoods, ever reached Gràcia.

That last day of August, so incredibly hot, a month after his father's death, Tino was observing the view from his terrace, wearing an undershirt and smoking, maybe thinking about the neighbor who had seen the application of the Law of Escape from her balcony. He lived on the second floor of a building on Venus Street, between Liberty and Danger. The Gràcia neighborhood maintained its ideology in its street names. Even today, just a bit further up, there's still Fraternity Street, and Progress Street . . .

The mechanic, Paco the Nut, came walking up the empty and badly lit cobblestone street from the garage where he kept his flamboyant taxi. He screamed, without consideration for the neighbors, who, because of the heat, probably couldn't sleep anyway: "Tino! Telephone!"

A customer. His number was on a list posted at different taxi stands throughout the city. There were people who preferred to hire private drivers rather than use the big companies or the collectives.

Tino came down to the street and ran to the nearby garage. Paco the Nut and some of his relatives were playing cards, all in undershirts. The receiver was off the hook.

"We'd like to rent a car for tomorrow," he was told. "We'd like to go to Mataró. Very early. At seven in the morning."

Mataró is a tiny industrial town on the coast, about twenty-eight kilometers from Barcelona. It was a long trip. At sixty cents a kilometer, he'd earn at least sixteen pesetas, maybe seventeen or eighteen with the tip. A good amount to feed his kids, pay his rent, and put toward the bank loan that had allowed him to buy the taxi and get his license.

"Just come by the corner of Cortes Street and Paseo de Gràcia. We'll be there. At seven sharp."

Euphoric, Tino turned to the garage employees: "The car must be ready by six in the morning, spotless, and with a full tank! There's a big tip in it for you!"

He ran home to celebrate his good luck with his wife.

"Will it be okay?" she asked him, her heart on her sleeve, always a little fearful.

"Of course it'll be okay."

"It's just that you still haven't transferred the title . . ."

"I've only had the car two weeks. It's being processed. What do you think will happen?"

The next day, dressed meticulously in his blue uniform with a flat hat and shiny shoes, Tino Orté waited next to his imposing white Studebaker 30 HP, license number 6205, at the intersection of the two majestic streets: Paseo de Gràcia, which is like a museum with the most advanced architecture, but also an arrogant exhibition displayed by the city's most notable families; and Cortes Street, which today is Gran Vía de les Corts Catalanes, and runs across the whole city, from north to south.

Two men approached him, one wearing a derby and the other a felt hat, both wearing suits, shirts with starched collars and cuffs, and dark ties, like businessmen. They looked very serious, as if their decisions could change the world.

Tino greeted them with his hat in his hand, a bow, and a

discrete smile, and didn't bat an eye when he saw the pistol on one of the men's belts. Back then, a lot of people carried pistols. For assault or defense, or both. After they made themselves comfortable in the back, he took the wheel.

"To Mataró?" he asked.

"To Mataró," said the man in the felt hat. Then he instructed Tino on the exact route he should take. "Go around Parc de la Ciutadella to the fish market on Icaria Avenue, then take Taulat Street to the highway toward France, along the seaside."

Tino might have taken the same route on his own, but the precision of the passenger's directions disconcerted him nonetheless, because it ushered him inexorably into a world he wanted to leave behind and which he did not like to visit.

They abandoned the wide boulevards, moved past the big modernist park, and immediately found themselves on Icaria Avenue, with its anarchist echoes. Icaria was the name of the utopian society that was founded here by Étienne Cabet, in which all people would be equal and money would not exist— such was his dream. Later, Cabet would go to the United States and make a new Icarian attempt in Nauvoo, Illinois.

Today, in the twenty-first century, Icaria Avenue is a pleasant road with trees and sculptures from that Barcelona which, in 1992, with the Olympic Games in mind, discovered the neighboring Mediterranean. That day, however, it was just the filthy and hectic main street in Catalonian Manchester.

During the First World War, Spain had been neutral and that created an opportunity to provide whatever was needed by both sides. Whatever the war destroyed, Barcelona's industry would replace. Especially fabric. Fabric for uniforms, for blankets, for tents. But also kegs, chemical and metallurgical products . . . Factories cropped up by the beach and the first railway in the Spanish state was laid to carry merchandise to nearby ports, where boats were waiting, and from there long trains would transport loads to faraway France.

Catalonian Manchester was what we called that hodge-podge of dirty, arrogant factories, and the little workers' houses that blossomed around it were called Poble Nou. The factories produced money, a lot of money, for the proprietors, providing huge Spanish-Swiss cars and fur coats and sumptuous feasts with tangos and the Charleston. And also spectacular buildings that are still admired by tourists from all over the world.

They drove alongside the train tracks, between the miserable shacks where dirty, naked children splashed in the mud made toxic by the industrial waste from nearby factories.

"It's infuriating how these poor people live and how the bourgeoisie live downtown," said one of the passengers in a shaky voice. "Two worlds, so close and so far away."

"Shut up, Manuel," said the other voice.

At the end of Icaria Avenue, there was the oldest cemetery in the city, with a façade that seemed like an homage to the most shameless masonry, with the eyes of God looking out at everything from five meters high, where the walls were washed with tar to cover the messages the authorities considered inappropriate.

They drove past the misery of cardboard and wooden-plank shanties and came upon the misery of dusty yards and what was once Horta's creek, which today houses the haughty Gotham that is Diagonal Mar, filled with skyscrapers like this city has never seen or wanted to see. Then there was a depressing wasteland of warehouses and train platforms and an artillery barracks with chipped walls, wilted tomato and lettuce plants, and a train crossing.

One of the men in the back placed the barrel of his gun under Tino Orté's ear.

"Now, go left. Down that road. Toward the woods up there."

Tino obeyed. Petrified. His mouth dry. It had to happen to him. In this cursed city of bombs, sooner or later, you were hit by shrapnel.

"Don't be afraid," the other one said, less aggressively. "We don't want to hurt you. We're workers, like you. This isn't about you. We need money for the Committee for Prisoners."

They arrived at the edge of the woods. Below them, the Mediterranean light yellowed the landscape.

"There's Jiménez."

A man smoked with ease next to the tracks, looking out toward the city of Barcelona.

"Here comes the train."

The train arrived, spewing smoke every which way, working up an infernal racket. It whistled long, warning the crossing guard to put down the barrier, like he did each day.

"If he doesn't do anything, it means there's nothing new."

"He's not doing anything. What's he supposed to do?'

"Take off his hat."

"Well, he hasn't taken off his hat, and there's the train. Run—what are you waiting for?"

The man in the derby leaned against the car window, his pistol still on Tino, watching him with the serene eyes of someone who wishes no harm but is willing to follow through on his threats if he's obliged to.

The man in the felt hat ran in the direction of the crossing.

The train cars were uncovered and carried five hundred workers toward the future, to build someone else's future, but they were happy and excited now because it was a payday. The payroll was in a strongbox guarded by two armed men.

The man in the felt hat reached the crossing guard, who was about to comply with his daily routine. Even from afar, Tino could see how he jumped a little when he saw the gun. Then Tino heard: "Quiet! Today the barrier won't be coming down!" The employee raised his hands and stepped back from the barrier.

The man named Jiménez, who had seemed to be basking in the sun, now fisted a pistol and ran toward the convoy, which was braking with an agonizing screech like the voice of a Greek tragedy's hired mourner before the disaster. That ferocious machine had the initials M.Z.A. engraved on its side.

Tino thought he glimpsed a man climb on top of the locomotive and then jump down to the cabin. What he couldn't see were the two men who'd come along disguised as workers in the multitude and who, guns in hand, were trying to scare the others so they'd go away. There was a hell of a commotion, shots, five hundred people trapped and scattering every which way in panic.

The only people who stayed behind, by themselves in one of the uncovered cars, were two armed men next to a trunk that was a meter long and half a meter tall. One already had his hands up, and even from two hundred meters away it was obvious he was shaking with fear and about to lose his balance. The second, however, was unbolting the safety on the Mauser, but not before the other three arrived and fired at him.

He fell like a sack of potatoes. In the distance, Tino thought it looked incredibly easy to kill someone.

One of the men who'd shot the guard, the most animated, dressed all in black and wearing espadrilles, threw the cash box on the ground. The man called Jiménez and the two dressed as workers picked it up. A fourth man jumped from the cabin and joined them.

The locomotive immediately sounded its alarm, but the shots continued, overwhelming the cries from the scattering crowd.

Tino realized then that some soldiers from the nearby artillery barracks were running toward the train and firing with each step. Right then, he felt like an accomplice to the assault and knew he was gambling everything in his life: his savings, his taxi, his family, his apartment in Gràcia.

His hand went to the wheel, he wanted to leave. But he was dissuaded by the man in the derby, with his serene eyes and his pistol.

"Be cool."

"For the love of God," Tino whispered.

"Not for the love of God, nor the homeland, nor the king."

The man in black, carrying the cash box with the guy called Jiménez, dashed toward the car, followed by the man in the felt hat, one of the men disguised as a worker, and the one who'd jumped from the cabin. The soldiers got to the train, climbed aboard, and took aim.

While crossing a patch of grass, the man in black suddenly tripped and fell, taking the cash box and Jiménez with him. The fake worker tried to help him and they all ended up on the ground. The man in the felt hat managed an epileptic leap and kept running. But the guy who'd been in the cabin stopped, turned around, and helped the fallen. The man in black was hurt and limped, and the guy dressed as a worker helped him along. Jiménez ran with difficulty under the weight of the trunk. Clearly confused and ashamed for having fled, the man with the felt hat, who got to the taxi first, demonstrated his impatience with a gesture that was worthless at this point.

The guy who'd jumped from the cabin, who was young and energetic, planted himself among the tomatoes, firing his gun, covering his friends' escape, until he fell helplessly between the lettuce heads.

By then, the others had reached the taxi and were climbing clumsily inside, five men and a trunk in what was designed for four, and one was hurt and howling. They piled up on each other, freaked out. "Fuck—let's go already!" And another voice, quavering, asked, "What about El Quero? Where's El Quero?" And another barked, "Fuck—they killed El Quero!" The treasure chest, metallic and secured with a thick lock, had the distinctive seal of the Aixelá security company.

"Let's go, let's go, let's go! Follow the creek to the highway to France!"

Tino had already started the poor car. They chugged along on the uneven ground, rocks popping against the Studebaker's underside, until they reached the highway.

"Turn right! Go back to Barcelona!"

Tino obeyed.

A captain with the civil guard was crossing the street and noticed the white car packed with troublemakers; it was stained with a red liquid, an alarming red like the color of blood.

They quickly guided Tino to Marina Street, where the man in the felt hat got out.

"Take me to María's house," moaned the injured man in black.

They continued to the city center, Plaza de Cataluña and its rounds, where the medieval walls used to stand and where the sentries kept watch.

"This way!"

They headed down Cera Street, which for many years had been a gypsy enclave in the city, and then reached Plaza Pedró, which still looks like it did in the '20s. Those walls, those sidewalks, those corners, those balconies with laundry on the line, all persist as if history was frozen in a static photograph.

That's where the trip ended. The man in the derby and the man disguised as a worker helped the man in black out of the car. They walked off in the direction of Botella Street.

Jiménez carried the cash box on his shoulder. He didn't seem too worried that he'd be seen with it. He moved down Carmen Street and turned at the first intersection.

The meter said forty-seven pesetas, which nobody paid.

Tino put the Studebaker in gear, and minutes later he was on Las Ramblas, always noisy, colorful, and jubilant, with its florists, the Boqueria Market, café terraces, and, at the end, Columbus's statue. Soon, he lost track of time and space.

He realized they'd pushed him into the furious war between the anarchist union, CNT, and the employers' union, which was called El Libre. But he'd been dragged into the wrong side—while the murders committed by El Libre had impunity, and were supported and protected by Arlegui, the chief of police, and all the powers in the city, Tino was sure that the men who'd assaulted the train would be viciously persecuted and most likely exterminated. And he had been an indispensable accomplice.

He didn't stop for his noontime meal. He arrived home midafternoon, left the car in Paco the Nut's garage, and went up to his place where his wife Elena was waiting for him and who started crying immediately when he told her what had happened.

"What will we do?" she asked. "What will we do?"

Tino made a decision. "I'll go to the police."

The captain from the civil guard who'd seen the white car and its red stain had immediately contacted the authorities, even before he found out there had been a train robbery.

Before noon, the police were already looking for the vehicle in question. Back then in Barcelona, there were no more than twenty-five thousand cars, most of them domestic. Foreign cars were rare, and American cars even more so, because they demanded a high level of purchasing power. A white Studebaker wasn't that hard to find. At sunset, when two undercover officers arrived at Paco the Nut's garage, the engine was still warm and nobody had cleaned the blood off the chassis. The mechanic told them the car belonged to Constantino Orté, who lived on Venus, between Liberty and Danger streets.

When the two inspectors got to his house, Tino Orté was just leaving, dressed in his best suit, and on his way to cooperate with the law.

They detained him.

"We'll talk down at headquarters," they told him.

They took him to the sinister building on Via Laietana, headquarters for the Barcelona police since the world began. In those years, it was a commercial avenue, perfumed by sea air. The building was a big black stain which distinguished itself by being set wrong, to the side, so as to break up the street's straight line.

Police Chief Arlegui came to see him personally. Those who knew the man said he had eyes colored by malice. He was the guy who'd come up with the Law of Escape. He'd planned a couple of attempts on the life of Martínez Anido, the civil governor, just so he could pin it on the anarchists and attack them accordingly.

"Three dead and at least three injured," he told Tino. "Forty thousand pesetas stolen. The worst act of vandalism ever perpetuated in this city. Do you think we're going to let you get away with that?"

Tino began to say he had nothing to do with those thieves, but the cops reminded him that his father had been such a dangerous anarchist that he'd been killed while committing a crime against the state. It also struck them as very suspicious that the car wasn't registered in Tino's name.

"Did you think that we'd never figure out it was you?" Arlegui laughed. He asked him who his accomplices were. The names Tino had heard during the doomed adventure echoed in his brain: *Manuel, Jiménez, El Quero, María.*

They beat him.

So he sealed his lips. He was muzzled by an irrational and suicidal fury. He shook his head and turned away when they showed him photos of the suspects. He refused to indentify even El Quero, the one who'd jumped from the machinist's cabin and then fell dead on the battlefield. He didn't blink when they showed him a photo of the man in the derby, nor the man in the felt hat, nor the guy called Jiménez, nor the man disguised as a worker, nor the one in black who'd been injured.

At dawn, the cops lost their patience and really let him have it. They broke the fingers on his right hand, they kicked him in the groin. His stubbornness convinced them that he'd voluntarily participated in the assault. When they threw him into a basement cell, his shirt was soaked with blood and his face was disfigured.

Sometime later, the police arrested two men who'd hidden the thieves, and the doctor who'd helped the man in black, and the railroad company employee who'd provided the details for the robbery, but they never found the loot. It's said that the man in black, who was named Recasens, was tried in France years later on assault charges and guillotined.

They say the money ended up with a guy named Ramón Arín, who chaired the CNT's Committee for Prisoners.

Tino's cell door opened and he raised his swollen eyes to the light.

"Get up," they said. "We're taking you to the Modelo."

It was a sad irony that Barcelona's city jail, where there had been so many horrors, was called Modelo; it pretended to be a model prison and an example for the rest of the world.

They took him out to the street.

Two cops with Mausers.

At that time, because there were very few cars and very few drivers, it was common to transfer prisoners on foot, even across the city, even to the jail on Entenza Street. But it wasn't very common to step out with the prisoners to busy Via Laietana, because it wasn't the breeziest image to offer to their illustrious visitors; ordinarily, they'd leave the station from the back, where the narrow streets of the old city awaited them, Ciutat Vella, a dark labyrinth, dirty and empty.

The arrested man in front, the police behind.

And back then, the detainee would sometimes realize he was walking alone. He couldn't hear the sound of the police boots at his heels.

And he'd stop and look back, all his vital signs on hold, and he'd see that the police were standing back at a certain distance, their Mausers at their hips.

And they'd say, "Go on. You can just go now."

BRAWNER'S SHADOWS

BY Antonia Cortijos

El Born

I t's been three days since I turned into his shadow. I sleep in the car so I won't lose track of him. I sleep in fits and starts, always aware of the door to the building.

Around seven o'clock, he steps out on the street and I immediately get out of the car. I follow him from a few meters back so as not to arouse suspicion.

All these sleepless nights are starting to wear on me and I notice that I'm moving slowly. He's getting too far ahead of me and I need to run to make up the distance. It looks like he's in a hurry. It's still dark out, though—they've just cleaned the streets and the water is getting in my shoes. My whole body shivers. I raise the collar of my coat and rub my hands to try to scare up some warmth.

He's nearing the Passeig del Born and, like every day since I met him, he goes in a little tavern at the corner of Calders Street. It's been open since six o'clock and a lot of the clientele are cab drivers finishing up the night shift and construction workers restoring houses in a neighborhood that's being rehabilitated. They pick at the walls of the storefronts and homes until the stones show, and then the structure's soul is exposed. You feel the vibration in your body and it tells the story of a neighborhood that was razed in 1714 by a vengeful king, who ordered the destruction of 1,200 homes so he could build his citadel, a military fort that dominated the city for more than a hundred years. Now, in its place, there's Parc de la Ciutadella, beautiful, expansive, green.

I wait a few seconds and, protected by the darkness outside, stealthily approach to see how he reads the paper and drinks his coffee. All three days, he's sat in the same place, away from the rest of the locals. I can't take my eyes off him, and I continue to contemplate him, the same as yesterday and the day before—the way he addresses the waiter, the small gestures with his elbows barely separated from his body, the wait until the coffee reaches the desired temperature, the pleasure with which he drinks it all at once. He's borrowed a newspaper that he holds near the coffee and, like every morning, I ask myself if it's yesterday's edition.

I breathe the salty fresh air with glee as light beckons dawn and profiles the silhouette of Mercat del Born, the old wholesale market, a modernist steel building that now stands empty and alone, with a sadness that comes from uselessness. It's easy to get your bearings in this neighborhood, since every street and plaza still echoes with the noises and smells that distinguished each artisanal specialty. The streets are named after them.

When thirty minutes are almost up, I hide in one of the nearby alleys. I know he'll cross my path at Sombrerers, a narrow street by the Church of Santa María del Mar; where there are now art galleries, wine shops, and restaurants, there used to be, from the Middle Ages until not too long ago, men's millinery shops. Later we'll go up Argenteria, where the smiths used to be, working silver, gold, and other precious metals. We'll move along Via Laietana, the neighborhood's southern border, until we arrive at the cathedral's plaza. Then we'll come to an ancient street, where a car can barely maneuver, and where there's a bunch of antique shops. I know which one he'll go in.

This is the time I use to get something to eat, and drink some coffee so the fog will lift from my brain.

Everything started about a week ago.

To me, it feels like an eternity.

The police came to my house to tell me, in a very frosty tone, that my mother had died.

They had found her body in the Botanical Garden at Parc de la Ciutadella, on a bed of white flowers, wearing a soft red silk robe which accented the pallor of her skin. The pose had been carefully constructed to make it seem as if she was enjoying a pleasant nap, and only her head, with abrasions on her neck and covered by a plastic bag, ruined the scene. The autopsy showed that Anna Brawner was already a corpse when she was deposited there, so an investigation was immediately initiated.

Inspector Gómez Triadó interrogated me twice but I couldn't tell him very much. She'd always been a very strange woman who never gave me access to her secrets: I never knew where she was born; she always claimed to be a citizen of the world. The only time I ever got anything out of her was in my adolescence, when I found out that her mother had died during her birth. But she never told me who my father was, or if he was even still alive.

I had to take care of the body and had it transferred to a funeral home where I held a solitary wake. Seated in front of her, unable to take my eyes off her face, I felt a short circuit in my chest, leaving me in absolute darkness. The connection had corroded, and I know now with absolute certainty that I'd never be without that gloom.

The funeral was the next day. Inspector Gómez Triadó was there, along with two men and a woman I didn't know.

One was an old man, surely more than ninety, who moved his very stately body with ease. That peculiarity, along with the high-collared, charcoal-colored, tailored suit that pretended to hide the ravages of age, and his immaculate and abundant white hair, gave him an aristocratic and seductive air.

The other man was in his forties, and he dressed and acted in a banal fashion.

The woman was the same age as my mother, but lacked her vitality, her love of life. Her gray eyes, covered in a haze, seemed to be asking for forgiveness.

Inspector Gómez Triadó hurried to take them in for questioning down at the station; it hadn't even occurred to me that those people could reveal hidden parts of my mother that would help me understand her and myself. I simply accepted their condolences and continued to stare at the luxurious coffin in which she rested.

But something bothered me during the brief funeral. I felt a slight tingling on my neck just as the ceremony was about to end, as if someone's gaze had been boring into me for a long time. An instinct made me turn my head, but I only glimpsed a shadow going out the door.

Nobody accompanied me to the small cemetery next to the funeral home, so I waited for them to finish preparing the grave and then I put the final touches on the burial rites by myself. I hadn't been able to cry, but the minute the workers walked away, I gazed at the huge bouquet of flowers on the headstone and tears came in a rush, unstoppable; I had to kneel because my legs couldn't hold the weight of my body, nor my pain.

When I opened my eyes, there was that shadow again. This time it vanished behind a white marble statue of a guardian angel. I don't know which part of me reacted, because I was lost in a world of memories. I went to the cemetery exit and waited a few minutes before sneaking back to my mother's grave. On the way, something made me detour toward the place where I thought the person who'd been watching me was hiding, as if breathing in the same air or walking on the same ground would connect me to him, would reveal his secret. I poked my head out, ever so slowly, from an extended wing, and then I saw him.

Completely overwhelmed, I had to turn away.

My eyes were lying, there was no other explanation.

Incredulous, I looked again and he was still there, erect, as if he were me, as if a mirror was reflecting my image back to me, with my arms crossed over my chest and my eyes fixed on the spot on the tombstone where the Brawner family name was written in gold letters on black marble.

I couldn't take my eyes off that tall man, his blond hair shining in the midday sun, his skin so white nothing reflected off it; everything had become light. But what caused a lingering, blurry, indefinable fear, what made cold sweat run down my back, was the expression on his face.

I've been following him ever since.

⸎

"I appreciate that you came right away."

"Inspector, I've always believed that a bitter drink is more difficult to swallow the longer you wait."

"I'm going to turn on the tape recorder but I need to tell you that you can say no."

"It's fine, I'm all yours. My name is Jacob Zimmerman, and I was born in Hamburg, Germany, ninety-two years ago. I've been living in Barcelona for fifty-eight years."

"Why did you attend Anna Brawner's funeral?"

"Because she was my daughter-in-law."

"So . . . are you related in any way to Julián Brawner?"

"Yes, he's my grandson."

"I'm surprised. I would have thought you didn't know each other."

"Yes, that's partly true. I'd never spoken with him until today, and I'm pretty sure she never mentioned me to him. It's an old family story. I decided to immigrate to Barcelona at the end of the 1920s, to escape from the economic crisis in my country. My wife, Edith Keller, had a boutique on the Rambla de Cataluña and I opened an antique store that I still operate. Anna Brawner's father arrived in Barcelona in 1942 when she was barely three years old. Back then, this city was a nest of spies of many different nationalities, but especially Germans. He was posted to the German consulate, which was then in the Plaza de Cataluña, and you can imagine his mission."

"Yes, I can."

"Those were very hard years for everybody. In 1942, I was forty-six years old, I had a stable life and five kids. The youngest was born here and had double citizenship. At the beginning of 1943, the oldest three were kidnapped, all under the auspices of that damned treaty that General Martínez Anido and Himmler signed in '39. Any German suspected of failing to support the Nazi cause could be detained and repatriated immediately without an extradition hearing or preliminary finding."

Jacob Zimmerman goes silent, as if he needs his memories to send him the strength to continue. The inspector is about to ask him if he feels all right when the elderly man picks up the conversation again. His voice is charged with a repressed anger.

"They never got to Germany! They were executed some-where on the French border."

Silence again. This time, Gómez Triadó just waits.

"My youngest son and Anna Brawner met about twenty years later. They fell in love a few months before her father died, and since she was left all alone, my wife and I asked her to come live with us. They were happy times that made up for the tragedy of the war years. When my son finished his stud-ies at the university, they got married, and before the year was out, she was pregnant. Excuse me . . . but could I have a glass of water?"

"Forgive my lack of manners. I'll be right back."

The old man is left alone. He puts his elbows on the table and rests his face in the palms of his hands. The darkness is soothing. He knows he needs to keep his head clear, his emo-tions in check. A few minutes later, the inspector is back.

"I brought you some coffee, if you're interested."

"No, thank you. At my age, a single cup means a lost night."

"If you need to rest, we can stop for a few minutes."

"No, no, I'm fine. The water will do."

As the old man drinks, Gómez Triadó observes his wrin-kled face. As he's been telling the story, sadness has been darkening his features.

"Everything changed when Julián was nine months old. For very strong personal reasons, she felt that she couldn't continue to live with us, and one night she vanished with my grandson. My son couldn't bear it, and he fell into a state of depression that ended with his suicide. We never heard from her again and then we saw the news article about her murder. I went to the funeral this morning to tell her how much I'd grown to hate her."

CR

I decide to sleep at home tonight; I've been following him for five days. I need to get some distance or I'll fall into the looking glass and be unable to come back. Everything is very confusing, as if I am slowly melting into him. He can sense my presence, he sees that I'm following him; I know that he knows because I'm slowly taking over the thoughts his mind generates. They come to me on a breeze that whirls around my brain, full of voices, noise, and hate.

I open the door but I don't turn on the light; I remember a childhood game of keeping my eyes closed, trying to feel the same sensations as a blind man. The blind have always fascinated me, and blindness is what I fear most, even more than death. Now I want to move in darkness again. I move toward the sink, feeling the walls so I can count the doorways. It's the third door. I go in. My eyes are getting used to the blackness and begin to make out blurry forms. The first thing I'll do is shower; I'm still carrying the sweat and dirt of the last five days, plus a thin film of resentment and rage which he has passed on to me.

I thought the water would wash everything away but the only things that are gone from my body are the dirt and sweat.

I try to sleep but my mother haunts me, I feel her near me, caressing my body with a deathly touch which filters into my brain with memories of lost moments and an image that repeats with the regularity of an advertisement stuck in my head. Sleep just turns it on. Darkness is near total, and in the background there's a thin light which attracts my gaze. I go toward it, passing leafy plants in the shadows at my sides, and I arrive at a small clearing completely covered by a bed of white flowers. It's from here that the light is emanating. A man with a woman in his arms approaches and when he gets to me, he kneels without seeing me, his eyes red from tears. He puts her down with great care amidst the flowers and the woman looks up at me, her face a mask of agony. I wake up in anguish, the sheets wet from sweat, and dawn's light is seeping.

I stay quiet, listening for the messages in my dreams, contemplating the dawn through the open window.

ભ

"I hope you're not thinking something's wrong because my husband and I attended the funeral."

"Don't worry," says Inspector Gómez Triadó, "that's why you two are here, to clear up that very point. It's just a formality. How did you find out about her death?"

"It was in the news."

"If you didn't actually have much contact with her, how is it that the company you run, Mr. Cánovas—which is owned by your wife—transferred 200,000 pesetas a month to the victim's account?"

"It was part of my inheritance from my father-in-law, it came with the company."

"And it didn't occur to you to stop doing it?"

"The terms of the will were clear: to keep paying until Anna Brawner's death. And that's what I came to do, to make sure she was dead."

"Quite a favor the murderer did you, don't you think?"

"Us and two other companies."

"We know, we've gone over the victim's accounts in great detail, Mrs. Cánovas."

"My name is Teresa Puig-Grau."

"I'm sorry, Mrs. Puig-Grau."

"It's the same old story. The two other companies are in the same situation. If we didn't pay what was due on time, first as indicated by the father and then by Anna Brawner herself, she had the legal power to take over our properties. In her defense, I must say that she never exceeded her authority."

"Are you saying she was blackmailing you?"

"No. What I'm saying is that Anna—actually, it was Otto Brawner—gave us three businesses before Franco could nationalize them during World War II."

"Could you explain that a bit . . . ?"

"I can tell you what my father told me."

"Please."

"We've been here since 1942, when Otto Brawner arrived to take over an important post at the German consulate on orders from Kart Resenberg, who was the consul in Barcelona then. Highly confidential official documents about businesses in the city working with Nazi capital passed through his hands. Unlike other German officials, who stayed at the Ritz or the Continental, Otto stayed at my grandfather's house, I suppose, so that young Anna could be raised in a family environment. The postwar period was very hard and many families had to rent rooms to survive. We felt like we'd won the lottery when Brawner moved in. He brought us coffee, butter, and cans of meat—and he always paid his rent on time. My father was about his age and they got along well. He accompanied him to the get togethers in Colón and to private parties organized at the Ritz. One day, Otto Brawner asked my father if he knew trustworthy people who could act as fronts for three enterprises that Johannes Bernhardt wanted to establish in Barcelona. He consulted with his father, who'd been a lawyer at the Generalitat of Catalonia, and my grandfather told him who Bernhardt was, which made him really reluctant to go ahead with it."

"Who was it?"

"It was the man who helped Franco win the war, the creator of a formidable economic and business empire that the German government established in Spain which included 350 businesses. In '36, if I remember correctly, that same German businessman, along with the Spanish captain Arranz Monasterio and other rebel soldiers, forced the pilot of a commercial Lufthansa flight to take them to Berlin, where they met with Hitler. It was Bernhartdt who got those military men ten planes, six fighter-bombers, twenty antiaircraft cannons, machine guns, and munitions, as well as the alliance with Franco that got him whatever he wanted."

"I'm surprised, I heard rumors but I didn't believe they were true."

"Now you understand my father and my grandfather's reluctance to get involved. But survival was more important then than pride or loyalties, so my father and two cousins acted as fronts for the duration of the war."

"Incredible! But let's go back to Anna Brawner. Tell me, Mr. Cánovas, did she ever threaten you in any way?"

"No."

"Do you know if she ever threatened either of the other two businesses?"

"Not that I know of, but I'd be surprised if she had. Whenever we were going through rough periods, she was the first to relieve us of the responsibility to pay until we were back on our feet."

Teresa Puig-Grau nods her head before addressing Gómez Triadó. "We both went to the German School, inspector. Anna was my friend until she discovered what her father had done. He was dead but she lived with her in-laws. It had been months since the birth of the twins—"

The inspector interrupts to make sure he heard right. "Excuse me, did you say twins?"

"Yes, identical twins. They weren't even a year old when Anna discovered, amid her father's papers, a list of the Jews that her father had turned over to the Gestapo and the SD. The real tragedy was that her husband's four brothers were on that list. That's when I saw her for the last time, when she asked me to meet her at the Samoa. She was completely destroyed. Her father was not only a traitor to his race but also the man who'd turned in her in-laws. She decided to disappear. I tried to persuade her, convince her she had nothing to do with any of it, but it was useless. Anna had always been a woman with very particular ideas about morality, about religion. She never spoke about her German origins, or about her Jewish heritage. She had created a lifestyle for herself, in her own way, and she followed its rules obsessively. I couldn't do a thing. And I never saw her again."

∞

I know that he killed my mother, our mother. It's still the dead of night and the rain is trying to wash the air. He walks ahead of me, under an umbrella. He isn't out for a meal and instead heads directly to La Palla Street, where he tries to hide at Zimmerman Antiquities, the store owned by his grandfather, my grandfather. He flees because he feels accosted. He reads my mind and finds a vengeful anxiety just as I read his for rage and pain. I want him to die the way he killed my mother, his mother. When I arrive, he has lowered the store's metal door and I know it won't open again until ten. I make my way to a tiny café with only five bar stools. There's barely any light, which is probably a tactic to hide the stuff on the floor, which sticks to my shoes, and the greasy gumminess of the bar itself, where I only dare to place my elbows. At first, I'm all alone. I order an expresso with a drop of milk, which I drink in small sips as I contemplate, through the glass, a few folks enveloped in shadows walking hurriedly toward their destinations. Slowly, the pedestrians begin to change and now they're kids on their way to school, alone or with their mothers. A ray of light cuts through the bar's window and bits of dust, robbed of their privacy, worry their way to the floor, the furniture, my shoes. My stomach demands solid food and I'm amazed I can still be hungry. I think about my mother and the question hits me again: why did she pick me? I could have been that other one, now tormented, filled with anger toward her and the chosen one. How could she do that? Make a choice! Condemn one of us to live in a world of absences, passed over, cornered, secret.

It's ten o'clock now. I get up, dropping a fifty-peseta coin on the bar. I wait for my change. When I go out to the street, the sun has completely taken over the alleys between the buildings.

I feel stupid with empty bags in my pocket. I bought them at the gas station yesterday. They're wide, made of thick plastic, and very manageable. I tremble a little and have to remember my hate in order to regain some strength. I've never gone inside the store though I've passed it without even a glance; it's still dark, he hasn't turned on the lights. When I open the door, a sound like a bell goes off and announces my presence. Then there's silence. I move inside with short steps, cautious; I have to calm down, every shadow cast by the furniture frightens me; I think of my dead mother to firm up my pulse. I grab one of the plastic bags in my fist. Suddenly, the lights come on and the brightness blinds me. I glimpse the figure of the old man who attended the funeral, my grandfather. He walks by some old cretonne curtains and stands in front of me, quietly, impassive, looking at what I can't see because I'm hypnotized before him.

The pressure of the plastic on my face and a quick jerk to cut my oxygen make my hands fly to my neck to free myself; I lose a few seconds before realizing all I really have to do is pierce the bag, but I don't have time to do it, my grandfather immobilizes me, circling me under his arms with the kind of strength produced only by hate or love. As he squeezes, he whispers in my ear a lullaby my mother used to sing: *"Mama sings you the loveliest song / you were born at night, like the stars . . ."* I try with all my might to get him off me. *"I love you, my son / my sweet light / you're the prettiest star in the sky."* When I'm just about loose, my brother kicks me and I drop to the ground. Pain races to my head and is transformed into a violent scream full of impotence and rage.

I remain inert and I hear my grandfather cry. There's barely any air left in my lungs and I can't distinguish anything through the plastic, just a milky fog that vanishes when I close my eyes.

THE PREDATOR

BY SANTIAGO RONCAGLIOLO

Barri Gòtic

At thirty-nine years of age, Carmen was resigned to her loneliness. She wasn't pretty but she wasn't ugly either, and averageness extended to every part of her life: neither rich nor poor, neither dumb nor exceptional. Carmen had such normal attributes—so few attributes—that she blamed her lack of having a partner on her demanding temperament and on luck. Not necessarily bad luck. Just *her* luck.

It's also not like she was a spinster or a prude. She'd had partners throughout her adult life. Some were quite pleasant. At the very least, they were steady. Most of her relationships had wasted away over time, and those that survived for several years tended to vanish when it came time to take the next step to marriage or parenthood. It wasn't, like her mother said with malice, that men refused to get married. It was actually Carmen who could rarely seem to make the commitment beyond six or seven weekends. She understood that she'd rather carry her tedium alone than share it. And if her sheets were cold, she preferred a hot water bottle to a tepid companion as a solution.

Anyway, to fill up her immediate world, she had her officemates. Carmen worked near Comercio Street in a travel agency. The biggest part of her job wasn't to send people out into the world, but to organize the tourists—each time more numerous—who came to visit Barcelona. In a way, the agency was not a starting point but rather a finish line, the last stop, which was underscored by its physical location: lost in the tangled alleys of Born, boxed into a dead end, under a vaguely ancient archway, practically invisible to the pedestrians; the office seemed like an enchanted cave in a forest.

The advantage in this was that clients tended not to even come to the office, which created a certain closeness among the staff. Carmen's four colleagues—Dani, Milena, Lucía, and Jaime—had established a warm camaraderie that was respectful of each others' private lives and allowed them to share their joys while avoiding intimacies. So when Milena's mother died, they all went to the funeral to be with her. And when Jaime got pneumonia, they all took turns bringing him soup at home. But when Carmen found out she had cysts that were affecting her kidney, she didn't want to bother anybody with her medical problems. And when her last boyfriend left her—Carmen remembered him well because he really hurt her when he split—she spent days locked in the bathroom crying, but never got it off her chest with her colleagues. She didn't even tell Daniel, the gay one, with whom she shared the most confidences. Carmen knew she could count on his support for small things but she was afraid that if she asked or needed more, it would cross the delicate line from collegiality to emotional blackmail.

The personal calendar at the office included festive events of which the most important were birthdays. Five times a year, after closing time, the group celebrated one of its members' birthdays. They would collect money among themselves so they could offer the honored one a significant gift, usually a bottle of fine perfume or cologne. And they blew out the candles on the cake, although since the girls were always on diets, the chocolate cakes had been reduced to muffins and coffee. Each time, these ceremonies included the retelling of the same jokes and, though it wasn't an orgy of fun, Carmen enjoyed them: she loved the certainty of small everyday rituals which made life easy to manage, free of surprises.

When she turned forty, the day coincided with Barcelona's Carnival and someone in the office—maybe Lucía, who could be a little over-the-top sometimes—had suggested dressing up in costumes and going out on the streets together, barhopping. Carmen thought Carnival was colorful and she'd been to it several years ago, but simply to watch, dressed as herself, protected by her normality while surrounded by the most extravagant and ugliest masks. She was willing to do it again on those same terms, with a kind of prophylactic barrier between her and the Carnival, smiling at the clever costumes in the same way she would smile at a spectacle on a stage. But the problem, to her dismay, was that the office staff had announced a *surprise*, which no doubt included a mandatory costume.

Carmen hated all that: surprises, costumes, and what she called "street madness." They struck her as childish entertainment wholly inappropriate for responsible adults. But to refuse would have meant introducing an element of confrontation to her secure work environment, and she wasn't willing to risk the stability of her tiny universe. Plus, to be honest, there really was no Plan B for that night. If she said no, she'd have to eat dinner with her mother. And she would do anything, even go out in the streets dressed as a monster, to avoid dining out with her mother on the night of her birthday.

As long as Carmen could remember, her mother had ruined her birthdays. She was a woman with an extroverted personality, who loved parties and party guests, and who always had a house full of people. As a result, she tried to turn each of her daughter's birthdays into a great social event for kids. She would move all the furniture out of the living room, buy tons of food and drink, and send out invitations every which way, even to girls who weren't Carmen's friends or, worse, who were declared enemies. If Carmen protested, her mother responded by saying that there's no better place to make friends than a party, and that there couldn't be too terrible a problem between girls her age anyway.

But Carmen—perhaps precisely as a response to all that— was a retiring and timid girl who would hide out in a corner while the other girls had fun and her mother bantered with the adults. Sometimes, while she tried to make herself invisible, she went from being a hostess to being her guests' victim. When the more seasoned girls would realize that she wasn't reacting to any of their verbal provocations, they'd come up with other ways to torment her: they pulled her braids; they shoved her; they laughed at her; they stuck jelly candies on her clothes; they stole her gifts. And later, when her mother approached them, they would pretend that everything was fine and force Carmen to smile and pretend as well. Of course, the first few times Carmen tried to tell her mother, but she just said, "Dear, you have to learn to relax. Your friends are only playing." With those words, she forced her to play as well. She told Carmen she had to learn to get along.

Since the human world was hostile, Carmen would take refuge in the toy world, especially the world of stuffed animals, which she loved. Her collection included a bear with button eyes, a zebra, a very fat cat, and a cow with a fat pink udder, among many that hung from her walls and filled her closet. Carmen treated these toys like friends. She'd gather them in a circle in the middle of her room and pretend to have tea. She'd let them decide what they wanted to play. She slept with them, and when there were too many to fit with her under the sheets, she'd give them her bed and sleep on the rug. They deserved it; at least they deserved it more than people.

Her favorite was a dark brown little wolf her father had brought her from Germany. She called him Max. When her mother once asked where she'd gotten such a name, Carmen replied, "That's what he wants to be called."

In fact, sometimes it seemed that Max the wolf had his own life, and he'd pop up in the most unexpected places: in the kitchen knife drawer, under her parents' bed, in the tub. At the same time, Carmen seemed to have a lot less of a presence. When she got home from school, she'd lock herself in her room with her stuffed animals and would have to be dragged out for dinner. When there were visitors, even children, Carmen would hide under the bed with her stuffed animals. As each day passed, she seemed to communicate more and more exclusively with them, delegating the role of spy in the outside world to Max.

If she had to communicate with adults, Carmen would do so representing the stuffed animals. She didn't ask for chocolates for herself, saying instead, "Max wants some." If she didn't want to go see her grandmother, she'd offer that the bear or cow was sick as an excuse. (The wolf was the only one with a proper name but he never got sick.) Even in her letters to the Three Wisemen, she only asked for gifts for her stuffed animals. The one she wrote when she was nine years old went like this:

> *Dear Wisemen,*
> *Please bring a scarf for the bear because he gets cold,*

and a hat for my giraffe who's very tall and bumps her head on the ceiling, and a girl wolf for Max because he'd like to have little wolves, thank you.

Her mother was really upset by that letter. For her, there was nothing worse than being condemned to isolation, and the girl was bringing it upon herself. To try and combat it, she took Carmen on excursions to Costa Brava, the volcano at Olot, the steam baths at Montbui. She would add other kids to the trips, as many as possible, until she filled up the family car. When they got to each place, she'd let them out, like a pack of hounds, so they could run all over the grass and hunt bugs—basically, so they could show off that they were full of life. But it was useless when it came to Carmen. The girl behaved with a proper but distant chilliness. She obeyed orders but participated in the games without complaints or enthusiasm, as if she were tackling a school assignment that wasn't too difficult. And she did this with her mind elsewhere—undoubtedly in her closet full of toys.

For her tenth birthday, her mother decided to try to use shock therapy. She organized the biggest party ever. She rented a local games place for kids and invited more than fifty people, quite a feat considering how few friends her daughter had. She bought the girl a pink dress and spent days teaching her how to look sociable and happy.

The day of the party, Carmen spent all morning consulting her stuffed animals about what to do. She'd gotten so enmeshed with them that their games were real meetings, with debates and turns to speak. That morning, a few of the animals suggested she get ill. Others, Max among them, advised straightforward insubordination: a refusal to attend.

But Carmen couldn't do that to her mother. She'd seen

her running around from one thing to another in preparation for days and knew how much this party meant to her. Besides, Carmen had developed a kind of protective shield that allowed her to function in the outside world in exchange for returning safely to hers, and she didn't mind using it when necessary. Frankly, that was the safest bet because it guaranteed that, as long as she knew how to behave, nothing would change between her stuffed animals and her. So, against her toys' wishes, she opted for the most diplomatic solution: she'd go to the party, then come back to her stuffed animal world, to hibernate until her next birthday.

The biggest surprise was that she actually liked the party. Busy with the trampolines and the rides, her guests didn't torment her, and she was able to get over her fears and play some of the games too. Aware of her love of stuffed animals, and unaware of her mother's worries, a few of the guests had given her stuffed animals as gifts: dogs, monkeys, chickens, deer. But, for once, Carmen was more interested in people and was able to have fun with them. That night, she came home with her heart swooning over her discovery of parties and her reconciliation with the world.

But when she went to tell her stuffed animals, they were no longer in her room.

Or in her closet.

Or under her bed.

Carmen looked all over the house. She rummaged through boxes. Peeked under rugs. Called aloud for each of her stuffed animals, especially for Max. Finally, fearing the response she already knew, she asked her mother what had happened to her friends. That's what she called them, *friends*, as tears rolled down her cheeks. And her mother's words hit her like anvils hurled down from the sky.

"You're too big for such things, dear. It's time you found other pastimes."

The day she turned forty, Carmen opened her eyes ten minutes before the alarm and let time ease by until the moment to get up. When she was getting dressed before the mirror, she realized that wrinkles were starting to show on her neck, her armpits, and between her breasts. She felt as though her body came with an expiration date. To celebrate the passage of time with joy struck her as a supremely tasteless custom.

As the day went on, her colleagues behaved with studious normality, which only made Carmen more nervous. Every now and again they exchanged complicit looks amongst themselves and she was tempted to pretend she was getting a chill and just go home for the day. In the afternoon, a client approached to wish her a happy birthday and winked at her. Carmen felt as if the whole city knew, as if she were walking the streets with a sign on her forehead that said: *Today I'm a year older.*

After doing the day's accounting and closing up shop, Jaime and Daniel turned off the lights and came out of the back room with the traditional muffin which was, in fact, Carmen's favorite: apple and cinnamon. It had two candles stuck in it, shaped like a 4 and a 0, which tenuously lit the scene while her friends sang "Happy Birthday." Carmen wished that everything would end right then and there and blew out the candles. But she knew the muffin would not grant her wish.

Due to the upcoming Holy Week holiday, they'd closed late, so they could simply change clothes and begin their *noche loca*, as Daniel had been saying with the heaviest gay accent he could muster. Then, the moment Carmen had been fearing finally arrived with a *ta-daaa* to spice up the occasion.

Milena and Lucía presented her with her costume, the irrefutable evidence that there was no going back, that she'd spend the evening dressed as someone else, surrounded by faceless people.

The costume wasn't even original. Worse yet, it was the most common of all: the prostitute. "A hooker!" Daniel squealed. It included platform shoes and high multicolored hose, a leather miniskirt, and a black top, which left broad swatches of skin out in the open. The good part was that, at least out on the street, she'd have to wear a coat. The bad part was the rest of it.

Her friends were prodigiously inventive and, without exception, were all better costumed. Each one took his or her turn going in the bathroom and, upon coming back out in costume, received applause and jocular comments from the others. Daniel wore a tunic and laurels like Caligula, and Jaime was going goth, with a nail-studded collar and leather accessories. Milena was dressed as Little Red Riding Hood. Lucía was a cop. Carmen tried to maintain her composure but had the sensation that everything was happening a million light-years away from her.

When they went out, they encountered vampires and astronauts parading down the neighborhood streets and tunnels. An imp and a witch stood in front of the wig store on Princesa Street comparing false noses. At the Plaza del Ángel, dogs and rats streamed out from the metro station. In the first few minutes, the five office workers felt a ticklish nervousness about their costumes, which Daniel tried to relieve with sex jokes. By the time they got to the Santa Caterina market, however, they felt much more comfortable in their new skins, which blurred under the multicolored tile roofs and the surreal atmosphere created by the other pedestrians. When they crossed Vía Laietana, a giraffe's long neck could be seen against the background of the buildings they approached. Carmen felt slight relief that her hussy attire was pretty conservative after all.

The Cathedral's esplanade confirmed this impression. Gargoyles that looked like they had just scaled down from the walls strolled by tourists and uncostumed pedestrians. In order not to get lost in the narrow alleys of the Barri Gòtic, Carmen and her friends followed Daniel's tunic single file to a bar. Once inside, maybe because of how anxious she felt walking down the streets dressed like that, Carmen relaxed a little, as if she'd arrived at a familiar, even cozy place.

The bar was decorated like a catacomb and the air was so thick with smoke that the guests looked like specters in the fog. Carmen asked for a double shot of whiskey. She didn't usually drink, but she also didn't know how to face a situation like this, and though Lucía was playing around with her handcuffs and everything seemed fun, she needed something to help her along.

"The bad part about Carnival," Milena said, "is that you could hook up with an ugly guy without even realizing it."

"No," responded Jamie, "the best part is that you can hook up even if you're ugly. This is a much appreciated day for thousands of people . . ."

Everyone had to practically scream to be heard. And half the conversation didn't even reach Carmen's ears, though she smiled so as not to seem out of it. She wanted to go to the bathroom but there was a mass of humans in the way. She tried but didn't get very far.

"Sweetie, you're getting looks," Daniel whispered in her ear.

At the bar, a wolfman had just ordered a drink. His body

was covered with hair and his furry tail wagged from side to side.

"He wasn't looking at me," Carmen replied.

"Sweetie, believe me. I know when a man looks at somebody. Even if it's not at me."

Somebody ordered another round and another drink ended up in Carmen's hand. The friends toasted and laughed, although Carmen didn't really understand what was going on. The wolfman was now closer to them and was suddenly speaking with Daniel. And soon with the others as well.

"You have a very good costume," Carmen said, just to say something. "You look like a real wolf."

"I *am* a real wolf," he responded.

And she laughed.

"Your costume is very good too. It's . . . inciting."

"I hate it."

Before she realized it, she'd embarked on a conversation with the wolfman. When she couldn't hear what he said, she simply admired the costume's perfection. She couldn't find the zippers or the seams, and the mask fit his face perfectly.

After a while, Milena asked: "Shall we go somewhere else?"

Almost automatically, they all began to push toward the exit. When they reached the door, Carmen noticed a bear wearing a scarf drinking in the back of the bar. It seemed to her that his eyes were like two buttons.

When they got out into the fresh air, Carmen realized she was slightly tipsy and the wolfman—by that point he'd identified himself as Fran—offered her a hairy arm, which felt like real fur to the touch. They lingered in a mob of skulls. When they turned a corner full of bows and crosspieces, Carmen bumped into a Che Guevara, who laughed uproariously.

There was a metal camera in the plaza in front of them that watched her with its single lens. It took Carmen a few seconds to grasp that it was a monument dedicated to someone or something.

"Where are we?" she asked her companion.

"It's this way."

They crossed a plaza bordered by columns, with a fountain in the middle, and palm trees. Carmen recognized Plaza Real, but it looked different. Maybe it was the people perched on the windows, who seemed to watch her in silence. When they got to Las Ramblas, Carmen realized she'd lost track of her friends.

"I swear they were right here," Fran said.

Then, and only then, did Carmen understand the true nature of her birthday surprise, a surprise that had Daniel's typical imprimatur and, maybe because of the warmth of the liquor, didn't bother her so much: it was a hairy gift, with big fangs, named Fran.

"Do you want to go to another bar?"

Carmen noticed how tall Fran was. She looked at him from below, with his profile silhouetted by the full moon. She smiled. A woman dressed as a cow with a giant pink udder walked by her, too drunk not to stumble into her.

Dear, you have to learn to relax.

They crossed Las Ramblas and went into El Raval. They passed by a kind of ancient jail with bars on the windows. Carmen thought she heard a scream coming from inside but when she turned, she saw only a man disguised as a cat with a very thick costume. Fran didn't bat an eye. He'd bought a beer from a Chinese street peddler and he offered her a drink. Carmen accepted. As they went on, the multitudes dispersed and some streets were completely empty. Further on, Carmen realized that people weren't dressed up as Moroccans. These were real Moroccans, and a few of them whistled at her when she walked by. The air smelled of kebabs and beer. On a corner, some graffiti demanded: *KILL THEM ALL.*

Fran came to a halt at a storefront with a locked gate.

"Damn," he said, "I didn't think it'd be closed today of all days."

"I'm cold," Carmen complained, feeling the air crawl in under her multicolored hose.

Without a word, Fran led her to a tiny street that emptied out to an intricate network of passageways. They entered the labyrinth and arrived at a building so narrow it couldn't accommodate an elevator. While they climbed the cramped stairwell, Fran mumbled something about his place and led her to believe he had liquor there. Carmen continued on, more because she was cold than because she wanted to. She felt heavy and clumsy, and she just wanted a couch to fall into.

And a girl wolf for Max because he'd like to have little wolves, thank you.

Fran's place proved surprisingly big considering the narrow stairs. It had a single hallway which extended to a central patio, while the rooms were off to the sides. The living room was just an extension of the hallway, which seemed endless. Carmen curled up in an armchair and accepted the brandy her host offered. When she brought the glass to her lips, she felt the warm and thick beverage, like a Turkish coffee.

"Fran, do you know you remind me of someone?"

"Really?"

"Can I call you Max?"

"You can call me whatever you want."

A thud, like a knock, came from somewhere in the hall, but Fran didn't seem to be aware of it. Carmen's feet were cold and she drank a little more. With each swallow, Fran would refill her glass with that liquid which seemed to her less and less like brandy. The room was spinning and she thought she heard voices other than her own, but she had a hard time figuring out if they were coming from inside or outside her head. Fran kept his costume on. The hair looked so natural. It was like sitting next to a giant dog.

"Max, why don't you take off your mask? I still haven't seen your face."

"You want me to take it off?"

Carmen nodded.

"You might not like what you see," he said, and she thought she saw a smile on his snout.

"Take it off."

He put his hands on his neck and struggled a little, as if he was having trouble finding the zipper. Carmen was seeing double and her eyes wanted to close but the anticipation kept them open. Finally, the wolf's face gave way. First, it went lax on his features, then absolutely amorphous. Fran grabbed it by the sides and pushed up. When the mask finally fell away, Carmen saw the face underneath. It was her mother's face. And now it was her voice, with thundering clarity, which seemed to come from every corner of the room.

"You're too big for such things, dear. It's time you found other pastimes."

In the next instant, Carmen saw only the open fangs coming toward her face. And darkness.

Carmen opened her eyes ten minutes before the alarm and let time ease by until the moment to get up. At first, it took her a few seconds to realize she was at home. Later, she tried to remember how she'd gotten back, but couldn't. She managed to believe momentarily that she hadn't gone out the night before, but her costume—that horrible costume—was thrown on the floor, like an annoying witness. She got up and shoved it under the bed with her foot. She wanted to forget she'd turned forty. That she'd ever had a birthday. The only thing that's really real, she told herself, is what happens in front of other people.

She was comforted knowing that nobody at work would ask her about anything. She had that kind of relationship with her officemates: respectful when it came to intimacy. She could decree that they'd never had a celebration with apple cinnamon muffins. Maybe the others wouldn't even remember it. Maybe they hadn't even taken note of yesterday and were just waiting for her today with a hooker costume, ready to go enjoy Carnival. When she undressed before the mirror, she realized that wrinkles were starting to show on her neck, her armpits, and between her breasts. She felt as though her body came with an expiration date. To celebrate the passage of time with joy struck her as a supremely tasteless custom.

THE ENIGMA OF HER VOICE

BY Isabel Franc

Poble Nou

T he clerk was surprised I wasn't familiar with the story. "Everyone in the neighborhood knows about it," she said, practically scolding me. I had recently moved into a very small apartment on Amistat Street that served as both living space and office for me. Since arriving in Poble Nou, I'd tried to gain the confidence of folks out in the streets, store owners and porters, if there are any (there are so few left); you never know when you're going to need information. I was curious about the name of the place, so I had decided to ask about it as a conversation starter.

"In 1957, a customer gave a parrot to the owners of La Licorería, the Farreras family. He had brought it from Guinea. It was a very likeable parrot, but a bit of a rascal. Streetcar 36 began and ended its route right here in front of the store. The conductor and the ticket collector would come in for coffee until the inspector blew his whistle to give the street-car the go-ahead. For a time, the whistle blew quite abruptly; the conductor and the collector would have to rush through their coffee and leave without paying to get back to streetcar 36 and take off, while the inspector would get annoyed that they'd left without him giving the official order. It took a while for them to discover that it was the parrot whistling. Its imitation was so perfect, and caused so much confusion, that the streetcar supervisor forced the store's owners to keep the bird inside."

"That poor parrot!" I exclaimed.

"Oh shush! It had such a mouth! And don't think it died of sadness, no ma'am: it lived until 1992, the year of the Olympics. It's embalmed in its cage, right in La Licorería. You can stop by and see it if you'd like."

As I was leaving the shop, I turned around to look at the lettering on the entrance: *El Lloro del 36* (*The Parrot of 36*). The shop doesn't exist anymore, just La Licorería; after Mr. Farreras's death, the women of the family rented the storefront and ended up closing it after a bit. They complained that it was too much to handle. Later, I stopped in to see the story's protagonist. It was a gray parrot, pretty big, with a mischevious face. They'd put a little hat on its head that looked like the inspector's, and a whistle hung around its neck.

There was also another story involving the parrot that nobody liked to mention: Twenty years ago, on a Sunday morning around breakfast time, with the store packed with customers, a man with a hunting rifle came in, walked toward the bar, and, without a word, unloaded two shots point blank in the stomach of a customer who had been peacefully drinking the house vermouth. The parrot must have been traumatized: first, being shut in, and then this event. I imagine that its larynx would have dedicated itself to brilliantly mimicking the two shots and terrifying the neighborhood. And I say *I imagine* because this wasn't anything the clerk told me; it was kind of taboo, as I discovered along the way, and it also led me to my first case.

I returned to my office thinking about the parrot.

Since I left the department—the police department, and the only job I've ever quit (all the others have asked me to leave)—my detective business has been my sole means of support. It didn't occur to me to do anything else; I don't know how to do anything else. At first, I thought of starting a GLBT-friendly agency. Since the passage of the same-sex marriage laws, a new market niche has opened up and specialization always guarantees a steady clientele. It's the usual: inheritance hassles, infidelity, divorce . . . With so much desire to go mainstream, they behave in every way like traditional couples. But I also feared that specialization might close some doors, and my priority is eating. I decided not to promote myself explicitly on my business card or on the door, but I did send out information to all the gay hangouts and organizations, web pages, and businesses, as well as all the neighborhood shops and strategic locations such as the courts, the unemployment office, and the bingo palace. G&R Detectives uses the initials of both my last names. But this way it makes it look like there are at least two of us.

That morning, after chatting with the clerk at El Lloro del 36, I got my first case. Around eleven-thirty, I received a call from a woman wanting my services; her voice was so sensual, it gave me goose bumps. It was certainly an intriguing voice. Since my office was a mess and something told me this potential client came from a good family, I decided to meet her elsewhere.

"If it sounds good to you, we can meet in a half hour in the patio at El Tío Che, in front of the Alianza Casino. I'll be carrying a copy of El País."

Without a doubt, El Tío Che had the best Cuban milkshakes around, creamy and with lots of cinnamon. The real Tío Che was originally from Valencia and passed through Barcelona on his way to America, but he missed the boat, and while waiting to catch the next one, he began selling his concoction. His shakes became so popular that he decided to stay in Poble Nou. On one of those afternoons when I was just hanging out in the neighborhood, the owner went on and on about it.

I was sucking on the slender sugarcane, forcing the sweet liquid into my mouth, when I saw a riot of curls, more fanning out than falling, and a huge pair of sunglasses in the middle. That couldn't be her, I thought, and then I watched—the little piece of cane stuck on my lip—as she walked directly toward me. An enigmatic face, with an overall feline aspect. Beautiful and tall. Like she'd just stepped out of a Botticelli.

What Diana Gallard needed seemed simple: she wanted me to protect a woman from a possible threat. Twenty years ago, this woman's husband had discovered she had a lover, had gone to look for him, and then shot him twice in front of a good number of people and a foul-mouthed parrot. Now he was getting out of jail, and the woman's niece—that is, this riot of curls—was afraid he would come for her. It was a well-founded suspicion, given the man had lost half his life due to that infidelity.

"Give me more details," I said.

"My aunt's husband was very jealous, and he'd already spent a good deal of time following her movements. Every afternoon, she'd go to a little house on Fernando Poo Street, where a couple, who they were both friends with, used to live. I think he also found some of her love letters and poems. One Sunday morning, he got his hunting rifle, went to La Licorería on Taulat Street, and . . . you know the rest."

La Licorería on Taulat Street, of course, I thought at once, but I was less struck by the coincidence than by the fact that the clerk had so quickly shared the story about the streetcar while keeping mum about this one. In any event, the story had finally reached me, and I needed to decide now whether I was going to deal with it or not. It was more of a case for a bodyguard than a detective. Still, I didn't think I could say no to my first case and, to be honest, I thought it would be stupendous to work for so fantastic a woman.

"So it's just keeping an eye on her?" I asked to confirm. "I only say this because sometimes I have very complicated cases and every once in a while it's good to get a simple one."

I had to make her think the agency worked at full tilt, and the truth is when I was on the force I did have very complicated cases.

I think it was when she responded that I noticed something for the first time. "Yes, just watch her," she said in a very low voice, so much so that I understood it only because of the body language that went with it. Of course, I didn't give it any importance then.

Before heading back to the office, I decided to take a walk along the seafront, between the beaches of Bogatell and Mar Bella. A stroll by the ocean always helps me concentrate, going over the facts in my head and coming up with a strategy. I ended up at Chiringuito del Moncho's and decided to have some chipirones and patatas bravas.

Diana Gallard had insisted she didn't want me to do anything about the man, just to keep my eye on the woman. "Don't lose sight of her," she'd pressed. And her voice was so quiet this time, I had to ask her to repeat it. And her insistence bothered me. I don't like to take orders, and when it comes to my cases, I like to figure out the tactics myself. But keeping in mind that I didn't want to get too tied up, and that I wanted to keep my client happy, I decided to follow her instructions. Although I didn't simply give in either. I called my friend and former assistant, Dos Emes (Two Ms—a pseudonym I gave her out of discretion, because she was still on the force), and asked her for details about the incident from twenty years ago.

"I'll look up the files," she assured me.

The next day, I posted myself in front of one of the buildings on Paseo Calvell at eight in the morning—it was the second building just off La Rambla de Poble Nou. At nine-thirty I went up to see the woman I was protecting, armed with a solid excuse.

"Good morning, ma'am. Acoustic inspection."

When you enter a home early in the morning, you usually find the wife in a robe or wearing an apron. But this woman was dressed to leave and was even lightly made up. She was in her late sixties and in good shape, though her expression was a little hostile.

She was suspicious from the go but I was convincing: "We're testing the levels of noise pollution in the neighborhood." I showed her a multiuse ID which I'd made myself. "If the noise in your home is greater than sixty-five decibels, the city has resources to assist with soundproofing. You know . . . double-glazed windows, cork reinforcement for the walls. May I come in to measure the sound?"

My purpose was simple: to see the woman up close so I'd recognize her and be able to follow her, and to get any kind of clue about her life. I also wanted to gain her trust, just in case I had to intervene later. A city inspector roaming the neighborhood can pop up anywhere without raising questions.

I pulled a walkie-talkie out of my bag and went through the whole apartment, focusing it this way and that, making it emit occasional sounds. It was a small apartment, probably no more than fifty square meters, with two bedrooms, a living room, kitchen, and bathroom; each room was miniscule. The terrace was square and overlooked the sea.

"You've done well since the cleanup, haven't you?" I said, trying to connect with her. "Have you lived here long?"

"All my life," she answered drily.

I knew those apartments had been built in the '50s by the city's housing department. Back then, Mar Bella beach was full of outdoor bars and, when the weather was pleasant, the neighborhood residents would gather there. But little by little, the space between the kiosks and the train tracks was taken over by little shanties that were washed out to sea on more than one occasion. During the next few decades, the beach became a great dump, with equal parts garbage and seashells. It was a black-and-white landscape in which only flames from the burning trash could be distinguished. It was the perfect place for metal scavengers, the homeless, and lonesome souls. The human and urban panorama eventually changed the way it always has in this city: with an extraordinary event. The '92 Olympic games brought color back to the neighborhood. It was completely transformed. Where factories had idled, parks and luxury apartments were built; some were turned into civic centers, like Can Felipa. They buried the tracks, cleaned the beaches, and built a sea walk; the day they opened La Rambla down to the water, people came down in a mad rush, like a procession, as if the way to illumination had been revealed. What had been a nest of shanties facing a gray ocean and isolated by the train tracks became a high-end neighborhood. And the modest building in which this woman had lived her entire life quintupled in value.

The interior of the home, however, did not appear to have gone through any modifications and still had the rancid air of the '60s; there was a deer scene overlooking the dining room, flowered wallpaper, faded tiles, and Formica furniture in the kitchen . . . as if time had stood still. There were also several ancient photos, but none showed a masculine presence that might be her jailed husband. I wasn't surprised.

The inspection completed, I said goodbye to the woman, headed out to the stairwell, and went up the last leg to the roof where I found the perfect watchtower. I pulled out a book, something light, and began to read: *The Intersection of Law and Desire* by J.M. Redmann.

Midmorning, the elevator stopped on the top floor and someone knocked on the door of the woman I was protecting. She was approximately the same age, and was dressed very simply in dark slacks and a linen jacket; she had gray-streaked hair that had been styled at a beauty salon. She went in and neither of them reemerged until the first hour of evening. I began to think this was going to be a very dull case.

At around four-thirty, a little after the end of the after-lunch soap on the Catalan network, they finally left the apartment. They strolled down La Rambla casually, arm in arm, looking like widows of a certain age who keep each other company. I followed them to El Surtidor bakery, well known for its coca de forner bread. During the stroll, they'd greeted several people along the way with a slight nod of the head and a cursory "buenas tardes." Soon they emerged from the bakery with pieces of coca de forner in their hands and I watched as they retraced their route until they got to the first rotunda, where they said goodbye with kisses on both cheeks. My protected woman did not go out again.

Yes, yes, a real simple case. And better yet: the next day, case closed. The woman's husband, the ex-convict who'd done time for the murder of her lover, had fallen to the Ronda del Litoral from one of the pedestrian bridges and thus ended his miserable life. Good thing he threw himself, I thought, because if it had been the woman I was protecting who'd pushed him, who knows what kind of future I would have had.

When I got the check from Mrs. Gallard, I told myself it

wasn't bad at all for my first case, although I was a little sorry about such a hasty ending, especially because I wouldn't have any more contact with her.

"It's a shame what happened, but now there's nothing to fear," I said.

"No, no, no—it isn't a shame," she replied.

"Excuse me?" Once more her voice was so tenuous I could barely hear her. I remember I got a little worried: maybe my ears were stuffed up.

"He was a despot," she said. "He would have gone after her for sure."

The patio at the Catamarán was quiet at that hour of the morning. A group of tourists strolled along the beach, and on the path, cyclists and runners crossed each other in opposite directions. It was a sunny day, windless, the sea as calm as a lake, and there was that woman who provoked a flurry of emotions whenever she was in front of me. She was intense, out of reach, and she wrapped me up in a fog. And she was imperfect: her nose was too big, her mouth too straight. That's what made her truly beautiful. I thought it was a real tragedy to never see her again.

"You don't need me anymore," I said, with just the slightest tone of disappointment.

She responded with a firm "No," and blinked behind her dark glasses while her long hands showed off three rings, one an antique, and a finger touched the edge of the glass in which the ice from a martini was slowly melting.

The ex-convict's accidental death seemed straightforward. Apparently, he was blind drunk as he headed to the Ronda, so he probably slipped. It had been eleven o'clock at night, when there's scarcely a soul around. There were no witnesses. He fell like a sack and was run over by a truck. Still, the idea of suicide, or less likely, that someone had pushed him, hadn't been entirely ruled out. The police completed the task of investigating without too much fanfare. Obviously, they interrogated the widow: if there was a possible suspect, it was her, but she had an alibi, and a very good one; I actually corroborated it. After a few days, it was confirmed that it had been an accidental death and that was that, case closed.

But I resisted the idea of having to stop seeing such an extraordinary woman. I guess I could say that my bloodhound instincts made me think something was off, that if it was a puzzle, it had missing pieces; I knew from my time on the force that all cases are like puzzles. But that wasn't what brought me back on the case. I was crazy to see her again, to reveal the enigma in her sensuous voice, to ask her to dinner, and . . . well, to shamelessly throw myself at her. Yet I hadn't found an excuse to see her until Dos Emes pointed out an important detail: the companion of the woman I was protecting, the lady from the afternoon prior to the ex-convict's death, was the widow of the man killed twenty years earlier in La Licorería.

"I was going over the file to get information for you when I noticed the coincidence," explained Dos Emes. "Everything happened so quickly I didn't have a chance to tell you before. To be honest with you, this death smells fishy."

"Fishy! Fishy!" I was furious. "What's the connection? The two women must have become friends after the tragedy."

"But, boss, doesn't it strike you as weird?" Even though I'm not her supervisor anymore, she's continued to call me *boss*. "Would you become friends with the woman who was your husband's lover, whose husband was killed by your husband?"

"What a mess!" I said. "But I don't know. For starters, I don't have a husband . . ." At that moment I realized I had the perfect excuse to see Diana Gallard again. "You're right," I added very quickly. "I'll call my client and ask her to clear up a couple of murky points about the case."

Late that afternoon, we met at the casino; this time I thought it was important to meet in a quiet place.

"What's there to clear up?" she asked, trying to mask her evident irritation.

"Did you know your aunt and her lover's widow are friends?"

Her voice changed again. "What's so strange about that?"

"Girl, you don't become friends with the woman who rolled around with your husband—the husband later killed by *her* husband!"

"Perhaps grief brought them together."

"What was that?"

"That maybe grief brought them together," she repeated, a little forcefully.

"Yes, that's exactly what I was thinking."

I have to confess, I really didn't want to work this angle. For me, the case was closed. Dos Emes is finicky, and the more I looked at Diana Gallard, the more I was attracted to her. That's why I soon changed the conversation and invited her to dinner at the best restaurant in the neighborhood.

"Do you know Els Pescadors?" It's an old-style bar with a kitchen, which has done very well thanks to a group of famous theater people, and has been turned into a fancy eatery on a charming plaza untouched by time, with three beautiful bella ombres trees for shade. "It's got the freshest fish in town, artfully cooked . . . By now you must know the quality of Catalonian cuisine."

I don't know why she accepted. The easiest thing would have been to disappear; I've always wondered if that was part of her strategy. After all, what could Diana Gallard see in me but a nobody who thinks of herself as a Miss Marple. You have your complexes, and at a certain age you know your possibilities and your limits—which doesn't mean that every now and then I don't get carried away by naïve dreams. In any case, the truth is that I very much enjoyed the dinner. We talked about her life and mine, what we liked, and though she was somewhat restrained, I got the feeling she had a good time. I think if that hadn't been for the case, she probably wouldn't have let slip a confession.

"I've lived in Florence since I was very little and the woman you protected isn't my aunt but my mother."

"Good god! Then the deceased . . . I'm so sorry."

"My mother sent me to Italy to live with her sister so that I'd be free of him."

"And when they jailed him, why didn't you come back?"

"I was an adolescent and it's not good for a kid to have her father in jail for murder."

I understood that, just as I understood why she wouldn't feel any special affection for her real father.

"My parents are in Italy," she said. "I've always stayed in contact with my biological mother. She's been honest with me; she's never lied to me."

"That's why you wanted to protect her now."

"She deserved it."

Given the serious turn the evening had taken, I didn't think it appropriate to suggest spending the night together. I've always been a little dumb about these things. And anyway, she was leaving for Italy the next day and I wouldn't see her again. In the end, the feeling you get for somebody you meet one day and instantly traps you, that desire to please them, to protect them, to care for them—it has no future. So . . . I contemplated her imperfect beauty one last time: the too-straight mouth, the too-large nose, and I thought: she hired me, I've done my duty, she paid me well, and that's the end of the story, with a wonderful meal and a kiss on the lips—the way you always say goodbye to impossible loves.

The next day, Dos Emes came to see me in my office. She was wearing her Mossos d'Esquadra police uniform and had that Colombo face she gets when she's onto something important.

"It's just that, it's what I said, boss, it smelled bad to me. I've been investigating and what I've found out is quite surprising."

"Whatever it is, Dos Emes, it's nonsense. And you watch too much *CSI*."

"No, boss, really! There's stuff here that will make your head spin. The two women are getting married!"

"What two women?"

"The widows . . . the widow of the murdered lover and the widow of the guy who died on the Ronda. Their names are in the registry, the wedding's next week. I found out by accident. I had to go to court to check all the files on a forgery case and there it was, their marriage document. Apparently, grief really did bring them together."

Now it really stunk. This was definitely a puzzle now and the missing pieces were starting to turn up. Dos Emes has a special talent for that.

"Boss, I have a feeling they didn't become friends after the tragedy but that they were friends before . . . and much more than friends. In the file there are copies of love letters that the murderer's widow received. They're signed with the initials

R.M. The assassin's widow and the friend of the woman you were protecting is named Rosa María. Everything fits. Imagine what it would mean to them if that guy were free. And the dead guy's cell had a call from an unknown number, from a phone card. My theory is that someone called and asked to meet him and—"

"He had a lot of alcohol in him," I interrupted. "The most likely scenario is that he slipped and fell."

"Precisely—with so much alcohol in him, it wouldn't be at all difficult to give him a little push and help him into the abyss. We'll also never know if he was hit in the head because the truck that ran him over fractured his skull. What can I tell you? The whole thing bothers me."

As usual, Dos Emes was right. Everything fit. In fact, the husband had suspected that his wife was cheating on him, and he was correct, but what he couldn't imagine was that his wife's lover was not a man but a woman. It must not have been difficult to find the rendezvous place, the little house where the couple used to live. For him, the rest held no mystery: if she was seeing someone, it had to be him, the other man, regardless of the initials on the letters; after all, clandestine lovers need to protect themselves. He went looking for the guy at the bar and blasted two shots straight into his belly. After that, the two women were set free. One dead husband, the other in jail, and a daughter in Florence; there was no obstacle to their relationship except the neighborhood itself: the people and what they'd say. They continued their love affair in secret. But the killer was going to be set free soon. Would he realize his mistake? The best plan was to eliminate him.

"But it wasn't either of them. They both have alibis and then there's my testimony."

"I know," lamented Dos Emes, and with a hint of cynicism

she quickly added: "And, of course, there's no other suspect."

I wondered, did Diana Gallard have an alibi? Why did she hire a detective instead of letting the police know about the possible danger to her mother? Had they spoken? Had they planned it together?

"Not that I know of, and anyway, what can I tell you? Nobody's going to ask questions. Let's let those two enjoy the last years of their relationship in peace, don't you think?"

Dos Emes sighed. "You said Diana Gallard returns to Italy this afternoon?"

"That's what she told me."

"And you don't plan to speak with her again?"

"What for?"

She looked at me with that face of hers that says, *Boss, I know you*, then sighed again. "Well . . . to find out, for example, if she's coming back for the wedding, although I'm certain that she won't. It's going to be conducted with absolute privacy. You'll see."

And, yes, I spoke with her, but only on the phone. I called her on her cell just before she boarded her flight. She was already at the airport. I'd returned to the patio at Catamarán and I was looking out at a serene ocean. I was trying to imagine it when it was more of a dung heap than a beach. I also tried to imagine the lives of those two women during the dictatorship, and in the post-Franco era, and through the transition. A secret kept in the deepest closet until there were no more obstacles. Their lives had changed just like their neighborhood, except that they were forty years too late. To reopen the case, interrogate Diana Gallard, and complete the puzzle would be to reimpose a black-and-white existence on the three of them.

I told her what we'd discovered (well, not me, it was Dos

Emes, but I didn't point that out). I told her the police were considering reopening the case.

"It's possible they may want to question you," I added, "but don't worry—in my statement I mentioned that you were with your mother that night. They'll probably drop it when they see that."

"Thanks," she said in that voice so low you almost couldn't hear it, like she always did when she was saying something compromising.

Planes were flying low, toward the horizon, en route to the airport. It was easy to imagine tourists and other visitors looking out the windows, contemplating the towers in the Olympic village, the new buildings, the port, the beaches . . . I wondered how many of those eyes realized that not so long ago, the neighborhood didn't exist in Technicolor.

IN THIS WORLD, AND AT THE TIME MERCEDES DIED[1]

BY LOLITA BOSCH

Sant Gervasi

I t wasn't like this in Barcelona in 1959[2]: on Saturday, September 12[3], the disfigured corpse of "a very well-dressed"[4] man was found in a Mexico City canal. Not far from there, "a radio cable electrocuted a little girl who was playing with her dolls. The little girl, who was one and a half years old, sustained the shock in her neck," ten thousand kilometers from Barcelona.

Fifty years ago, fifty years from me.

Two decades after Francisco Franco rose against the legitimate republic, won the Spanish Civil War, and imposed a

---

[1] For Héctor Tenorio Muñozcota, a friend.

[2] Barcelona had already been occupied for twenty years by illegitimate Francoist forces who had usurped power from the republic after three years of civil war. The world was a gray place, and the neighborhood of Sant Gervasi, where the protagonist of this story comes from, was a repulsive place, for more than any other reason because it always stayed exactly the same. It was the same no matter what. Seemingly safe, bourgeoisie, flexible. Everything was understood. It was very similar in its warmth, its tranquility, and its silence to many other neighborhoods in other cities in the world. This is the main setting for this story, though war, exile, and fascism have expelled it very far away from itself. Now Sant Gervasi is in Mexico. At the time of the story, Barcelona was both here and there. Sant Gervasi was a place divided by those who left and those who stayed: twenty years after a war between brethren.

[3] Ten years after Germany declared itself the Federal Republic of Germany.

[4] Unless it says otherwise, all the quotes are from the Mexican newspaper *El Universal*. They come from the B section published between September 14–20, 1959.

fascist regime that would cover the entire country with a gray darkness that would blur everything.

On Sunday, September 13, 1959, a day before vacation started at the Universidad Nacional Autónoma de México, a Soviet rocket sped to the moon at three thousand kilometers per second. That same day, just as the patriotic celebrations to honor the Child Heroes[5] began, the newspapers proclaimed that there would not be a scarcity of tortillas during the strikes in nearby Mexico City.

The next morning, September 14, 1959, Russia confirmed its rocket landed on the moon, though the United States denied it.[6] Spain sided with the U.S., of course, because in the fascism of our youth, communism was a social cancer. And while the two countries spent the day arguing, with Barcelona's population unable to listen in on the arguments, a literacy campaign was launched in the Mexican state of Guanajuato and three notices appeared in the papers honoring Mr. Ricardo Ochoa Faist, head of public relations for Gillette Mexico, a European business. Abroad, Indonesia's attorney general was arrested and accused of being a communist. There were tributes to Simón Bolívar in Caracas, London observed Anti-Nuke Week, and the Brazilian army threatened to expropriate cattle if the meat supply wasn't reestablished. In Mexico City, America's soccer team beat Atlante 0 to 1. And in Barcelona, ten thousand kilometers from the Mexican capital, two weeks by boat, fifteen hours by plane including the layovers,

[5] The name given to six of the cadets who fought in defense of Chapultepec Castle during the War of Intervention against the United States (1847–1848). Their names, which we can all recite from memory, are Agustín Melgar, Fernando Montes de Oca, Francisco Márquez, Juan de la Barrera, Juan Francisco Escutia, and Vicente Suárez. The cadets' deaths, like so many other historic events, are enveloped in all sorts of legends.

[6] Both countries were right, though neither ever acknowledged this. In fact, the space satellite Lunik 2, which had left earth September 13, 1959, with the goal of landing on the moon, crashed into the Sea of Serenity. So, in a way, it did get to the moon. But it didn't actually land.

forty years of dictatorship, an infinite political distance, Barça scored four goals against Bilbao's Atlético.

Final score: 4 to 1, much emotion, Catalonian, restrained at the start of the playoffs. A sigh.

A little bit of a breather for Barcelona.

Joy in the transported neighborhood of Sant Gervasi in Mexico City.

On September 15, as Khrushchev[7] was flying to the United States and the world debated the truth regarding the Soviet rocket's moon landing, international legislation sought to establish rights to the moon to avoid old conflicts, Mexico was celebrating its national holidays, and a two hundred–kilo tusk from some prehistoric animal was discovered in the Olive Valley in Chihuahua.

An intact souvenir from a disappeared world.

Two days after the national holidays[8] and the subsequent hangovers, on September 18, 1959, Khrushchev condemned capitalism "but tasted and enjoyed it," 1,500 candidates for parliamentary office presented themselves in Great Britain, and typhoon Sara left behind "a wake of death and destruction" on American shores.

Nothing happened in Barcelona because there, or here,

---

[7] Nikita Sergeyevich Khrushchev was born April 15, 1894, in the mining village of Kalinovka, and died September 11, 1971, in Moscow. At twenty-three, he had joined the Bolshevik Revolution of 1917. And from that point on, he fought with the Red Army during the Civil War (1918–1920), had a political career in the Ukraine, was first secretary for the Moscow region and the Ukraine, tried to suppress Ukrainian nationalists, directed resistance against the Germans during World War II (1939–1945), and was elected prime minister of the U.S.S.R. He used his power to reconcile with Tito's Yugoslavia, to break with Mao Zedong's China, to settle Siberia, and to aid the Hungarian government against an anticommunist uprising. In 1962, he was accused of encouraging a cult of personality, just as had happened with Stalin, and he was expelled from the Communist Party and forced to resign from his post.

[8] Since 1825, September 16 has been officially celebrated as the beginning of Mexican independence: El grito.

the world was turning more and more into a place like any other.

And abroad, in spite of the Republican efforts to take Barcelona and Catalonia in a journey to exile, everything was being transformed.

The world was lying in wait.

And on the following day, September 19, 1959[9], as Khrushchev proposed retiring all the world's armies in four years and Mexico debuted a new system to light public areas in the capital, Barcelona continued slowly darkening. It was turning into something opaque, hermetic, authoritarian, and fascist that was getting harder to move away from by the minute. It was harder to feel safe. It was more unimaginable to flee, to fly, to escape.

Francoism had been in power twenty years, which is why one Barcelona remained living there and another had left. And this story[10] is about a famous crime in Catalonian high society, abroad. The one in the other Barcelona, in the other Sant Gervasi, so cozy and pleasant, which had needed to escape.

But then, on September 20, 1959[11], in the Mexican newspaper *El Universal*, a woman named Amalia published her recipes for pastries to accompany tea: marion cookies, nut pastries, almond croissants, and tropical bread. A woman named Amalia published a breath of fresh air in the midst of all that reality and alienation.

A pause. A cookie + a hot sip.

---

[9] Twenty-six years later, in 1985, an earthquake shook Mexico City, killing between ten thousand and forty thousand people.

[10] Lolita Bosch: "In This World, and at the Time Mercedes Died" ("En este mundo y en aquel tiempo en el que murió Mercedes").

[11] Ten years before Argentina had satellite communications, and twenty years before Bokassa I was defeated in what is today the Central African Republic.

Slurp. Napkin. Thanks.

Just as the press confirmed that field mice were devouring babies in Mexican towns, it also reported that in Santa Cruz de Juventino, Guanajuato, a little girl named Elsa Medina Huerta had died: Elsita.

Amen.

Amen for this world, and for that time in which Mercedes Cassola died; she was born long before Francoism, long before the war, long before the republic, exile, the frozen world in which both of us were born that was what Sant Gervasi had become, and which she took with her ten thousand kilometers away.

Amen for Mercedes Cassola, who had to leave the sunny city in which she was born.

Twice as close to me.

And amen for this world, and for that time in which Mercedes Cassola died so far from home and from how things might have been. Amen at last for Mercedes Cassola, far from History and from the inertia of the Barcelona neighborhood in which she grew up, and in which she lived through the war, and from which she escaped when they locked her in and she realized that she had to leave because she wouldn't be able to do so later. Everything would turn into Mary Nothing-Going-on-Here Poppins. Instantly, her world would be closed off. Asphyxiating. Claustrophobic. Constantly the same. Repetitive. The environs kept purifying itself until it turned into the placid neighborhood it had been before, and which it wanted to be after the war, and even later: today. A peaceful and quiet neighborhood in which its inhabitants took refuge when Barcelona was under siege. Even though today, again, the wind whistles between streets, parks, balconies, houses, one-story buildings.

I was born in this neighborhood. And these continue to

be our streets, our parks, our balconies, our homes, our one-story buildings.

Not so before. Before me, fifty years ago, Sant Gervasi was an immovable place in which those who stayed wanted to believe in the feeling that they were safe. A beautiful Mary Poppins world in which things had only one meaning which defined their context, a world into which I was born eleven years later.

Then 1959 arrived.

That's when the Cuban Revolution triumphed and the first photos were taken of the dark side of the moon. Then—still 1959—Francoist forces celebrated twenty years in power, the United Nations declared the Rights of Children, the Inter-American Development Bank was established, and Sukarno[12] installed a dictatorship in Indonesia.

Boris Vian, Camilo Cienfuegos, Buddy Holly, and Lou Costello died.

But Robert Smith, Rigoberta Menchú, Jeanette Winterson, and Evo Morales were born.

In this world, at that time, Mercedes Cassola[13] died far from her home, from her past, and from the simple world that she'd left behind so as not to suffer within it. A world she'd wanted

---

[12] Ahmet Sukarno (Surabaya, 1901–Jakarta, 1970) founded the National Indonesian Party. As punishment for his nationalist audacity, the Dutch colonial authorities detained him and he spent two years in prison. In 1939, he was exiled to the island of Sumatra, where he was liberated by the Japanese in 1942, during one of the battles of World War II. When the conflict was over, he declared Indonesia's independence on August 17, 1945. And thus began a war against the "low countries" that wouldn't end until 1949, when Indonesian independence was finally recognized. In 1956, Sukarno suppressed all political parties, and he established a dictatorship in 1959 which he called *directed democracy*. In 1966, General Suharto removed him from power, then replaced him as president of Indonesia in 1968. Sukarno spent the rest of his days in isolation, under house arrest in Jakarta, where he died June 21, 1970, on the first day of summer.

[13] Almost fifty years ago.

to take with her when she left Sant Gervasi: leaving Barcelona.

This was ten years before the murder of Roman Polanski's wife in California[14].

In that world, and at that time, things happened this way: On September 13, 1959, Mercedes Cassola was killed in Mexico City in an eminently Republican neighborhood that could have reminded her of her hometown of Juárez in Mexico— "eighteen stab wounds made by a slender knife plunged from the tip to the bottom of the blade."[15] She lived in a house she owned on Lucerna Street, number 84-A[16], which would have reminded us of a building in her native Sant Gervasi, our Sant Gervasi, a solid and safe neighborhood that managed to be flexible enough to imagine itself in America, flexible enough to imagine itself in Mexico. Far from that broken neighborhood in Barcelona in which Mercedes Cassola got the impression that people were too much alike, more and more so all

[14] On an August night in 1968, Sharon Tate, wife of film director Roman Polanski, was having a party at her home with her friends Abigail Folger, Jay Sebring, and Wojciech Frykowski. All were brutally murdered by followers of Charles Manson; they called themselves *The Family*. Sharon Tate was eight months pregnant and the killers wrote the word *pig* with her blood on the walls. Charles Manson, who had been in and out of prison frequently over the previous eighteen years, had moved to San Francisco in 1968, where he found followers to make up *The Family*. Allegedly, among his closest followers was Dennis Wilson, one of the Beach Boys. In 1971, Charles Manson was sentenced to life in prison after the death penalty was abolished in California. Four years later, Lynette Fromme, another one of his followers, would try to assassinate Gerald R. Ford, president of the United States.

[15] From here on, unless noted otherwise, the material in quotations continues to refer to *El Universal* (see footnote number 4) but relates to the investigation by Eduardo Téllez, *El Güero*, a legendary crime reporter who worked at the time for the aforementioned newspaper.

[16] The house where Mercedes Cassola was killed was among those that collapsed during the earthquake that flattened Mexico City at 7:19 on the morning of September 19, 1985. In the place where it once stood, there's now a public parking lot, where it costs about twenty-five pesos an hour to park, or about two and a half dollars.

the time, and a feeling that Francoism was going to bury them up to their necks.

Especially before.

Because before, when Mercedes Cassola was born, before the war, before the dictatorship, and before exile, Sant Gervasi—especially Sant Gervasi—was a kind of "old neighborhood" that in Barcelona is referred to as a barrio-de-siempre, a forever kind of place: peaceful streets, families with familiar surnames, similar lives, parks with playgrounds, small hills that are really centuries-old private gardens, low buildings, open skies, guards keeping watch, solid steel fountains, trees. Kids.

A pleasant place. A peaceful world. Safe, pretty.

Time passed the same as always, because it was the only way everyone knew to feel safe. That *we* knew. Because what's certain is that we, all of us, aliens in a devastated Barcelona, were a little safer. A little farther away from that city depressed by the impunity of the fascist authorities which surrounded it with big, invisible eyes spying on everyone all the time.

Huge Eyes Watching Everyone.

But not Mercedes Cassola. She was able to leave at the right moment, to flee barefoot until she was found many years later by one of her two servants—María Luisa Monroy—when she went to wake her on the morning of September 14, 1959: "I awoke at six and went to the mistress's bedroom. I saw the light was on. I found it odd and thought she'd already gotten up. But when I went in the room, she was stretched out on the bed and covered in blood. I screamed in terror and Amelia came running. I told her I couldn't look anymore and we went out together. Amelia, who is braver, is the one who found the lifeless bodies."

Mercedes Cassola had been planning to travel that very

day to the United States[17]. Her brother Pompilio[18] had agreed to pick her up at seven p.m. to take her to Benito Juaréz International Airport in Mexico City, although he later told the authorities he had no idea his sister intended to fly with a companion that day.

They didn't know each other well. They were siblings, but different. Yes, they'd left Barcelona together, but for different reasons. Yes, they both missed the war. But Pompeu went to Mexico because he thought he could continue living his life there exactly the same way he had in Sant Gervasi. As if everything could be the same and he could be safe that way. Mercedes, too, but not in the same way. Mercedes left, not just by lifting her city by a corner and packing it all up, but because she wanted to shake things up. To discover the empty spaces she'd missed. To win back the destiny she'd lost in the war. To build a world. To make plans, with her wings spread over Mexico, feathery and accessorized with bells. To

[17] A country that borders the Mexican Republic on the south and that bicultural space called Canada on the north. And whose president, Ike Eisenhower, visited the Francoist dictator, Francisco Franco, when only the Peronist authorities from Argentina, Salazar from Portugal, and, a little later, the Holy See, had done so. With this visit Eisenhower influenced the international community, which didn't take long to surrender, almost completely, before Franco's government. He was treated to a tribute during his visit to Madrid that included sixty thousand flags, twenty thousand posters in which he was shown alongside Franco, one million bulbs and 360 lights illuminating Madrid, and many wreaths of glory. They also made him honorary mayor of Marbella, and an honorable member of the Spanish Baseball Federation. Ike Eisenhower stayed at Moncloa Palace and dined with the dictator at the Palacio de Oriente, where Franco dared to say, "Our two countries are together at the front of peace and freedom."

[18] Pompilio is the translation of the Catalan name Pompeu, which is rarely used in Spanish. A fairly common name among Catalonians (in honor of Pompeu Fabra, Barcelona, 1868, exiled to Prada in 1948, an industrial engineer, the linguistic normalizer of Catalan and author of the reference dictionary *Diccionari general de la llengua catalana*, 1932). Pompeu also refers to one of the legendary kings of Rome and means "solemnity." Although some say it refers to the Sabine numeral *pompe*, or *five*. From this point on in the story, his name will appear correctly in Catalan.

draw Sant Gervasi from the sky and take refuge in it. Yet in America—here, she, it—all was different. More free. That's why, among the many things strewn across the house on Lucerna Street, there were two passports with American visas and this other information:

• *Mercedes Cassola Meler, 39, Barcelona, Spain, naturalized Mexican citizen, divorced, living at 84-A Lucerna Street.*
• *Ycilio Massine Solaini, 23, Uruapan, Michoacán, single, businessman.*[19]

The rest was a chaotic and incomprehensible mess, like so many other things: the phone line was cut, "various curiosity seekers managed to get in," a bag of jewels disappeared during the investigation, ashes were found on the dining room floor, "two open suitcases and all their contents thrown about the floor." And in the main bedroom—furnished with European wood like their native Barcelona home, although painted in tropical colors typical to Mexico's south—two lifeless bodies.[20] Far from everything.

María Luisa Monroy and Amelia Martínez Pulido, both twenty years old, had worked for a long time in Mercedes Cassola's home, and when they discovered the murders, they

[19] Ycilio Massine was the son of Doña Albina Solaini, who had been widowed a couple of years before when her husband went to Italy because of an illness and died on the operating table. Ycilio lived with his mother at 31 General Cano de Tacubaya Street; he'd dropped out of school and led a life that his relatives described as "not too decent." Although he claimed to be a carpet salesman, he was in fact unemployed. It was his mother who maintained the household, thanks to her job at a boarding house that primarily served Italian immigrants who came to this part of the Americas looking for work.

[20] Death: cessation or end of life. In traditional thinking, the separation of body and soul. (*Dictionary of the Real Academia Española, Vol. II*, Madrid, 1992.)

called a neighbor and then the police. Nobody wanted to touch the dead. Not without permission. Ycilio Massine had forty-seven stab wounds, almost all from the shoulders up, with three on the right arm and another on his belly. Mercedes Cassola was still in her negligee on the bed and had two rings on her fingers which the killer(s) apparently hadn't been able to remove. That's how the bodies were when they were transferred to the police department and then to Juaréz Hospital for an autopsy.

The bodies were transferred together.

Supervising the investigation was attorney Ana Virginia Rodríguez Miró[21] and her secretary, Armando Zamora Negrete. Only one suspect could be considered responsible for the murder at 84-A Lucerna Street: the victim's ex-husband, Felix Herrero Recalde. He was also Catalonian, also from Sant Gervasi, also a resident of Mexico, also far from home.

Also because of a lost war.

He was a man with whom Mercedes Cassola shared origins, codes, wings.

But it was just a theory. And Pompeu Cassola himself rejected it that very morning, after he went to the police when he got to his sister's house and saw the bodies and the authorities and the two maids and the neighbor who didn't want to touch anything.

After a few days, Felix Herrera Recalde himself proved the theory wrong, since he had been visiting in Catalonia when Mercedes Cassola was killed and returned to Mexico to make a statement to the police.

[21] When it comes to the murder of a Catalonian, it's hard for the surname of the chief of investigation not to remind us of Joan Miró (Barcelona, 1893– Palma de Mallorca, 1983), painter, sculptor, printmaker, and ceramicist. Considered a master of surrealism. According to André Breton, "the most surrealist among us." His work, according to Miró himself, was about "killing, assassinating, erasing" the formal approaches to painting in order to find a new, contemporary form of expression.

He declared he had returned to Mexico of his own accord.

He said he hadn't killed anybody.

He said he had returned to his native city for the first time with a reentry permit and now had to leave again.

After their separation, Mercedes and Félix had not hated or resented each other, or felt anything close to that. They'd simply divorced ten years before and he'd moved to the port of Veracruz. They both had great fortunes and neither of them had any desire to kill anyone.

They'd both fled from death.

When Mexico opened the door of exile to them, together, Mercedes and Félix made a great deal of money in construction. And though they divorced later, they divided everything equally and remained friends.

Friends who led different lives.

Nothing more.

There was nothing else to it.

And now another pause, but without tea and cookies.

Another pause because the police really don't have a clue.

Negligence? Desperation? Indifference? Prejudice?

Later, they performed autopsies on the two corpses, together, at Juárez Hospital.

Then Mercedes Cassola's father went to Mexico to reclaim his daughter's body[22]. He was a gentleman from Sant Gervasi, who looked like those men who walk their dogs in private parks in the afternoons, who live quietly waiting for the world not to darken completely all of a sudden, for the

---

[22] Although there's no clear link between the two incidents, I'll add here that almost two years after the death of Mercedes Cassola, on May 2, 1962, somebody pushed her father at the corner of Insurgentes and Bajío, in the Roma neighborhood of Mexico City, at the very moment a truck was passing by. So it was that Mr. Cassola died in Mexico, run over by a truck, though I have no idea why he was there and what he was doing. In the end, Pompeu inherited all the family money. If any of you think

Mary Poppins Time to turn into a burst of light, to turn silent again, to turn away again from this absolute fear that anything can happen. He was a man who never managed to distinguish with any exactitude the Sant Gervasi that stayed behind from the Sant Gervasi that left, and which the government had allowed him to visit with a special permit so he could retrieve his daughter. Mercedes Cassola's father arrived in Mexico City a confused stranger, and waited for the autopsy report with the patience of a man who'd lost a war. Later, he sent his daughter home in a sealed coffin and buried her in the cemetery in her native city, our native city. The real neighborhood.

This was eleven years before me.

The discreet funeral consigned Mercedes Cassola to the orchard, the forest, the world, the garden from which it was a scandal to escape without seeming different.

The dead woman returned in silence: she was already home.

No obituary in her hometown paper, in our hometown paper. Not a word about Mercedes Cassola's death in America, nor in Barcelona. The daughter of the Cassolas died far away because she had business there with her husband; she was buried in Sant Gervasi because that was the place where she grew up, where she lived, and from which—in spite of the flexible wings with which she wanted to fly to Mexico with, taking her city with her, folded up and held by a corner—she couldn't leave. She couldn't escape from it.

And, now everything stops. Just like that, without a pause.

So that in spite of the time, this story, and her colorful wings, feathers, and bells, Mercedes Cassola ended up inheriting a tainted city, a wounded city, that same old neighborhood.

Alone.

this is enough to judge these two unsolved crimes, you're obviously within your right to do so. But as the narrator, I'd suggest that Pompeu's pain not be forgotten. And that stories without contradictions are incomplete.

There's practically nothing to add. The autopsy performed the morning after the murder—when they were finally able to get the two rings off Mercedes Cassola's right hand so they could give them to her father—only yielded two facts:

1) There were two different weapons used in the killings, of different sizes, and Mercedes died after she was knocked out. But not Ycilio Massine, no. That robust young man, the Michoacán-born son of Italians, fought for his life.

2) There were no signs of forced entry in the house. But Mercedes didn't appear to have any enemies in the family.

That's when, empty-handed, the police and the press visited El Frontón México[23]. In search of a social explanation to

---

[23] El Frontón México was built in 1929 and is considered one of the most beautiful buildings of the era. It's situated on more than three thousand square meters of land and has been the site of various world championships, including Pelota Vasca, martial arts, and the national boxing title, the Golden Belt. In 1939, it was the birthplace of the Partido Acción Nacional.

El Frontón closed its doors on October 2, 1996, after the site's operator, Miguel del Río—who owed over three million dollars for more than seven years of rent to the owner, Antonio Cosío Ariño—asked Ramón Gamez, the leader of the Sindicato de Trabajadores del Frontón México (STFM), the workers' union, to put off a strike so he could continue operating until an eviction notice arrived.

In May of the previous year, after the union's workers had decided to join the Confederación Revolucionaria de Obreros y Campesinos so they could rid themselves of their "charro" leader, the strike had ended and the workers symbolically gave the building back to its owner, who announced that he was going to remodel and open again. But the secretary of governance didn't renew the owner's sport and gaming license, a necessary requirement for El Frontón México to be able to operate. The workers begged the owner as well as those in the offices of the SEGOB (Secretaría de Gobernación) to get the license issued so El Frontón México could open its doors again. In the meantime, its facilities were ransacked and destroyed by thieves and the homeless, and water damaged its roofs, floors, and walls.

The building's interior now resembles a trash heap: broken furniture, take care of everything. It was a place where people went to have fun, where there were few prejudices, and where Mercedes Cassola, finally, looked like a fish floating in the stagnant lake that's hidden under Mexico City.

And even so, in that place taken advantage of by everyone: nothing. And in spite of the raids, the back-and-forth accusations, and the different connections published in the press every day, the crime committed against Mercedes Cassola and Ycilio Massine was eventually filed away for lack of evidence. Nothing came from the chauffeur named Clemente, who'd driven the couple from El Frontón to Lucerna Street the night of September 13, 1959, nor the young men of Italian lineage detained by the police in various raids, nor Mercedes's former lovers who might have been angry over losing the money and freedom that Mercedes had given them. Nothing.

The tips they got after the murders were useless.

And this is how occupied-Barcelona and that Mexico of another time tried to forget the 1959 crime. They buried it. Nonetheless, what happened at 84-A Lucerna Street had a deep impact on Mexican society, while the Francoist steel curtain was able to keep the story out of the press.

Now drawn to new headlines in the newspapers[24], the sad

---

cut cables, random clothing, gravel, and garbage, as well as gallons of paint thinner and gasoline covering the floors, which in some places are flooded due to leaking. Humidity has weakened the walls and most of the ceilings have come loose from their moorings. The marble floors in the lobby are flooded, and the Art Deco which distinguished it is gone. (Mael Vallejo, October 23, 2005: "Agoniza el Frontón México," *La Crónica de Hoy*.) As I write this, El Frontón México is still abandoned.

[24] After September 20, 1959, there was nothing published in the Mexican press about the double homicide. Following the description of the incident on the 14th, the rest were allegations: random tips, autopsy reports, interviews with those close to the deceased, and Doña Albina Solaini's sadness. Nothing else. The murder of Mercedes Cassola and Ycilio Massine was never solved. And their bodies, loveless I suspect, finally said their farewells: they buried Ycilio in Mexico and Mercedes was repatriated to the world from which she'd been expelled.

and violent deaths of the two lovers slowly disappeared from the public's attention.

Soon after, the bodies had already been separated.

Both were far from home.

A last pause: a minute of silence for the dead.

So, after all that, there was practically nothing. Later, later meaning now, later, after the bodies were no more, after I was born in Sant Gervasi and traveled to Mexico, after Francoism, dictatorship, exile, and those huge scissors which can cut off colorful wings with bells and feathers, the 1959 double homicide was revisited in three texts[25] (four counting this one)[26], and the Mexican writer Carlos Monsiváis turned it into one of those standard tales in the fight against homophobia in Mexico, a Let's-Not-Forget-How-Things-Really-Are-Here.

It started because Güero Tellez, the Mexican investigative reporter, said, "This type of crime, as we all know, is characteristic among homosexuals, whose passions are infinitely more robust than other people."[27] He concluded, "The answer might be the following: the killer's body type probably resembled Massine's, and he was prepared, with a different knife in each hand, so that it was probably easy for him to overpower Mercedes Cassola and her lover."

Everything was left like this: in the hate felt by a powerful and oblique homosexual octopus that extended its tentacles with a knife in each fist. An inhuman apparition that, in the final act, cuts up the bodies and writes something on the walls.[28]

[25] José Ramón Garmabella: "Reportero de policía, ¡el Güero Téllez!, ¿Quién asesinó a los amantes de Lucerna?"; Carlos Monsiváis: "La impunidad al amparo de la homofobia."

[26] Lolita Bosch: "In This World, and at the Time Mercedes Died" ("En este mundo y en aquel tiempo en el que murió Mercedes").

[27] José Ramón Garmabella: "Reportero de policía, ¡el Güero Téllez!"

[28] I haven't been able to find anything anywhere about the word, or words, that were supposedly written in blood at 84-A Lucerna Street in the early hours of September 13, 1959. Ten years later in California, Charles

Like what happened, years later, to Sharon Tate[29].

Unfortunately, the death of the lovers on Lucerna Street, Pompeu's exile, and the victim's father's patience, like a man who'd lost a war, were transformed into Let's-Not-Forget-How-Things-Really-Are-Here so that we could talk about the Big World Mercedes Cassola grew up in back in Barcelona. In Sant Gervasi.

She took the city with her, flying.

Amen for Mercedes Cassola.

Amen for Ycilio Massine.

And amen for us too, because we don't really understand what infuriated the killer(s), why the victims were judged so harshly by the authorities and the press, the pain of trying to dig out the truth that the parents of the victims had to deal with in that neighborhood where families all know each other, as was the case in Sant Gervasi, there in the heart of Barcelona. Amen because we don't know what Charles Manson's "family" was based on but we can follow the clues to the crime[30]. Until now. Until now, because we—those of us who

Manson's gang wrote *PIG* in large letters on the front door of the Polanski family home.

[29] Roman Polanski's wife.

[30] Charles Manson founded *The Family* in 1967, in Haight-Ashbury, San Francisco, two years before they killed Roman Polanski's pregnant wife. *The Family*, whose violent philosophy is still followed by some satanic worshipers, had no rules other than those imposed by Charles Manson, who had managed to pull together a group of devoted fanatics; he called himself Satan, Jesus, or God, without distinction. And *The Family* revered him as such: at his last trial, some of his followers told how they'd seen Manson bring a bird back to life after taking it in his hands and softly blowing on it.

During its first few years, *The Family* committed various murders that helped the group's leader polish his philosophy. And in 1969, Manson announced the coming of the Apocalypse: the time had come for the black race to rise against whites. In the end, only 144,000 survivors would remain, taking shelter in a subterranean world from which they could only emerge if led by a new global king: Charles Manson. This is how he are here—now know that Charles Manson was judged because of his philosophy, and that the crime committed against Mercedes Cassola and Ycilio Massine was, in turn, almost buried by prejudice.

Two prejudices: one in Mexico, the other in Barcelona.

So Mercedes Cassola lost twice.

As Carlos Monsiváis tells it, the case had so much resonance because of "the unique circumstance of a woman from Catalonian high society who lived as she pleased" during Francoist times. And so: reporters, agents, elected officials, and detectives all agreed—the victims deserved what they got. And so: amidst the thousands of murders of gay people, the public only remembers the case of this *fruit fly*[31] and her bisexual lover, the story told in lurid detail."[32]

This is what the Francoist authorities would have said: Why did she leave? She would have been safe here.

That was in 1959.

Mercedes Cassola dared to flee from the Sant Gervasi in which I was born eleven years later. In time, I too went to Mexico and then returned and wrote this story and understood that, unfortunately, time is implacable; I can't say any more.

(Silence.)

Time doesn't make the world a different place.

tried to convince various African Americans that they should embrace their destiny and kill whites.

[31] *Fruit-fly* is the name given to women who look for bisexual lovers in gay circles. In the '50s in Mexico, this was a very tight community "with its fashionistas, painters, jewelers, Porfirian landlords, movie stars, mid-level bureaucrats, writers, all determined to live as freely as possible. The police focused on that community, especially after they found out that Massine was a male prostitute" (Carlos Monsiváis, see footnote 32). That's something else we didn't know until now, but which hasn't made the crime committed on Lucerna Street seem any less terrible. The result is that the rest is just gossip and prejudice. The story just about ends here, except for one phrase.

[32] Carlos Monsiváis: "La impunidad al amparo de la homofobia."

That's why I searched the Barcelona telephone directory for some relative of Mercedes Cassola's whose tale might make it possible for me to finish this narrative[33] in a gentler fashion: bringing flowers to the dead, writing that I did in fact return. I realized that the crime against Mercedes and Ycilio can only be summarized like this: impunity, history, judgment, homophobia, freedom, fascism.

I look for Mercedes Cassola in Barcelona so I can take her away. Again, as if she were flying. I want to take her with me back to Mexico and hang her wings on the dead who we do remember.

The dead who did in fact receive pity.

But there's nothing, even though I did manage to find some Cassolas[34] in the city of Barcelona. And even though I visited their home in Sant Gervasi, I haven't come across anything, yet I've seen everything: and everything was practically the same. The same quiet place in which I grew up, in which she grew up. And when I stood there, in front of the Past, I didn't dare knock on the door to ask about a killing that took place more than forty years ago.

That's why I haven't said or written anything.

I returned home, where I went on the Internet to send this story exactly as it is[35]. Without a clear understanding of whether I had managed to open any locks to a spiraling world able to absorb everything. Without a sense of whether I had reached the exact point where the dead rest in This World and At That Time when Mercedes Cassola and Ycilio Massine died[36]. And thinking, in my heart of secret gardens, that

---

[33] Almost fifty years after the murders on Lucerna Street.

[34] Which means *saucepan* in Catalan, although I haven't found any metaphoric connection with the ideas or incidents in this story.

[35] www.mail.yahoo.com.

[36] It's possible that if I were to look over this text again, I might include another footnote. Nonetheless, I think those in the final version are

the world is like that sometimes, and that it stays that way in small spaces. There's nothing I can do about it.

And as I understand it, more or less, this continues to be a world without me.

Without any of us.

representative of its finality. So the only thing left, then, is to be grateful for your careful reading and to wish you a good day. Take care of yourself.

PART II

Sheltered Lives, Secret Crimes

PART II

SWEET CROQUETTE

BY DAVID BARBA

El Carmel

W hen I found out about the disappearance of Swiss gourmet Pascal Henry, I had no doubt that his body had become part of the larder for the liquid croquettes offered on the degustation menu at El Bulli. It happened June 12, 2008, when he went out to get his wallet and never came back for dessert; he left his hat, a notebook filled with gastronomic observations, and the bill, which was yet to be paid. He was never seen alive again.

I decided to investigate the crime the minute I read the article about it in *La Vanguardia* while I was having my breakfast of café au lait and a Chester cigarette at the Delicias bar, across the street from the Montaña Pelada. Later I took a walk on the hill in order to get the facts of the case straight, especially because I couldn't get that damned gourmet out of my head. Up there, I could sit and contemplate the city's putrid sky and delight in the Sagrada Familia's spires, the San Pablo Hospital watchtowers, the Cathedral's needles, and the rail tracks along the port, not to mention the swarm of phallus-like glass-and-steel towers which have, in the last few years, smudged the kind face of Barcelona that I've known since childhood.

Pascal Henry also had a kind face. I remember a picture of him next to chef Paul Bocuse, in which they're both smiling and a little flushed from wine, their cheeks so puffy that a couple of quick slices would have produced a pair of succulent pork chops. After all, meat is meat, and anthropology long ago proved that if we've put aside cannibalism, it's only because it's been turned into a cultural taboo. In my opinion, we humans will end up eating each other sooner or later, and we'll season the filets with fine herbs. We're all gourmets.

What I have in common with Ferran Adrià is that we were both born in a squalid neighborhood on the edge of Barcelona. As a kid, I also played with my chemistry set and my sister's toy kitchens. So, with a little bit of luck, I too could have become a star chef. Unfortunately, fate also bequeathed me a fine palette and a certain taste for exotic meats. And I say "unfortunately" because, instead of being born in the bosom of a bourgeois family from Guy Savoy's Paris, or Pierre Gagnaire's or L'Arpège's, I was born a boy in the Reyes Robledo family, an illustrious clan of short, pigheaded day laborers from the Cazorla Mountains, immigrants to Barcelona along with hordes of other cheap workers who came to fatten the industrious factories of Catalonia in the '60s. Here, in the Carmelo neighborhood, my parents opened a butcher shop on Santuarios Street, in the same place immortalized by Juan Marsé in *Últimas tardes con Teresa*, that famous ode to the neighborhood that was always my home, or, in other words, the vulgar place from which my restlessness rose. I'm not from here or there; just an anonymous charnego, that pejorative that so well captures the traditional disdain that tried-and-true Catalonians had for the descendants of Andalusians, at least until the arrival of all these blacks, Moors, Chinese, and South Americans who now make up the lowest rungs of our feverish and multicultural social ladder.

Yes, I'm a racist. But no one should confuse me with the usual sociological profile of the uneducated child of immigrants who embraces xenophobia. I studied Spanish philology at the Universidad Central. With a little bit of luck, I might have been able to avoid my fate among pork chops, but nobody opened that door for me. If I'd been more of a trouser snake with one of those girls from college, I might have carved out a future as a landlord. But I couldn't get rid of that outsider air about me and I preferred the comfort of marriage to Maruja, my lifelong sweetheart. When she was twenty-eight years old, she still had the big, perky tits I fell in love with; her ass was like a cow's, and it only got better and better over time, as the composition of her muscles swelled. And better yet, my fresh-faced girl made a Córdoba-style salmorejo sauce to die for. Too bad that someday she'd want more out of life.

Things went awry when they inaugurated the Juan Marsé Library a few steps from our house. Maruja signed up for a book club in which, inevitably, she discovered all of his novels. I suspect that quarrelsome charnego universe chock full of heroes made her reconsider our mediocrity. All of a sudden, she developed an enormous curiosity about the other face of Barcelona. She sought it out in novels like Eduardo Mendoza's *La ciudad de los prodigios*, Juan Miñana's *La playa de Pekín*, and Francisco Casavella's *El día del Watusi*, which had the same effect on her as Don Quixote on chivalry: it alienated her from our modest food business. I wasn't worried until the Sunday she didn't tend to the chicken roaster so that she could lay on the couch and read. Although it's true that it was our third week without a day off, I did think it was a bit much to simply declare, while painting her toenails a fiery red and never once lifting her gaze from a book of poems by David Castillo, that I shouldn't count on her help with the business anymore. What kind of intellectual crap had she begun to believe? Did she think books were going to put food on the table? I'd had similar thoughts when I graduated, when it still hadn't sunk in that everything was already foretold, and that in Catalonia, without the right surname or relative, you can't get very far. There's nothing worse than a cultured peasant, than being aware of the glass ceiling above your head that will impede all your professional advancement. At first, I went to all the publishing houses, bookstores, and cultural centers in the city. I must have handed out two hundred resumes, but it was futile. I gave up a year and a half later, thanks to my father, who never quite got over looking at me as if I were a lazy ass and reminding me of the security that came with inheriting the business. The day I decided to put on an apron, I also decided I'd never read another book.

Life went on, I kept cutting filets, until that notorious fall, when my stupid wife began wearing a Palestinian scarf, avidly watching Lorenzo Milá's newscasts, and supporting the gay marriage law, obviously under the influence of her new friends from the book club. It was just a short step from there to reading Manuel Vázquez Montalbán's work.

"What are you thinking?" I asked her one afternoon when I went upstairs wearing my bloody apron and found her working her back into some absurd yoga pose while reading the adventures of Detective Pepe Carvalho.

"I just want to get some culture," she answered. "It seems like all I do is go up and down the stairs from the house to the butcher shop."

Maruja had always read, but not much more than what was given as gifts to her parents, a pair of immigrants from Córdoba, and maybe a best seller by Dominique Lapierre or Jorge Bucay, and, inevitably, *The Da Vinci Code*, after which she began to show some bizarre tendencies like refusing to greet Don Victorino, the priest who married us at the parish of Mare de Déu del Coll.

"Maruja, I meant your back," I said, feigning concern. "You have scoliosis."

She shifted her body and brought her eyes up from *Los mares del Sur* like a cheap femme fatale. "Manolo, I'm going to study humanities," she spit at me.

Our marriage began to drift after the last New Year's Eve we spent with the family. My parents barely spoke—they never had anything to say aside from things like "Slice up two hundred grams of jerky" and "Debone some pig's feet." But Maruja, who'd always been our family's joy, didn't say a word either, and after we were done with our coffee, she had the nerve to go throw herself on the couch to read another one of her novels, while the rest of us had to deal with Spanish TV's New Year's Eve special with the comedy duo of Cruz and Raya. Every now and then, Maruja would smirk while we laughed heartily. But the worst came when it was time to unwrap the gifts and I found myself with a recipe book by Ferran Adrià in my hands.

"Let's see if you smarten up and get the business up to date," she said in a derisive tone.

"Now you're going to knock my cooking?"

"It's just that your ham croquettes are so common."

"What's wrong with my croquettes?"

"They're dry. I dare you to try making El Bulli's liquid croquettes."

This was too much. With a gesture that signaled I was offended, I went to my room, which upset my mother. At first, I just left Adrià's recipe book on the night table. But after a while, curiosity got to me and I broke my vow against reading to see what in heaven's name a liquid croquette could be. That recipe book was my undoing! Reading it robbed me of reason. I didn't understand a thing. All of a sudden, my world of oxtails, sausages, and veal steaks came crashing down faced under Adrià's techno-passionate cuisine, spherification with alginics, oysters with carrot, fake melon caviar, hot water gelatin dusted with agar . . . After going head to head with the ovens belonging to the messiah of modern liquidity, how could I continue the daily heresy of cooking dry croquettes? The first symptoms of depression arrived that spring.

The same day I was coming back from the doctor with a prescription for headache medicine and an unemployment certificate in my pocket, I ran into Maruja sitting on the windowsill, with her back up against a wall, her feet bare, and her thighs obscenely escaping from under her dress. She was so absorbed in her reading, she didn't even ask why I wasn't at work at the shop.

"What are you reading?" I only said this to break the ice.

"It's called *La lectora*," she responded enthusiastically. "It's by a friend from the book club. A genius! He even won a prize at the Semana Negra in Gijón. It's about a student in Bogotá who's kidnapped by a bunch of lower-class delinquents so she'll read them a book. It's because . . . they don't know how to read."

I was stunned. What was this bitch telling me? Couldn't she see she'd ruined my life? Hadn't she noticed me utterly defeated before the ovens, trying desperately, in vain, to copy the damned postmodern liquid croquette recipe? Why did she have to engage with me now, after months of ignoring me, just to tell me about some asinine criminal plot birthed in some third world hut in the twisted and odious mind of some Latin American?

Techno-passionate cuisine was my refuge as my marriage degenerated. I was soon making secret reservations at restaurants run by copycats of the star chef—and I discovered there were dozens of them, hundreds, most of whom destroyed the liquid croquettes as badly or even worse than I did. They all had something in common with me: they dreamed of setting foot one day in El Bulli, the exclusive restaurant on Cala Monjoi, which only serves eight thousand diners per season. My attempts to make a reservation were in vain. *We're sorry, please call again next year,* they'd tell me over and over. A wall of gourmets and half the world's plutocrats, all with wallets thicker than mine, moved in front of me. My frustration was growing at a dizzying rate and the headache medicine barely had an effect. It didn't take long for me to start drinking, and on more than one night I ended up sleeping it off at the bar counter, crying on the shoulder of some obese dropout from the culinary school.

One afternoon, everything came to a head. I had been strolling down Cala Monjoi, as I often did in those jobless days, so I could revel in the envy provoked by diners leaving El Bulli in their big cars, with a blonde as arm candy and a belly full of deconstructed tortilla española. I'd spent the afternoon planning to buy a rifle with a telescopic sight so I could fire above the diners' heads; later I thought an AK-47 might be a better way to get a table without a reservation, like a Vietnam vet, and I got so excited at the thought that I almost killed myself on the highway, pushing my old SEAT Panda to the limit of how fast it could go. As I sped up the Carmelo highway and turned toward my house, a certain scent of burnt lamb made me think it might be better if I stopped at the mechanic's on Santuarios to check the car while I calmed my nerves with a couple of drinks at the nearby bar, El Pibe.

I was attended to by a young indigenous man with lips as thick as Mallorcan sausages. He had an air about him like a juvenile delinquent and, given the tiresome salsa music that was spilling from the speakers, I figured he was Colombian.

"What's up, bro? The spark plugs are practically dead!" he declared after a simple peek at the engine. "I'll have it ready for you in a half hour."

I was on my way out the door when I happened to glance at the speaker delivering that relentless musical torture and saw a framed university degree, a master's in philosophy and letters from the University of Cartagena de Indias. Another aspiring South American intellectual working like a peon in Barcelona, I thought as my gaze moved around the mess in the office and bumped into a familiar-looking book under some papers. It was a copy of *La lectora*. That's when I realized the smell of burnt lamb wasn't coming from the engine but from my own head.

"Do you like to read, buddy?" the mechanic asked when he saw my eyes fixed on the book's cover. "I'll give you a copy of my novel. I just work here to put food on the table for my eight kids, but my real vocation is literature."

I left in a flash, with my stomach turning and the book in my hand. My wife was cheating on me with a South American mechanic with intellectual pretensions! That's the thing about Spain: you pick up a rock and uncover a writer underneath. We're a country of Quixotes, poisoned by novels. It starts by abusing literature and ends by cooking with liquid nitrogen.

After that terrible blow, I felt the moment had come for me to act but I contained myself: vengeance is best served cold, like a gazpacho frappé.

I came up with my plan that very night: the next day I drove my SEAT Panda to an isolated curve on Aguas Road. I walked down to a phone booth on Avenida de Vallvidrera and called the mechanic.

"Hello?"

"Don Sergio, my car stopped working again."

"Don't worry, buddy, I'll come get you right away."

Everything went according to my plan: I killed time smoking one Chester after another, looking out at the city's detestable new skyline, until, forty-five minutes later, the indigenous guy showed up, loudly honking the horn of his rickety tow truck.

"Okay, bud, we'll see what happened to your ride."

It was getting dark as he stuck his nose in the engine. A car went by, then another. Then it was deadly quiet. I took the knife for slicing ham from the car, hid it behind my back, and slowly approached. I'd lifted my arm toward his neck when, all of a sudden, a car flew past at top speed and blinded me with its lights. I couldn't repress a hysterical scream. My heart was beating out of my chest and, with my nerves on edge, the knife fell to the ground. The Colombian, alarmed, jerked his head up and hit it on the hood of the car.

"Goddamnit! That hurt! Why are you screaming?"

I realize I lost it at that point. I should have gone for the knife and done things right, but, afraid I'd lose the advantage I had with the element of surprise, I decided to slam the hood down on his head with all my might. The first blow smashed his face against the engine. But it wasn't enough: I pounded him fifteen, twenty times, until he quit screaming and ceased moving. I'd made enough noise to wake up the entire city. But when I finished the job, not even a fly was buzzing.

After that I only remember flashes, until I got the damn Indian naked on the counter of the butcher shop. His face was a bloody mess and he wasn't moving. I went to sharpen the machete, and when I came back to hack him to pieces, I found him sitting up, glancing around.

"What am I doing here?" he mumbled.

There was no time to waste in response, which consisted of a sure blow with the machete, leaving the instrument embedded in his head just above an ear. He died instantly, with a great spasm but without unnecessary suffering. I'm a good guy: I don't like to drag out anybody's agony. When animals suffer too much, they get poisoned with adrenaline and then don't taste good.

That morning at the Delicias bar, reading about Pascal Henry's disappearance, I decided to give Maruja another chance. To celebrate the end of the betrayal and rivalry with the Colombian, I invited her to dine with me at Can Fabes, the famous restaurant owned by Santi Santamaria, which was much more accessible than El Bulli. On the back page of *La Vanguardia*, I had read an interview by Ima Machín with one of the survivors from the plane crash in the Andes, a guy who rebuilt his life by creating an ostrich ranch in the Pampas. When they asked him why ostriches and not cattle, he said that, to his surprise, he found ostrich meat much closer to human flesh. Both were sweet, almost porklike, and very, very tender.

That same night, sitting at a table in Can Fabes, I wanted to try an ostrich filet. The waiter was quite taken aback with my demand but decided to ask in the kitchen if it'd be possible to satisfy my caprice. After a few minutes, all the waiters were staring at me as if I'd killed someone. Maruja got tense and asked if we could leave, but it was too late: we were already sitting under Santi Santamaria's round shadow with carving knives in our hands.

"I understand that you'd like a dish of exotic meats," a raspy voice whispered a few centimeters from my wrinkled nose.

"It's okay, just bring us the degustation menu," I said apologetically.

"Why don't you try my râble cuit au moment with cocoa sauce? If you don't like it, no problem at all . . ."

"Ah, well, unfortunately, I'm allergic to cocoa."

The chef lifted his own carving knife in a compulsive gesture while muttering terrible threats in a barely comprehensible Catalan, as if he were the witch doctor in an African tribe about to stuff a careless explorer into the pot. Finally, he bellowed: "Get out of my restaurant! Go home, cut your own leg off, and have some pig's feet!"

No other phrase could have suited me better. I took it as culinary advice from a master on the subject, and also as proof that Santamaria must have engaged in some kind of ritual cannibalism. I left smiling, but Maruja was very upset that we'd been kicked out and misunderstood my quick retreat as an act of cowardice. I drove home as fast as I could and dropped her off without paying any attention to her recriminations or insults and offering no explanations. Once alone at the butcher shop, I grabbed the best of my slicing knives, opened the industrial freezer, dropped the Colombian's semifrozen cadaver over my shoulder, and deposited him on the chopping block. With an expertise that's totally mine, I managed to cut off a leg without much blood splatter. Then I lit the stove, put a pot over a low flame, deboned the limb, and cut up a bit of onion. I sliced the meat in uneven pieces, dropped them in the water, and set it to boil. With a bit of butter and cream, I poached the onion and added it to the meat and its broth. After twenty minutes over the fire, I ran it through the food processor until I got rid of all the lumps. Later, I heated up the croquette mix and put the mass in spoons which I'd dipped in alginics. I fried up some bread crumbs and battered the croquettes. Finally, the result of all of my sacrifice was there before my eyes, challenging my palette, saying, *Eat me.* And so I did: I ate three in one shot! I couldn't believe the results: the croquettes exploded in my mouth, filling all my taste buds with a torrent of flavor. I'd found the star chef's best kept secret!

Energized with curiosity prompted by the Swiss gourmet's disappearance, I began outlining a new strategy to get a reservation at El Bulli. This time, I pretended I was a respected German gastronomist on vacation in Spain. I thought the Henry case might have caused a rush of cancellations—no diner wants to think they could die at the table—and two days later I received a call from Cala Monjoi.

"Mr. Jürgen Klinsmann?"

"*Jawohl!*"

"We have a free table on Thursday."

Maruja was very happy that I was finally taking her to dinner at the most distinguished restaurant in the world. She was radiant that night in her ethnic dress and bead necklaces. She looked like a Spanish-gypsy version of the Queen of Sheba.

"The Klinsmanns, I presume," said the kindly maître d' when we arrived at El Bulli.

"No," said Maruja.

"Yes," I said.

"Who is Klinsmann?" she asked as they led us to our table.

"A literary pseudonym."

There was no more conversation that evening. Maruja didn't know how to even begin eating those spherified yogurt knots with ficoïde glaciale, and I couldn't wait to taste the famous liquid croquettes. When the sacred moment of communion with the master finally arrived, my hands were trembling with excitement. But everything fell apart with the first bite—not a trace of Pascal Henry in that toasted bread crumb! No matter how hard I concentrated, I could not find the characteristic porklike taste of human flesh in the liquid croquettes or in any of the other dishes I ordered from the degustation menu.

This being the case, where was the gourmet? Who had eaten him? *Santi Santamaria probably kidnapped him*, I thought as I descended into this new abyss of depression. *He probably ended up in the pots at Can Fabes.* Pascal Henry had dined at Can Fabes exactly two nights before his disappearance from Cala Monjoi. Santamaria's calculations would have been as simple as they were perverse: wait for the gourmet to leave El Bulli before striking like a bird of prey—I wondered if he'd sent some underling from the kitchen or if he'd kidnapped the man himself. The consequences would fall on his competitor: a media frenzy, clients vanishing, perhaps a city inspection that would unveil a dangerous arsenal of chemicals and gels . . .

Upon arriving home that night, only one thought hammered at my temples: to slice Maruja's neck with the ham knife to quiet her constant recriminations. She was going at me the whole way home. "You didn't say a word during the entire dinner; I'm sick of your bored and boring personality; your lack of consideration has no limits." To be honest, I was used to her criticisms. What really enraged me was that she asked for a divorce. And all because of that asshole Colombian and his book.

After I took my shoes off, I quietly opened the box of kitchen utensils where I'd hidden the weapon and, with cold blood, went looking for my wife. She too had taken her shoes off to snuggle up with the cushions on the couch and surrender to the final pages of Andreu Martín's *Prótesis*. She never got to the end. So absorbed in the book, she only realized she was going to die when she felt the traitorous blade on her neck and I whispered: "No more reading at home."

As I wrapped her up in plastic and cleaned the stairs that

went from our apartment to the butcher shop, I mused how the next day I'd take all her damn detective novels to the San Antonio market and see if a bookseller would give me a decent price for all of them.

I decided to begin by cutting off her head, since part of the work had already been done. When I managed to separate it from her neck, I held it high, in a kind of *Hamlet* pose.

"No more cheating on me with some South American!" I yelled, and I laughed with all my might.

Later, I ripped open that stupid ethnic dress, which was now soaked with blood, removed her underwear, and began to slice off her arms and legs. I figured I'd use them to give the business a boost. Next weekend, instead of roasted chicken, there would be liquid croquettes!

That radiant summer Sunday, I wrote a brilliant advertising on the butcher shop's board: *Try Ferran Adrià's cuisine without leaving El Carmelo!* Half an hour later, the place was full of diners, retirees, and Andalusian widows dressed in black. Trays of croquettes just flew out the door and I realized that what was left of my late wife's and her lover's bodies would not be enough to satisfy more than a week or two of demand. I needed to find myself some other spacey Pascal Henry type. But I didn't even have to go out to look for him: that same evening, my mother-in-law called from Córdoba to tell me she was about to get on a train to come visit. I'd told the whole neighborhood that my wife was with her parents, so that crazy old woman actually posed quite a threat to my story. I went to get her at the station, and as soon as we got home, I didn't even give her a chance to take her coat off before I'd sliced her neck and dragged her down the stairs. I realized right away that this one wasn't such a good idea: an old hen will make a good broth but has little meat. I saw quite clearly that, at my current sales pace, I'd be out of provisions in no time.

Then I remembered my hateful neighbors from across the street and I decided to kill two birds with one stone: I'd become famous for my haute cuisine while ridding the neighborhood of immigrants. There, just a few meters from my door, was the illuminated sign of my biggest competitors: the Chinese owners of Tiananmen Segundo Restaurant. Nobody would ask uncomfortable questions about a couple of "yellows," so that very Monday I decided to have a "happy meal" to lure them to my store. All those things fried in MSG made me want to vomit, but in the end I decided to try what was most in accord with my exotic tastes: shark fin soup. But the maître d' made me change my order.

"It doesn't taste like much, sir. Allow me to recommend a specialty that's not on the menu."

"Interesting. What is it?"

"Giraffe meat, sir. Just arrived from the African savannah."

"Now we understand each other, China boy."

That week, I found myself eating at Tiananmen Segundo every night. Mr. Hu Jintao offered me a truly personalized service: before my astonished eyes, he paraded dishes of succulent zebra filets, savory wild feline ribs, delicious turtle soups, and other delicacies made from animals en route to extinction that I savored unquestioningly. The prices were reasonable, especially in comparison with the incredibly expensive restaurants of the great chefs. And to top it off, this was across the street from my house. My nascent friendship with my former enemies allowed me to closely observe these restless beings, destined to be used as my raw material. It was still too soon to think about a kidnapping. But I knew it wouldn't be long before I lured one of these slanty-eyed anthropoids to my shop.

Everything was going smoothly until Mr. Jintao heard about the growing popularity of my liquid croquettes and wanted to try one. At first, I tried not to give it too much importance, but in the face of his insistence, and the shots of rice liqueur that he served me after each screaming monkey foot or rhino back, I decided to give the Oriental a little taste of my delicacy. The following Sunday, a feverish day in terms of sales, I went over to Tiananmen Segundo with a tray of liquid croquettes. Mr. Jintao was at a table with about seven or eight other Chinese guys eating rice and spring rolls.

"Don Manolo, would you like to join us?"

"No, thank you—I've put myself on a diet," I said as I uncovered the tray to offer my goods.

All at once, and with appreciative grunts, they launched their little yellow paws at the croquettes; I waited for these to explode in their mouths so I could take pleasure in the looks of satisfaction on their faces. But that wasn't exactly what happened. Instead, Mr. Jintao began to gag, he turned green and then purple. Finally, he spit with a disgusting noise and a slew of curses in his native tongue. The other diners were aghast, not sure whether to chew or spit, until, one by one, they followed their host's example. What had gone wrong? Was my most recent larder of lesser quality than the previous ones? What was wrong with my mother-in-law? Did I use too much alginic? I didn't get a chance to ask because Mr. Jintao, like an enraged Bruce Lee, screamed and grabbed a knife, coming after me with the clear intention of killing me. Luckily, the table was long enough to give me a head start and I was able to make it to the door.

When I finally turned back, just about when I reached the middle of Santuarios, I saw all the diners staring at me with hate from the door of Tiananmen Segundo: they had all kinds of knives in their hands, baseball bats, bottles, and even guns. This was pretty serious. *How did they discover my secret?* I asked myself over and over as I locked myself in my house, totally freaked out, and with the added fear that they'd call the police. Later, a bit calmer, I realized they wouldn't call: it was perfectly clear that Mr. Jintao knew the taste of human flesh as well as I did. That gave me a bit of time: for the rest of the afternoon, I used my furniture to barricade all my doors and windows, then sat down, filled with anxiety, to wait for the yellow horde to come for my head like gremlins in the night.

But instead of being subjected to all their firepower, at eleven o'clock I heard the light rapping of knuckles outside. Then I heard the little Chinese man's familiar voice.

"Don Manolo, I've come in peace. I only want to talk, and to make you an offer."

"Why should I believe you, Mr. Jintao? You just tried to kill me!"

"I am so sorry, Don Manolo! It was a moment of confusion. I beg your eternal forgiveness for my censurable act. I give you my word that nothing will happen . . . if you cooperate."

"Just tell me what you want and let's get this damn farce over with!"

"Don Manolo, I merely want to buy all of the supplies you might have of your, ahem, excellent exotic filets. I need them for my restaurant. I promise there won't be any reprisals. My organization will pay for your goods at a price you won't be able to turn down."

I vomited just then. Not because I suddenly knew Mr. Jintao had been feeding me human flesh all those nights, but because I must have eaten a bunch of old Chinese dudes who probably couldn't have passed a simple health inspection. And with all those diseases out there! How could that

Chinese man have fooled me so badly? Where was my gastronomic knowledge? Where was my palette? And, more impor-
tantly, how had Mr. Jintao managed to make it seem like it was
a different meat every time? What was his secret ingredient?
Damnit, I thought, *I'm going to have to ask him for the recipe!*

"Look here, Don Manolo," Mr. Jintao said as soon as I
dared to unlock the door, "we've had a great increase in clientele in our chain of restaurants. Spaniards like our products.
You're a barbaric people, bloody and cannibalistic, as is evident in your sausages, your bullfights, and your tomato fights
in Buñol."

"Fine, it's a deal. Take it all and cook it up! All I want is
for you to leave me alone."

"That we can't do, Don Manolo. You have a special talent, a talent as a provider, and you're going to work for us:
ever since the economic crisis, fewer people are coming from
our country. We can't allow such an abrupt drop in supplies.
From now on, consider yourself employed by the Red Dragon
Triad."

"No, no, never! I don't want to be a contract killer with
the Chinese mafia, I'm strictly a killer on an as-needed basis."

"You don't have a choice, Don Manolo. If our restaurants
go empty, you'll be the next one in the freezer. Consider yourself lucky to be alive and go get us some good meat. If not, you
might wind up as chop suey."

Since that day, my life hasn't been the same. It's true that
that demonic Fu Manchu lookalike paid me very generously
for the arms, heads, and ribs I still had in the freezer. But I was
overcome with fear, and now my days aspiring to be a star chef
are over. Where am I going to find my next victim? How long
until the cops get their hands on me? I suspect that, sooner or
later, Mr. Jintao will be true to his word and I'll be eaten like

some vulgar duck l'orange. But this week, I intend to survive: I've been hanging around El Bulli again and I've noticed that Ferran Adrià likes to stroll on the beach every day at sunset. It'll be easy to take him from behind by surprise, slice his neck, and stuff him in the Panda's trunk. I'm also going to try to get the Chinese to include my delicious liquid croquettes on their menu, since I'm the one who copies them best. Adrià is chubby and well-formed, he's going to have a lot of meat: we'll prepare him in soy sauce and a serving of Three Delicacies rice. Then it'll be Santi Santamaria's turn. They'll all be licking their fingers when they taste my star chef râble.

[Editors' Note: all characters and places in this story—even those based on real people and restaurants—are fictional or used in a fictional context.]

THE OFFERING

BY TERESA SOLANA

Sant Antoni

Translated from Catalan by Peter Bush

T
hat morning when he got to the Clinical Hospital and saw the medical record for the body that had just come in, he didn't give the name a second thought. Eugènia Grau Sallent. Twenty-nine years old. Circumstances surrounding death: possible suicide caused by an overdose of diazepam, no signs of violence. The victim hadn't left a note. The autopsy was timetabled for the following day and he was the forensic scheduled to perform. As one half of the staff was on holiday and the other hadn't a spare moment, it was only reasonable for him to be assigned the case, though he was hardly idling. Fortune had it that no corpses had been admitted for a couple of days and he'd been able to spend some time on his backlog of paperwork. But the party was over. Experience showed that when one dead body came in more would soon follow.

The name of the woman whose autopsy he'd have to perform made him think of another Eugènia and the bunch of reports he had promised to take her that morning. Eugènia was one of the secretaries who worked for the forensic pathology department and she'd been expecting that batch of overdue files for weeks. He glanced at the dossiers piling up on his desk and sighed. The bureaucratic procedures of the judiciary never failed to put him in a foul mood, but he decided he might as well complete the files that were almost finished. At the very least, he'd give Eugènia something to be getting on with. A couple of hours later, feeling pleased he'd dispatched some of those tedious reports, he hummed his way to her office with a sheaf of files under his arm.

Marta, the other secretary, was on holiday and nobody was around. Eugènia's computer was switched off and her table was neat and tidy, as if she'd not come into work that morning. It was strange because in the six years he'd worked as a forensic doctor at the Clinical Hospital in Barcelona he couldn't recall that girl ever missing a day. Had she perhaps also gone on holiday? Not likely, the secretaries took it in turns and one couldn't go off until the other was back. Besides, he'd seen her the previous afternoon behind her desk, as quiet and efficient as ever, and she'd said goodbye with a barely audible "see you tomorrow" when he nodded in her direction. She'd not mentioned any holidays, so she must be ill. He left the reports on her table and walked glumly back to his windowless cubbyhole. With a little luck, nobody would bother him and he'd be done by midday.

How old was Eugènia? About his age? He reckoned she was well past thirty, although he'd never actually asked her. In fact, the two of them couldn't be said ever to do small talk. *Hello. Good afternoon. Thank you. Here are those papers . . .* and that was as far as it went. Eugènia was dour and introverted, and they had very little in common. And she was ugly, incredibly so. Her unusual structural ugliness derived from a range of small blemishes that weren't easily sorted. In her case, genes had dealt her a bad hand and made her the repository of all the physical flaws of her ancestors. Poor Eugènia had simply been very unlucky. She was short and stout with stumpy legs propping up an overlong torso. Her breasts were

massive in relation to her height, and she was round-shoul-
dered. She was dark-haired and swarthy, but in a coarse dingy
mode, not to mention extraordinarily hairy. When she depil-
ated, her legs and arms were a mass of tiny red scars that only
disappeared when her hair started to grow back. A real mess.
As for her facial features, she hadn't been let off lightly there
either. Flabby cheeks, large bulbous nose, bulging eyes, and
greasy spotty skin she tried to conceal beneath a thick layer
of face cream. She dressed unpretentiously, normally in dark
colors, but nothing she wore did her any favors. Though she'd
never worried about her appearance, she'd long ago given up
trying to look pretty and now merely tried to pass unnoticed.

He had found Eugènia off-putting from day one. When he
had to go to the secretaries' office to return a file, he always
tried to deal with Marta, because her colleague's unsightly appearance put him on edge. He couldn't help it.

"Hasn't Eugènia come in today?" he asked one of his
colleagues.

"Eugènia? The poor thing's downstairs. Didn't you see her
record?"

"Record? Which one? You mean the one for the woman
admitted this morning?"

So secretary Eugènia, nature's joke in poor taste, whom
he'd been working with for six years, was the woman who'd
committed suicide currently going cold in the basement. He
put on his gown and went down to the room where they kept
the corpses to take a look. According to her record, Eugènia
was in cooler number ten. When he opened it, he came up
against her misshapen body and familiar acne-splattered face.
Yes, there she was, as white as marble except for her face that
had a good color to it. How odd. The girl had felt spirited
enough to make herself up before taking her own life. Pow-

dered nose, rouge on cheeks, liner on eyes, red lipstick . . . She wasn't wearing earrings or any other jewel, except for a small, apparently antique ring on the ring finger of her right hand, and she had gathered her hair up with a blue ribbon. One thing in particular caught his attention: the sweet scent given off by her body. A fresh, strong flowery fragrance, though he couldn't say which flowers. All he was able to distinguish was the smell of roses and violets. But the odor emanating from Eugènia's body wasn't one of violets or roses, or perhaps it was but mixed up with others. All in all, it was extremely pleasant. He sniffed her legs, her belly, her breasts, her arms, her neck and hair. No doubt about it. She had splashed perfume all over herself, every fold and cranny, as if she'd wanted to ensure she would smell sweetly after death.

According to the preliminary report, she had been dead ten or twelve hours. If she'd not been pale as marble from the neck downward, you'd have said she was asleep. He glanced at her card again. Twenty-nine when he'd have guessed thirty-five or -six. Yes, after looking at her close up, that girl wasn't over thirty. It was really strange: she looked younger now that she was dead. The report said they'd found her at home, stretched out on her bed in a supine position, stark naked but covered by a blanket. Next to her they'd found a white summer dress yet to be worn and, on her bedside table, three empty boxes of Valium, a glass, and a bottle of mineral water. She had taken the trouble to send her neighbor a note so she'd find her early on and ring 061, and she'd also had the forethought to leave the door unlocked so the firemen wouldn't have to force it open. Everything indicated that before swallowing the pills, Eugènia had seen to every last detail. Even to the point of choosing the dress she wanted to be buried in. You didn't find many young suicides with such sangfroid.

Of course, he had never autopsied anyone he'd known. Forensics, like surgeons, never open family or friends. They leave that to someone else. In Eugènia's case, the girl had been working at the hospital from the age of twenty and everyone knew her, even if the two of them had never hit it off. Anyway, he knew next to nothing about her. Whether she had a boyfriend (he thought not) or friends or was happy at work. As far as he was concerned, Eugènia was merely the secretary he greeted politely when he went in and out of the clinic, and to whom, every so often, he handed reports to be sent to court. In the six years they'd worked in that department, they'd never had coffee together or commiserated over setbacks in their lives. The truth was, Eugènia was a completely unknown quantity.

Even so, it felt strange to think that tomorrow he'd have her naked and defenseless on the autopsy table. He wished the case had been assigned to someone else. He did remember *one* thing about her: she was very shy and quick to blush. Whenever he poked his nose into the secretaries' office, Eugènia would immediately turn red and hide her less than attractive face behind hair that was as rough and black as coal. *Poor girl*, he thought, genuinely moved, *she was so ugly that no man could ever have given her a second look.* Of course he never had. He had just treated her like a piece of the furniture and avoided sitting at the same table when they were both in the cafeteria. As far as he could remember, he'd never paid her a compliment or smiled at her beyond the call of politeness. And he'd never done so because she was ugly and her ugliness made him feel uncomfortable. He regretted that now.

He shut the door to the cold room and decided to put her out of his mind. He must concentrate on the paperwork. He went upstairs and straight to his office, determined to bury himself in his private backlog of bureaucracy. However, before doing so, he switched on his computer to take a look at his e-mails, as he always did midmorning. And saw it. A message addressed to him from someone he wasn't expecting to hear from at all. Name of sender: *Eugènia Grau*. His heart missed a beat. It was a short message, barely two lines. It started *Dear Doctor* and signed off with a *Yours sincerely*. In a neutral polite tone, Eugènia asked one thing of him: that he personally carry out the autopsy on her when she was taken to the morgue. Nothing else. That was it. Taken aback, he read that concise text several times trying to decipher a possible hidden meaning. Eugènia had left no suicide note but, for some reason that escaped him, before ending it all she had taken the trouble to perfume herself, make her face up, and e-mail him that highly unusual request. His stomach felt queasy. He didn't know what to think.

He decided not to say a word and spent the rest of the morning sitting in his office pretending to work. Just before two o'clock he informed his colleagues that he had a headache and was going home. It was true his head was throbbing. He was on his way, walking past the secretaries' office, when he stopped in his tracks. He'd had a hunch. In a flash he went inside and started rummaging in Eugènia's desk drawers. He soon found them. There they were. A set of her house keys, with a note of her address. Yes, it was the address that was also on her card. After ruminating for a few seconds, he put the keys in his pocket and rushed out. As soon as he hit the pavement, the light of the midday sun dazzled him and he had to shut his eyes. A motorcyclist almost knocked him down. What the hell was he up to? Almost unaware, there he was, in a taxi and asking the driver to take him to the address attached to the key ring. His heart was racing and he found it hard to breathe. Let alone think. The girl lived by herself, on Floridablanca Street, very close to where they worked. The taxi got there in only a couple of minutes.

Eugènia's flat was near the Sant Antoni market, in a district on the left of L'Eixample that had never lost its noisy working-class character. The market was the first to be built outside the city walls when they were demolished in the last third of the nineteenth century, and it retained its spectacular iron structure and bustling atmosphere. It was still the center of the busy commercial activity that characterized the neighborhood where Eugènia's family had lived for nigh on a century. At the end of May 1909, Eugènia's great-great-grandparents had moved there with their burden of children, belongings, and debts, and the expectation they would find home comforts that were nonexistent in the tiny dismal flats in the old part of the city. Little did they imagine that the streets of their new neighborhood would very soon be transformed into one of the scenarios of violent conflict between workers and troops in the Setmana Tràgica and that smoke from burning churches would blacken the sky over their new start in life. It had been a short journey from where they used to live, a brief ten-minute exodus on foot, but far enough to leave behind that labyrinth of damp narrow streets prey to overcrowding, dirt, and poverty. Unlike the well-off middle classes who had migrated further, to the distinguished buildings the architects had erected on the right of Balmes Street, more modest families like Eugènia's were forced to settle for those humbler flats on the borders of their old district. Now, together with the Raval, it was one of the most densely populated parts of Barcelona and home to most of the immigrants coming into the city. You only had to look at the headscarves worn by the Arab women or listen to the melancholy voices of the men conversing in remote, incomprehensible tongues on street corners or sitting on benches. The frantic Babel of streets in Eugènia's neighborhood was awash, as they had always been, with hope and rage, honest folk and hoodlums, next-door neighbors from way back and newcomers. Blocks and sidewalks harbored prostitutes and old dears going to their daily mass, pimps and shopkeepers, informers and plain-clothes police. Traffic was nose-to-tail and car fumes polluted the air. There were few tourists strolling thereabouts. They preferred the beach or air-conditioned museums.

The block where Eugènia lived didn't have a concierge. It must have had one once because there was a concierge's cubbyhole, but at some point the neighbors clearly decided to install an automatic entry system and save money. Concierges are expensive, and it was still a modest neighborhood, however much the prices of flats had rocketed in recent years. It wasn't difficult for him to find the front-door key, because there were only three on the ring. It was a narrow gloomy staircase, which at that time of day reeked of boiled cabbage. As it was summer and the windows were open, he could hear mothers shouting to their children to come and eat, and impatient, grumbling men demanding their dinner. Eugènia lived on the fourth floor (which was really the fifth) and there was no elevator. He gritted his teeth and started on the steep ascent.

Once he was at the top he opened the door and went into the girl's flat, trying not to make any noise to avoid alerting the neighbors. What he was doing was probably not altogether illegal, but at the very least it was rather unorthodox. Forensic pathologists don't visit the scene of the crime after the coroner has removed the corpse. It's not part of their duties. Why was he doing it then? What was he hoping to find?

In all the time he'd been a forensic it had never entered his head before. Was he perhaps hoping to find a clue to why Eugènia had committed suicide? With those unprepossessing looks that life's lottery had awarded her, it wasn't difficult to imagine her leading a lonely life, being chronically depressed, or not feeling she belonged to a world where beauty and the attributes of youth seemed to determine the rules of the game. Eugènia must have tired of looking at herself in the mirror every morning and seeing only a reflection of her ugliness. She must have given up the struggle. And as she had been working at the morgue long enough to know that suicides always pass through the Clinical Hospital, she must have thought it preferable for the autopsy to be performed by the doctor she'd had least to do with. It was all a question of tact. Yes, that explained the message she had sent him. It couldn't mean anything else.

The flat was light and strangely tidy, like her work desk. Not a speck of dust to be seen. It was a small flat, barely sixty square meters all told, but Eugènia had good taste. The few pieces of furniture she owned were solid and made of fine wood and the décor was sober without seeming characterless. There were rugs on the floor and plants by the windows, and books as well. Hundreds of books. Bookcases galore. Eugènia was a well-read girl, then. She was no ignoramus.

The kitchen was also tidy and the fridge was completely empty. Somebody had unplugged it. Nor was there any rubbish in the bin. Eugènia had had the forethought to empty the fridge and take the trash down to avoid leftover food rotting and stinking the house out: farsighted to the bitter end. He entered her bedroom apprehensively. The curtains were open and sunlight was pouring in. The forensic police must have taken the glass, bottle of water, and boxes of Valium because they were nowhere to be seen, but there was a slim volume on her bedside table. The book was open and a postcard marked the page. It looked vaguely familiar.

He took the postcard and turned it over to see who had sent it. A shiver ran down his spine. It was the postcard he himself had sent his colleagues at the hospital a couple of summers ago, when he was on holiday. He remembered it now. He'd spent three weeks touring the Balkans with a colleague who was an orthopedic surgeon, although their relationship had been short-lived. All the women he got close to did their best to take over his life, but he wasn't ready to make commitments and in the end they all left him. He glanced at the postcard rather nervously. It was one of those typical cards that tourists like to send to friends or relatives, a landscape of the region of Thracia with a few ancient ruins in the background. The image meant nothing special. In fact, he could have sent that card or a dozen others. It had been a polite gesture. He put it down and picked up the book. It was a modern edition of *Phaedrus*, a translation. He dug into his memory and tried to disinter texts he'd read and forgotten in high school. Wasn't *Phaedrus* the dialogue about beauty? Or was that *Phaedon*?

He was forced to sit down when the room started to spin. His body was drenched in sweat, a cold, unpleasant sweat. He was a doctor, and though his special interest was forensic medicine, he could still recognize when two symptoms were connected. That Eugènia had used this postcard to mark the page in the book on her bedside table the moment she committed suicide, and that she'd sent him the unusual request, couldn't be two isolated acts. Perhaps the book indicated something as well. Had Eugènia chosen it to kill time while she waited for the pills to take effect, or had she decided to commit suicide as a result of reading it? If he recalled aright and *Phaedrus* spoke of beauty, the book reinforced his first hypothesis. Yes, that must be it. Eugènia had committed suicide because her ugliness made her tremendously unhappy.

He picked up the book and went off to the dining room. When he finished reading it was six p.m. He was right. The book was about what Eugènia wasn't. Or maybe was, because right now he couldn't be so sure. Wasn't Plato really saying that beauty is independent of the physical world, a quality of the nonsensory world that doesn't necessarily correspond to the one captured by our senses? The thought was highly disturbing. Reading the book, you could hardly say the philosopher was pouring scorn on ugly people; rather, he was warning of the error of trusting in appearances. On the other hand, Socrates's ugliness was proverbial. The old philosopher was no Adonis. So what if there was beauty after all in Eugènia's misshapen body? But what kind of beauty? An inner, purely intellectual beauty, like the one Alcibiades had praised in Socrates in *The Symposium* and the one Eugènia cultivated with all her sophisticated reading matter? Yet if that was so, why had she committed suicide?

When he walked into the hospital the next morning, Eugènia was already on the autopsy table. Her body still gave off a flowery scent. They'd followed his instructions and taken off her ring and the ribbon with which she'd tied back her hair. They'd washed her face, her makeup was no longer visible, and she was now a pallid white. Her lips and nails had acquired the blue tone poisoning that diazepam brings, and she no longer looked if as she was asleep. She was frankly very ugly. He unhurriedly pulled on his gloves and put on a plastic apron, and cheerfully asked the assistant he'd been assigned for the day to proceed to open the back part of the skull while he took his scalpel and prepared to extract her other organs.

He wasn't expecting any surprises. Experience told him that they were dealing with a conventional suicide and that all they would find would be a general collapse provoked by the overdose of tranquilizers.

Normally, when he was working in the dissection room, he did so to music by the Beatles, the Rolling Stones, Tina Turner, Michael Jackson, Madonna . . . Some of his colleagues preferred to listen to classical music, but he'd rather his head be filled with upbeat melodies and songs that invited you to hum along and not think. On this occasion, he said he wanted silence and was in no mood for jokes or chitchat. A little solemnity was the least he owed that ugly girl who'd remained a stranger while they worked together for six years. His assistant nodded, shrugged his shoulders, and started to saw bone.

He had slept badly that night with one nightmare after another. He'd woken up exhausted and soaked in sweat. In one of those dreams, the only one he could remember, Eugènia, dressed like a bride, had smiled at him with her chubby, spot-infested face. Her hair was tied back with that blue ribbon and she was holding a hand out beckoning him to follow. He resisted.

On his way to work, he thought how in essence there'd been nothing in the dream to justify the unpleasant, anguished feeling he'd woken up with. Standing in the morgue, preparing to stick his nose inside Eugènia's body, the memory of that nightmare upset him again and made his pulse race. He took a deep breath and tried to regain his composure. He was a professional who had performed thousands of necropsies. He must chase off those ridiculous images and concentrate on the task. While he was cutting the skin on her trunk and proceeding to detach her thorax, he suddenly realized where he'd gone wrong. His scalpel fell to the ground and for a few moments it was as if he'd turned to stone while his brain strove to come to terms with the consequences of the discovery he'd just made. It was too sinister, too twisted. His assistant observed the scene in silence and retrieved the scalpel without opening his mouth, but he could see the doctor's face was as white as the corpse he had just opened.

He'd got it completely wrong. Eugènia's request had nothing to do with any sense of tact, or with the fact they'd barely interacted. It was quite the opposite. Eugènia had died because she wanted him to look at her and touch her, as he'd never have done when she was alive. The girl was offering him her body the only way she knew he'd be prepared to receive it: stiff and cold. After all, she'd decked herself out with the attributes of a bride. She had understood that ending her life was the only way to be intimate with him, the man whose polite silences had slapped her ugliness in her face every day. That's why she'd kept that postcard and sent him the strange message disguised behind such prosaic words. Had she also foreseen he'd visit her flat, or wasn't that part of the script she'd written?

He tried to control himself. He set her different organs down one by one on the table until he had gutted her. First he examined her brain. It weighed exactly 1,270 grams. It was entirely symmetrical and flawless. In fact, one of the most perfect brains he'd ever seen. There was no bruising, no minor hemorrhage, no imperfection, and it possessed the uncanny beauty of harmonious proportion and unusual refinement. That was what caught his attention. In all the years he had been working as a forensic, he'd never seen such a well-formed brain. It was riveting, a prodigy of undulating tissue that few eyes could have been privileged to contemplate over the centuries. He then went on to examine her remaining organs.

They were all intact. No sign of edemas or blocked arteries, as if Eugènia had never swallowed the pills or the passage of time had left no trace in her insides. Each of her viscera was exquisitely proportioned in a way that was rare to find in a human body.

Eugènia's immaculate organs were the repositories of such extraordinarily sublime beauty that he was continually forced to catch his breath. Her entrails irradiated a hypnotic, luminous quality and the smell they gave off was in no way unpleasant. There were no signs of putrefaction. In some sense, it was as if Eugènia's body allowed him to contemplate the great secret, the primordial model of absolute perfection. Once more, the thought paralyzed him.

He stayed like that for a long time. Ecstatic. Astonished. Silent. However much he tried, he couldn't take his eyes off that pure, unanticipated beauty. His assistant was frightened to see him in such a state and offered to accompany him outside, but he refused and vigorously ordered him to leave. The assistant was used to obeying and left the room without protesting, but he was sure the young man would soon be back with one of his colleagues. He barely had time. He now thought the body wasn't at all deformed or monstrous, but a prodigy of beauty and perfection. He picked up the needle and thread and lovingly began to sew up Eugènia's empty body. He personally wanted to look after it. He then put the ring back on her finger and the ribbon in her hair. Blue brings brides good luck. Finally, he put his lips next to the girl's cold lips and kissed her.

When they eventually found him unconscious on the ground, he said he had just fainted.

In the months to come everyone noticed something was wrong with him. He hardly slept or ate, and the purple circles now established around his eyes made the pallor of his face even more alarming. He'd grown thinner and his hair had turned gray from one day to the next. Now it was almost white. He drank coffee all the time, and his left eye twitched nervously and forced him to blink compulsively. His pulse trembled and stuttered. His head of department was worried and repeatedly begged him to take sick leave or go on holiday but he refused, laconically asserting that he was fine. Despite his gradual, quite visible deterioration, despite his sickly, aged appearance, he continued to arrive punctually and nobody had any complaints. After all, he worked more hours than ever, as if he never had enough to do, and he engineered it so he was always on call. For the last few months he'd been a silent presence at every autopsy and always volunteered to give a helping hand to the less experienced forensics. Everyone avoided his company and few dared say a word to him.

One night he was left all alone. The other doctor on duty was forced to go home suffering from a bad bout of summer flu. The rest of the staff had finished their shifts. The security guard was dozing as he did every night sitting in his cubbyhole with his radio blaring, and now and then he'd glance at the monitors that kept a watch on the entrance and sides of the building. Despite the apprehension the man had felt initially, when he'd been assigned to the old site of the Institute for Forensic Anatomy, experience taught him that problems always came from outside. He didn't like the dead, but at least they never gave him any headaches.

Recently there'd been a constant stream of bodies. Suicides, accidents, drug overdoses, bodies stabbed to pieces, anonymous faces no one could identify . . . The coolers in the basement were crammed with corpses patiently waiting their turn before they could be sent to the cemetery or medical students' lectures, and the staff was complaining. If that rate were maintained, they'd have to do overtime. They didn't even know what to do with the bodies. And couldn't cope with the workload.

There'd been no incidents that night. No calls, no emergencies. The next morning, shortly before eight, the head of service arrived. He liked to be the first and used that period of quiet to organize the day's schedule and shifts before the phone started ringing. He wasn't surprised not to see his colleague, because if it was a quiet night the forensics on duty got bored and often joined the nurses for coffee. He was probably upstairs in the library taking a nap or had gone to the cafeteria for breakfast. While he was rummaging in his pockets for his keys, he thought he heard a noise in the basement. It was a kind of feeble, barely audible moan, like a continuous sobbing. No doubt somebody had left the radio on. He sighed, put his coat and briefcase down, and took the stairs to the basement where the dead were stored. The door was just pulled to. As he opened it, he instinctively gave a start. The panorama in the autopsy room chilled him to the bone.

He tried to shout but was unable to articulate a single sound. For a fraction of a second he thought it might possibly be a hallucination caused by the shadows in the morgue, a sly trick played on his brain by stress, but then he understood immediately that what he could see was for real.

Decomposing bodies piled up on tables, on the floor, anyhow, open down the middle, with viscera chucked all over the room. It was impossible to take a step without treading on livers, encephalic matter, kidneys, or poorly dissected hearts. There were also intestines tossed in every corner, like macabre streamers decorating a lugubrious party where the guests were dismembered bodies and heads severed from their torsos. The stench was unbearable, as if hell itself had thrown its gates open. The only spotlight in the room barely lit the central table where they placed the bodies when they were performing necropsies, but the phantasmagoric skin of the mutilated corpses absorbed that light and projected a sad, sinister set of shadows. The moans were faint but could still be heard. They came from a man crying facedown on one of those disemboweled corpses, his gown dripping blood. No doubt about it. It was one of his doctors. He seemed to be holding something. And there was lots of blood. Lots. But the dead don't bleed.

He suddenly recognized her. She was one of their pediatric nurses, a particularly pretty girl with wonderfully blond hair. It was difficult not to notice that svelte well-proportioned girl and her bright cheerful eyes. It was less than a fortnight since she'd come to tell him how worried she was by the state of health of the man who at that moment was sobbing over her bloody, opened body. Now she was naked and completely still, somehow strapped to the table with plasters and bandages. The ball of cotton in her mouth must have suppressed her screams, but not asphyxiated her. She had undoubtedly resisted. Her blue eyes were wide open, but no longer smiling. Her vacant expression was one of panic.

She'd been cut open from top to bottom, her ribs pulled apart and various organs wrenched out. As he closed in, he thought the man was holding something that pulsated rhythmically. Suddenly, he retched. It was the girl's heart. Still beating.

The doctor didn't even notice he was there. Beneath the tears, his gaze wandered aimlessly. The startling beauty he'd discovered inside Eugènia's body had made him lose his reason. From that day on he'd searched every corpse that passed through his hands with the fury of a man possessed. He'd examined hearts, livers, brains, uteruses, kidneys, each of the organs capable of hoarding the secret, dazzling beauty that had emerged unexpectedly from Eugènia's imperfect body. In his despair, he had decided to look for it in the prettiest woman he knew, only to meet with failure once again. He now knew he would never again contemplate that golden mean of harmonious proportion, that unusual and extraordinary beauty Eugènia had generously given him as a present when she'd offered him her already deceased body. And such certainty meant the solitude overwhelming him at that moment was immense and irremediable. He had embarked on a journey into the deepest darkness, a prisoner of an ancient and tragic wisdom that would never again be within his reach. A journey on a one-way ticket from which he would never return.

A HIGH-END NEIGHBORHOOD

BY JORDI SIERRA I FABRA

Turó Parc

P elayo Morales Masdeu is ten years old and a bastard. Short, rather fat because of bad eating habits, black-haired, bleary-eyed, with a small nose and mouth (a wreck of a face dominated by cheeks, chin, and forehead, four cardinal points of excess). When he smiles, his eyes shrink until they turn into horizontal slats. When he speaks, almost always shouting, he raises his eyebrows extravagantly. But the worst almost always comes when he does neither of these things. Then the whole world shakes.

Pelayo Morales Masdeu was a child once upon a time. Now he's an old man.

A ten-year-old old man.

"I want to go to the park."

"It's late now, master."

"I want to go to the park NOW," he says calmly and emphatically.

"Don't you think that after yesterday . . . ?"

"Whose side are you on, you stupid cow?"

"Don't talk like that, please."

"Let's go to the park then."

"Look, come out to the balcony. The same mothers are there."

"So what?" He begins to get angry. "I didn't push that moron down the slide! And I didn't throw sand in the other kid's eye! The first kid fell and the second is an asshole!"

"The girls' mothers are there too."

"Why do I care if they're all jerks? All girls are the same!" His anger grows. "If you don't take me to the park, I'll go by myself!"

"You know you can't go by yourself. Your father has forbidden it."

"Who's going to kidnap me? I'm going, I'm going, I'm going!"

"Master . . ."

"Then come with me. You're supposed to be here to serve me, right?"

"Among other things, master."

"You're so stupid . . . Sometimes I understand why they kicked you out of your country."

"They didn't kick me out. I came to Spain to—"

"Oh, go to hell! Are we going or what?"

He's already in the vestibule. Felipa doesn't know what to do. He's quite capable of opening the door and running downstairs. It wouldn't be the first time. Then he'd hide and scare her to death. What he'd said about kidnapping were not just empty words. His father wants her to keep an eye on him at all times. His mother too.

"Are you coming or not, you moron?"

"Why don't you play with your PC or with that little gadget—"

"The little gadget, the little gadget," he says, then bursts out laughing. "The PlayStation, stupid! Now leave me alone!"

He opens the door and Felipa only has time to grab her jacket to cover her maid's uniform. Pelayo is already one floor down, taking the steps two-by-two and three-by-three.

"I'm telling you again: don't talk to me like that, master, please! What will the neighbors think?"

She hears his voice moving away from her: "What do I care what those old people say?"

She catches up with him on the street. It's useless to try to take his hand. He says that she sweats, that she smells, that she's nothing but an Indian, like all of them. And when she reminds him that in the Philippines they don't have Indians, he says he looked it up on a map and they're all Indians, because they can't live that far from North America and Europe and not be Indians.

At least he looked at a map.

They get to the park and people stare at them quite blatantly. Looks of disgust, looks of rejection. Looks. A woman calls her daughter and, grabbing her hand, starts to leave the park through the gate on Pau Casals Avenue, toward Francesc Macià Plaza. Another mother tells her son to stay away from the newcomer. A third mother hesitates for a second, and it's just enough time for Pelayo to jump the pigeons, rock in hand. She stands up, calls both her children, and makes her way to the northeast exit, the one toward San Gregorio Taumaturgo Plaza with the round church in the middle.

It's a beautiful day to stroll down the Turó.

Pelayo goes to the swings. He doesn't have to wait too long. One of the kids jumps off right away, scared by Pelayo's killer look. Felipa lowers her eyes. At times she still asks herself how someone can rip the wings off a fly just to witness its suffering, or sit there and watch a pigeon with torn legs and wings struggle to rise up and take flight.

"Master, do not swing so high!"

"Shut up, you idiot, or I'll tell Mother you didn't let me play!"

Other nannies don't come near her anymore. Mothers don't talk to her. She's alone.

Pelayo Morales Masdeu flits from one place to another.

The Turó Parc playground empties little by little.

Vanesa Morales Masdeu is seventeen years old and a slut.

Attractive, slender, almost anorexic, her black hair flows down to the middle of her back; she has light eyes, sensual lips, a pointy chin, an exuberant body, and beautiful hands. Young men, and some not so young, have been courting her like wolves for three or four years now, and she's one of those who plays and plays well. Like a halfback on a soccer team. She plays the game and even allows herself the luxury of scoring a goal or two.

Felipa sometimes asks herself why Vanesa's parents spoil her so much, why they allow her so much freedom.

She's a mere girl.

A devil too.

At night, when the house is sleeping, Felipa leaves her room and walks barefoot to the enormous balcony overlooking Turó Parc. She is so tired, so exhausted, that at times she can't get to sleep. If the weather is good, she goes out to the balcony and gazes at the dark and silent trees, so close at hand, so far from her life. People in Barcelona say Turó is the city's most beautiful park: small, triangular, cozy, with plenty of places in which to get lost, to sit down, to read the paper, to absorb the sun in open spaces, to walk the dog, to play, or to amble about under the shadows of the tall trees and all the well-manicured shrubs. It's a park for prosperous couples, rich old men aided by assistants with sad faces full of longing, and children with governesses and uniformed maids, all foreign, just like her.

A park in a high-end neighborhood.

She likes to look at it, especially at night.

The south end, the narrowest and most open part of the

triangle, opens to Pau Casals Avenue. On the sides and north, it's straight, barely a hundred and fifty meters long by about two hundred. The pond with the invisible fish, because they're rarely seen, is over to the left; the playground is just down from there; a tiny beverage stand with barely half a dozen tables is located in the center. There used to be a small theater. Once upon a time. The buildings bordering and trapping the park on the north and along the sides, to the left and right, are noble, regal, from when the rich began to move in and the neighborhood blossomed. Structures with ten or twelve stories, built in the '50s and '60s, solid, with uniformed porters instead of old doormen and women in aprons. From the top floors, it's possible to glimpse the sea in the distance, and also the Tibidabo, with its Luna Park, the communication antenna put up for the '92 Olympics. But only from the top floors.

Like hers.

Suddenly Felipa sees her, as if emerging from the night. The car moves too fast along Ferran Agulló Street and brakes sharply in front of the house. Felipa leans out a little, just enough to see her, running, tossing her black hair. The figure of a young man exits from the other door. He takes her under the streetlight and they kiss in a singular fashion, as if eating each other up.

Then he does something else.

He sticks his hand under her skirt, up the back, then the front.

The girl opens her legs, offering herself, squeezing against him.

One minute, two, five, until they separate and she enters the building.

Felipa miscalculates the time. She should have gone back to her room right away. But she's still hanging around closing the window. Vanesa is already inside the enormous

400-square-meter duplex apartment. An apartment you can lose yourself in.

"Good evening, Miss Vanesa."

"Oh God, you scared me! What are you doing here?"

"I couldn't sleep. Shall I fix you something?"

"What would you fix me at this hour of the night?" She takes a quick glance at her watch. "And you . . ." She struggles for the right words. "Are you spying on me?"

"Me?"

"Shit, Felipa. If you tell Mother, I swear I'll make your life a living hell!"

Felipa's about to tell her that she couldn't make it any worse, but ends up not saying anything. It can always get worse. There's always a way. The laundry that's not washed on time, and the blouse that, although she has ten others, is precisely the one she needs to wear that afternoon; hot meals, cold meals; searching pockets before the wash and sometimes finding incriminating things such as condoms . . . She has lied for Vanesa so many times, to protect her, but ultimately also to protect herself.

"I have never told your mother a thing, miss."

"Of course . . ." Vanesa crosses her arms.

"What?"

"You people were already doing it when you were like eleven or twelve, right?"

"Doing it?"

"C'mon or I'll smack you. Doing it like rabbits."

Felipa thinks she knows what Vanesa's talking about but doesn't want to get into it. After all, she'd found the girl one day with a boy, in her own bedroom, when she was barely fifteen. Her parents weren't home, like always, and though it was her free afternoon, she'd come back early because she wasn't feeling well, didn't have any money to spare, and knew all too well she had nowhere to go.

"If there is nothing you want, I'm going to bed," and she tries to leave.

"May I ask you a question?"

From the look of contempt on the face of this know-it-all, Felipa is sure the question won't be to her liking. "Of course."

"What are you doing here?"

"Working, miss. Working."

"You're revolting." Her face stresses the disgust. "You come to Spain penniless and take care of other people's children because you can't feed your own. Why do you have them then?"

"Children are a gift from God."

Vanesa bursts out laughing. "Go on with that nonsense." She almost spits the words out. "Mother told me that your first husband left you and that you didn't even have time to hug the second one before he knocked you up."

"My Manuel died, miss."

"Who takes care of your children?"

"My mother."

"How long has it been since you've seen them?"

It's hard for her to speak the words. Sometimes it's too much, much more overwhelming than usual.

"Almost three years, miss."

Vanesa Morales Masdeu holds her gaze.

Then Felipa looks down, unable to resist. "Good night." She starts to leave.

The girl says nothing.

A few steps.

"Don't go making noise in front of my room tomorrow. Clean somewhere else, okay?" she hisses suddenly.

Felipa nods and walks on. When she gets to her room, she knows exactly how difficult it's going to be to fall asleep.

Laia Masdeu Porta is forty-seven years old and a slave driver.

A natural blonde with two liposuctions and three face-lifts, she's a Botox addict, does four or five hours a day in the gym, a sauna, massage, and intensive care; always corporal, never intellectual; almond-eyed, generously siliconed lips, an adolescent's body, large breasts, well-manicured hands, and expensive clothes. She rarely smiles so as not to provoke un-necessary wrinkles. She never voices strong opinions because she doesn't have any. Her hourglass is perfect.

As solid as her amorality.

The first thing she does when she crosses Turó Parc on her way home from the gym is to look up to see her wide balcony. It's not the first time she's surprised to find Felipa up there, doing nothing. But, of course, it'll be the last if she catches her again. The most amazing thing is that she always says she's cleaning the windows or sweeping. For God's sake, they're all alike. A herd of beggars. Although Felipa has been with her for a long time. Years now. But it doesn't mean she's the least bit fond of her . . .

They're nothing more than third world animals living like rats in a society that's beyond them.

Laia Masdeu Porta goes up the elevator by herself and enters her apartment without making a sound. She takes off her jacket, looks at herself in the mirror, the front and sides, all mechanical gestures, and then walks away with the same circumspection.

Her maid is in the bathroom, on her knees, scrubbing the toilet.

Laia relaxes, although not too much.

First, the kitchen. She opens the fridge. She keeps tabs on the food, because recently she's discovered that sometimes there's a missing steak, or yogurt, or custard. She hates to be robbed. But all those wretches steal. They can't help them-selves. That's the way they've been brought up. Deep inside, she knows she should feel sorry for them.

But she doesn't.

They know well enough to send their money back to their countries.

And then they complain. They complain! The day before, she'd had a talk with her and made things clear.

"Look, Felipa, if you're not happy, there's the door, under-stood? I just have to tap my foot and fifty more like you come rushing out. But not even like you! Cheaper! We've done quite a bit for you. What more do you want?"

She goes to the dining room. The mail is waiting on a large cut-glass platter on top of a little table, next to the door, so everyone can pick up their own. She glances at the letters from the bank but doesn't open them. José María will take care of them. She grabs hers, all junk mail. But she does take a look at the phone bill. She rips open the envelope and stud-ies the calls.

None to the Philippines.

She sighs.

It's not about the charges for two or three euros that she finds on the bill. It's the actual fact, the detail. Aren't there telephone centers for immigrants? Let them talk from there! What if there's a truly important call for her while Felipa is chattering or whimpering with her children or her mother?

And Felipa calls them every week.

Well, it's hard, but she's already taken her in hand.

The poor thing can't cope with more—

"Felipa!"

Laia sees her emerging from the bathroom almost bent in two, rubbing her hands on her apron and wearing her eternally frightened face.

"Yes ma'am."

"Anything new?"

"No, no."

"Calls?"

"No, no."

"Oh, girl, please wipe that look of horror from your face. Good heavens! It's not the Gestapo questioning you!"

The maid doesn't know what to say.

She doesn't know what the Gestapo is, of course.

"My God." Laia Masdeu Porta sighs. "You're such a sad person, eh?"

Felipa doesn't move; she holds the same expression.

"I am going to my studio to relax. I'd like a salad for lunch, but careful with the vinegar. And scrub your hands well. You just had them in the toilet!"

Laia goes to her room. First, she changes into something more comfortable. She opens the dressing room and checks out her clothes. Half the things in it aren't good anymore. It's impossible to wear them anywhere. Even less with the staff watching her. Mariano, Alberto, and Andrés's wives are really something . . . and the "new ones" are much worse. Ignacio's is a twenty-two-year-old kid. Although she's already thirty-five, Francisco's wife also looks like a supermodel.

She'll clean things out this afternoon.

Everything in the trash.

She doesn't want to see Felipa, like that other time, a year ago, when she caught her rummaging through the cast-offs for a sweater, a blouse, a skirt . . .

This cheapskate behavior makes her shudder.

She undresses, looks at herself in the mirror again, the one in the dressing room, from the front, the side; she tucks in her belly, lifts her breasts, strokes her behind with both hands. Everything's solid. José María doesn't touch her anymore, but that's because her husband's impotent and stupid. The young man at the gym, the one at the door, didn't take his eyes off her. He was checking her out. She can still make anybody scream in bed. She just has to decide to do so. She's going through the best period of her life. The age of wisdom.

Too bad sex is so exhausting, so sweaty . . .

She puts on clean clothes. House clothes, but classy, because you never know when someone might call or come over. Dignity is in the details. Her mother used to say: "Hold your head high, even when you step in shit."

She leaves the room and goes to the studio that serves as her oasis. She hears Felipa singing softly to herself. Laia hates it when she does that. She's asked her not to do that, but if she starts to argue about it she'll end up with a migraine and that's not what she needs right now: a wretched headache because of that idiot. So, for once, she lets it go. She closes the studio door and opens a window. Turó Parc immediately restores her peace of mind. This is her world. The rest can go to hell. That green patch and the surrounding buildings. That is her Barcelona, exclusive, unique, her own.

The world works, in spite of all the damned Felipas.

Laia Masdeu Porta lets herself drop into her favorite armchair and, just before picking up a fashion magazine, closes her eyes for a few seconds and relaxes.

José María Morales Moreno is fifty-five years old and a son of a bitch. He combs back his increasingly thinning hair, which is shiny and somewhat out of control around the back of the neck, where there are black cowlicks that make it seem just a touch trendy. Tanned complexion, the eyes of a lynx, straight lips, an incipient double chin that will soon vanish with surgery, a big body, the body of an entrepreneur, a powerful body. After he was mugged by some Moroccans, in the very center of Barcelona, and they took his gold Rolex and two rings— one, to his relief, his wedding ring—he never wears anything ostentatious. It's not necessary, either. His mere presence sets off the staff's neurons wherever he goes, from a restaurant to the hairdresser's where they take care of his image. That and the armored car do the rest.

The world has gone crazy.

And sometimes, like this afternoon, especially so.

"Damnit, fuck! What are you talking about?"

Felipa stops in the middle of the stairs at the upper part of the duplex. Her boss's voice comes through the half-open door like a gale-force wind. She hesitates and rubs her hands. They are sweaty from fear, from what she's daring to do, from everything. She thought this was the best moment and now, suddenly, she hesitates.

She's about to go back down the stairs.

But a hint of anger stops her. It's taken her so long to make up her mind . . .

The voice is loud and clear again: "Then give him half a million, goddamnit! With everything we've got on the line, we're going to get caught up with details now? I know he's not fit to be seen and he's a pig, but what do you expect? Calm down, we'll get rid of him in less than a year, I'm telling you! Now we have no choice but to put up with it. Just make him sign the receipt, okay? And careful on the phone, damnit. Everything's taped now. Idiot judges and their fucking mothers!"

Felipa is on the other side of the door, trembling, wondering for the second time whether to come back later or wait. The problem is that if he leaves the office and goes downstairs, it'll be difficult to get him alone. It's not that there's much interaction between the people in the house, but if Master Pelayo, Miss Vanesa, or Mrs. Laia show up in the middle of her request . . .

Through the door's small opening she sees him, red with anger, furious, incensed. The force of his power is clear from here.

If her need didn't outweigh her fear . . .

"And that other one wants a hundred thousand?" José María Morales Moreno's voice intensifies. "Fuck him! Why is it that in this fucking country nobody lets you lay a brick without asking for something? Tell him fifty, Eloy, and make it work! We're not going to just throw money away like that! At this rate, we won't even have ten million!"

This isn't the first time she overhears him on the phone. Last time it was with Gemma. Gemma has been to dinner with them a couple of times. She's very good looking, younger than Mrs. Laia. José María's sweet nothings left no doubt about what was going on between them.

But that's none of her business.

Perhaps that's part of the game among the rich.

Besides, Gemma is not the only one.

Her boss's trousers are a well of surprises, a stream of secrets. His audacity is astonishing. The week before, she'd found a pink card with a woman's peculiar name, perhaps French. The card described the many things she could do with a man in bed. A month before that, she had found a receipt from a no less conspicuous club.

Felipa isn't clever, but neither was she born yesterday.

Sometimes she thinks about the four of them and doesn't understand a thing.

"Look, you know what? A couple of our guys will break their legs for four euros, okay? Then it'll be fine to can half the staff, to throw all of them out on the fucking street!"

The phone conversation ends.

Felipa counts to ten and rubs her hands on the apron again. She takes a breath and slows down her heartbeat. Now. Now or never.

Then she knocks on the office door.

"What do you want?" roars the voice of the owner of the house.

"Excuse me, sir . . ." She puts her head through the opening.

"Oh, it's you. What is it?"

"Sir . . ."

"Come in, come in. I don't have all day."

She has to jump right into the issue, heart on her sleeve.

"Sir, it's just that . . . well, the last time you gave me a raise was . . . more than a year ago, you know? And now . . ."

"What do you want? More money?" His eyes are big as saucers now. "Are you out of your mind or what? Do you think they just give me money, like a present? We're in a recession, do you understand? Yeah, I know you have no fucking idea what I'm talking about, but that's the way it is. And what do you want money for, Felipa? For the love of God, you have everything you could want here."

"I want to visit my family for Christmas and—"

"For Christmas? This year? Are you thinking of leaving precisely when there's the most work, with all the dinner parties and . . . ? C'mon, c'mon, Felipa, don't mess with me, okay? Leave me alone; just take it up with my wife."

"But your wife—"

"Felipa." He looks at her sternly and his dry gesture signals the end of the conversation.

She lowers her head and leaves the office.

For some time now, she has stopped crying when she feels worse than a rat, but this time she shuts herself in her room and weeps until she's called and has to run out to see what her masters want. Any one of her masters.

Felipa Quijano Quilez is thirty-five years old but looks more like fifty. She's short, with olive skin, eyes painfully tired, a sad expression on her face, worn-out hands, worn-out hopes.

This day, this afternoon, she calls home from a telephone center.

"I'm coming back," she declares.

Then she holds back her tears, talks with her mother, with her children. She says the same thing to all of them.

"I was lucky. I won the Spanish lottery."

At night, she makes dinner.

Cool. Feeling nothing.

She doesn't sweat now, she feels no fear. She's worked everything out. Now her will is firm.

She cautiously distributes the rat poison she bought at a drugstore downtown, not overdoing it, so they won't notice its bad taste. The exact amount in the soup, and a little more in the wine and the meat sauce. She found out what she needed to know about it. She had asked the druggist what would happen if people imbibed it by mistake and the man was graphic and generous in his explanations. A person will notice the flavor unless the soup is strong and salted, unless the wine is dark, unless the sauce has mustard. A human being can't eat it without detecting its bitterness, but a little at a time in soup, wine, sauce . . . The druggist said that more than one writer of detective novels has asked him about this and he's become an expert.

But she wants it to kill rats, right?

This is the first night in over a month that the four of them are eating together at home. Generally it's the husband who's missing, but the wife also has her dinners with friends, and Miss Vanesa sometimes "studies" at a classmate's house. This is her chance, after so much patience these final weeks. A royal dinner. She's a good cook, although they hardly value her work and at times they even get angry or laugh at her. She consults the wife, but she just shrugs and tells her not to make her dizzy with details, to do whatever she wants.

Whatever she wants.

The only negative comment comes from the head of the family.

"This wine seems sour," he says.

But Miss Vanesa is somewhat kind. "The sauce is very good today, Felipa. It was high time you learned to cook. It's rather strong . . ."

She goes back to her room after doing the dishes and clearing the table.

Then she packs her bag.

That's it. That's it. That's it.

So close to freedom.

She doesn't want to sleep. She believes it's better to be awake, to keep the tension calmly within her, but she drifts off. She doesn't know exactly when her eyes close. Well, that's the proof she's relaxed. Very relaxed. So relaxed she dreams of happy things, her house, her children. No agitation. Nothing startling. More than surprising, this is all extraordinary. When she wakes up, she finds the first light of day entering her window.

She goes to the master bedroom first.

The wife, Mrs. Laia, is there just like always, lying on her back, with her face mask and one of her silk robes covering her cold body. Her husband, however, must have felt sick because his body is half on the bed, half on the floor, as if he tried to get down or crawl after the life that was escaping from him. His expression is bitter.

Painful.

Felipa looks at him for a while without moving a muscle.

She doesn't feel a thing.

Nothing.

She goes back to the wife and spits on her. Oh yes.

Then she goes to Miss Vanesa's room.

And then to Master Pelayo's.

The girl evidently felt the pain too. She lies on the floor, on her stomach, her hand hooked, a nail chipped. But the boy, just like his mother, seems to be sleeping, seraphic, innocent.

An innocent devil.

Convinced she's got nothing to fear now, she goes back to the master bedroom and takes some clothes suitable for herself and her mother. She leaves the jewels. She prefers money, the large sum of dirty money hidden in the office. And she doesn't even grab it all. She doesn't want to arouse suspicion at the airport. She takes just what she needs to start anew. With the clothes in a bag belonging to the couple, she returns to the children's rooms and picks through their closets.

The last thing she does before leaving is look out at Turó Parc, the poet Eduard Marquina's gardens.

This she will miss.

It's undoubtedly the prettiest park in Barcelona.

She exits the building without anyone seeing her, not even Tomás, the superintendent, who at that time of the day is having his sandwich, away from prying eyes, down in his hideout in the basement. She hails a cab and the driver helps her with her three bags. Destination: the airport.

Felipa Quijano Quilez looks for the last time at the park, at the city to which she'll only come back if God, in his infinite goodness, wills it. Her face shows no emotion. She doesn't feel guilty either. In her country, they kill pigs in less pious ways. The only thing she knows, and this certainty increases by the minute, is that she is free.

Free.

For the first time in a long while, there's a hint of a smile on her face when she sees the airport in the distance.

There's no problem buying the ticket. There never is if you're traveling first class. Like a lady. She waits in a comfortable VIP lounge where there's no lack of anything. And in no time, she'll be flying back home, to her mother and children.

At long last.

Life isn't always unfair.

Fucked, yes. Unfair, no. It depends on the person.

She finally laughs when the plane takes off, almost two hours later.

She doesn't know whether the Philippines has an extradition treaty with Spain, but she doubts very much that they'll find her in the mountains west of Kabugao, no matter how hard they look.

THE CUSTOMER IS ALWAYS RIGHT

BY IMMA MONSÓ

L'Eixample

Translated from Catalan by Valerie Miles

D on't you ever just let your mind wander?" her husband had asked when they first met. "Wander?
Where to?" she said, surprised. He fell in love with
her that very instant. He had been married for years to a pe-
rennially dissatisfied woman and had come to think it was a
trait shared by all females. When he met Onia, it was hard for
him to believe he had been wrong. Onia never said things like
If only we would do such and such, and even less: *If only we had
done such and such*. He could count on his fingers the times
that Onia had begun a sentence with the words *if* or *maybe*.

They'd never had any children because she couldn't imagine herself as a mother. And because most of the things attached to childhood seemed to her both foolish and silly. She
had never believed for a moment that the three Kings came
from the East bearing gifts. She had only ever cared to watch
the feet of the Gegants*, and from a very early age she had
wondered how much they paid someone to wear them and
how heavy they were. When she was asked to write things at
school she found it an impossible task. Reading stories with
even the slightest dose of fantasy was like torture for her.

"I'll tell stories to the children myself," her husband would
say, since he had wanted to become a father. "But I just can't
imagine what a child of ours would be like," she'd respond. He

---

*Large wooden carnival figures brought out during festivals and important
occasions to dance with and impress children

was a silver importer; every two years he travelled to Zacatecas, Mexico, and came back overwhelmed by the poverty and the orphaned children there. A friend of his had taken a few of them in so they wouldn't die of hunger. It was 1980, during the time when Cervantes Corona couldn't finish his gubernatorial acceptance speech because his voice had broken with emotion at the state of desolation in which his predecessor had left the region. His friend's wife told him the children needed a family. They were able to provide food and shelter, as if the kids were abandoned kittens, but that wasn't enough. And so one day, when they were already well into their forties, he said to Onia: "If you can't imagine a child of our own, then you no longer need to. She already exists." He told her about the children of Zacatecas, the mining orphans: "Any one of them, or more than one." Each time he came back from one of his trips to Mexico he told her about the starving children. She had a hard time getting her head around the idea, but since she had no real imagination, she couldn't find a pretext to oppose it. So she acquiesced. Living with her was easy, everything was so overwhelmingly logical.

They lived in L'Eixample and so they thought they should look for a quieter neighborhood for a child—or even better, a house in the country near Lleida, where Onia was born. But the task of finding the house of their dreams fell to her husband, as she didn't do such a thing as have dreams. In Sitges: "It has an enormous rooftop terrace with views of both the sea and a pine forest." When they went to see it together, the art nouveau details weren't much to her liking. But the views were very nice and it was basically fine with her. They put their apartment in L'Eixample up for sale.

The week they were supposed to sign the mortgage contract, she found a job that allowed her to put her accounting studies to good use. It was a well-paid job near their home, for a pest control company. It put a stop to their plans: they couldn't go live in Sitges if her job was in Barcelona. At that time it was still a long commute. So they put off their plans to move indefinitely. As time went by, they also dropped the subject of adopting. So they stayed in L'Eixample and didn't act on the one and only big decision that could have changed the course of their lives.

It took him a long time to give up the dreams he had built around the house and child. For the first time, he was seriously bothered by the fact that she didn't have any dreams of her own, that her feet were so firmly planted on the ground. But when he would reflect on the horrible life he had shared with his ex-wife, he would go back to admiring Onia. *What incredible common sense she has,* he often thought. One time he asked her: "I already know that you never daydream, but what about when you sleep?" She told him that she rarely remembered a dream. And when she remembered anything, it was entirely uninteresting; fumigating fleas, adding up invoices, retying her scarf. To her, not dreaming at all and dreaming such things were one and the same.

Thirty years went by after the decision that was never made. This year Onia would turn seventy-nine. She had no regrets and thought very little about the past. She had just remodeled her dining room, which opened out on the corner of Passeig de Gràcia and Passatge de la Concepció. It had previously remained closed. Now she spent her days there, as she could no longer walk around without help and so tended to go out very little. Despite the fact that she'd just bought herself a brand-new wheelchair. "The Ferrari of wheelchairs!" the salesman exclaimed. "Just imagine all the things you can do now!" She shot him a stern look and replied, "Why, imagine it yourself, young man."

* * *

One afternoon, and quite unexpectedly, Onia felt as though there was something missing inside of her, like there was a great big hole in her life. She had never really noticed this empty space before, and if she hadn't lived for so many years, she would have died without ever feeling it. But that afternoon, all of a sudden, perhaps because she now had unlimited free time (she couldn't imagine that she'd actually die one day), she decided for the first time ever to follow her teacher's advice, the one who had made her write about trees with secret doorways and daisies that zoomed away from their flowerpots on rollerskates. She was never able to just come up with these sorts of things, and so the teacher used to tell her: "Start with reality and then go beyond it. Change it, distort it, don't write things as they are, but as they could be, or as they could have been."

So she started that very afternoon. She sat down in front of the window that looked out over Passatge de la Concepció, not over Passeig de Gràcia, which she loathed because it was so lit up and conspicuous. Luxury stores, tourists, colors, everything en masse and uncontrolled. In the Passatge, however, things were less hectic. There were only a few stores. From her window she saw the corner façade of Santa Eulalia; customers went in through the doors that open onto Passeig de Gràcia, so there wasn't much of interest to observe there. She could also see the restaurant Tragaluz, where celebrities often showed up with their court of paparazzi. But Onia didn't think this would do much to stimulate her thoughts and set them wandering. In any case, the restaurant was closed in the afternoon, which was when Onia spent time looking out her window. There was a small store between Tragaluz and Santa Eulalia which sold sweaters. It had belonged to her husband until he passed away six years earlier and she had decided to sell it. Shortly afterward they opened Tot Cashmere, which is still there today.

She sat down at three o'clock in the afternoon and didn't move from her spot. The method consisted in watching any person who entered the Passatge and trying to imagine their name, their job, their family, their origin, and their future. She tried with more than twenty people but nothing occurred to her. It's supposed to be quite easy, something a five-year-old can do. But no, not for her. She just couldn't see herself doing these asinine things. At five-thirty she decided to give herself one last shot. A tall woman with a long black braid and sunglasses turned the corner from Passeig de Gràcia and entered the Passatge. Onia tried to imagine which one of the stores the braided woman would enter. She had stopped in front of the show window of Santa Eulalia: Onia had a few extra moments to call up her fantasy, but the woman walked into the sweater shop. Onia didn't give up hope. Since the woman would be in the shop for a bit, she had some time to make up her story: Who is she? Where does she live? When will she come out? What will she buy? Why? Where will she go when she comes out?

Twenty minutes went by and Onia still couldn't find any answers to these questions . . . She searched for a way to open her mind with visions of this unknown woman's immediate future, but she couldn't do it . . . When over an hour had passed, the woman with the braid had still not come back out. This fact alone would have given anyone else plenty to imagine. But Onia simply felt surprised. She had stopped trying to stimulate her imagination twenty minutes earlier. She didn't feel like fantasizing: now all she wanted was for the woman to come out.

Cristina's voice called from the kitchen: "It's eight-thirty, do you want me to make supper now or wait until later?" Onia didn't answer her, she was suddenly feeling extremely curious. She knew the shop space very well—it was tiny and there was no other exit. The sales clerk had turned out the lights and was preparing to leave, alone, peering at herself in the window. Cristina walked into the dining room to ask the question again. "I'll have supper later," Onia said distractedly. But then she turned to the girl and asked, "Could you do me a small favor, dear? Would you go down to Tot Cashmere and see if there is a woman with a black braid inside? Go quickly because the sales clerk is closing up." Cristina, who immediately imagined a dozen motives for such a strange request, hurried down the stairs two-by-two, crossed the Passatge as fast as she could, and reached the store just as the sales clerk began lowering the metal security grille. Onia saw the two women talking, and the clerk immediately raised the grille again, opened the door, and they both went into the store. Ten minutes later, the two of them came back out and closed up the shop.

"There was nobody inside," Cristina said.

"Then how did you convince her to open the door again after she had already closed it?" Onia asked.

"We used to greet each other when I was working in the café next to the store . . . so I told her that I needed a green sweater to match a purple skirt with green trim to wear to a party tonight where I'll see some old school friends—"

Onia interrupted her: "You could simply have told her that I asked you to check something for me, you didn't have to go into so much detail."

"But it isn't true, I don't have a purple skirt with green trim or anything like it, I just thought it would be more believable than if I told her that you had asked me to go running down and stick my nose into her business."

Onia grew impatient: "Did you check to see if there was another door? Maybe they remodeled the interior . . ."

"I checked everything," Cristina said. "I didn't see a single door. Why?"

Onia took a deep breath and told her the truth: "A woman went in two hours ago and never came out."

Cristina's face went blank. "Don't take this the wrong way, but I think your imagination is playing tricks on you," she said. Onia didn't take it the wrong way. But neither did she take it well. She'd clearly never had an imagination. Her sight or her memory could trick her, yes . . . she was seventy-eight years old. But no doctor had ever mentioned any such problem, and since nobody had ever mentioned one, she couldn't imagine there being one. The next day she continued watching the store and she saw two more disappearances. After a few more days, she was absolutely sure there were some people who had walked into the store and never walked out.

"What do you know about the sales clerk in Tot Cashmere?" she asked Cristina.

"Not very much. I know she works during the day, and then in the evening she takes care of her son who is in a wheelchair and who doesn't like to leave the house. She came from Mexico years ago and began working in the store when she finally got her papers. The son is seventeen, I think. He didn't come around very often when I worked in the café. She complained often about having problems paying her bills."

Onia didn't know what to think. She didn't have the resources to judge the story: she never went to see thrillers or read mystery novels. She never read science fiction, didn't believe in ghosts, and had never been interested in people who disappeared, except for the real cases she heard on the news. It was still very hard for her to believe what she had seen. So one afternoon she grabbed a paper and pencil: she counted the people going in, and when they came out she crossed them off the list. By evening she realized that there was something still stranger yet: not only did some of the people who went in never come back out, but some of the people who came out had never entered in the first place. Contrary to what she had suspected, more shoppers had come out than had gone in.

Since she had no fictional references to help her unravel the strings of the story, the next day she decided to go see the sales clerk herself and ask questions point-blank. She went straight into the store and without beating around the bush declared: "I am an old woman who is overwhelmed with curiosity."

The store attendant said: "What do you need?"

Onia explained everything she had seen through the window, and for reasons she couldn't quite understand, the clerk was effusively kind and attentive in a way that seemed entirely out of place.

Finally, she responded: "I know you will keep my secret."

And Onia answered: "You can be sure of it. I am as silent as a grave." The young woman pushed the wheelchair to a spot behind a stack of pashminas. Onia could see into the dressing room through a tear in the curtain. Not even a minute later, she heard the happy sound of a door opening and her heart began to beat quickly.

A middle-aged woman with red hair asked for a cobalt-blue cashmere sweater. The clerk went straight to the shelf and took down a very large green garment.

The customer said: "I think it's too small." The clerk looked her straight in the eyes and said: "No."

But the woman responded: "Don't you know that the customer is always right?"

Then the clerk grabbed a cobalt-blue sweater from another shelf. It was very silky, with a high neck, and was as ample as the first one. The woman brought it to the dressing room while the clerk locked the front door. Through the tear, Onia saw her arms search out the sleeves with a little difficulty, and for a minute that felt like an eternity, she watched as the woman appeared to be choking inside the sweater. From behind the pashminas, Onia could hear her breathing hard and saw that her head still hadn't appeared through the collar. *So that's it. They suffocate to death inside the clothing. But then what happens?* she thought.

Finally, a shock of red hair shot through the wool neck. The hair was dry and discolored. Then a piece of yellowed parchment emerged, which turned out to be an ear. Suddenly the whole head emerged, an aged head, followed by a second one. Two heads. And two bodies. Twins. Old twins.

The two women finished removing the sweater and smiled at the clerk. One of them approached the cash register and signed a check. The clerk put the check in the register but kept the sweater. Onia watched as one old woman put her checkbook away, while her twin left the store, moving aside for a young man coming in to buy a scarf. When the young man exited the store, Onia came out of her hiding place.

The clerk took her time explaining to Onia that she had a son who never left their house. "His whole life revolves around looking out at the sea and the pine trees from the rooftop terrace . . . But a year ago, they put the land in front of the house up for sale to build an apartment building. I've been afraid of this happening for years. Moving to another house would be his death. I felt helpless, desperate . . . Then one Christmas an angel visited me. A stranger came into the store and asked me for a blue sweater. I had a cobalt-blue cashmere sweater that was two sizes too big, but she took it anyway. She came back the next day. 'It's not my size.' 'I told you it was too big for you.' 'You're wrong. It's too small. Lately, everything is too small for me,' she said. I must have had a puzzled look on my face, because she followed with, 'Yes, it's true, don't look at me with that expression on your face: the customer is always right.' I processed her return and she left. That very afternoon, another woman came in and asked for a cobalt-blue sweater. When I showed it to her, she said: 'It's too small for me.' I argued with her until she finally said: 'Don't insist: the customer is always right.' I thought it was so strange, but what came next was far stranger. I saw three heads coming out through the neck of the sweater, each one about twenty years older than the girl who had pulled it over her head . . . While signing a check, one of the triplets said: 'Am I the first customer who is always right?' 'I don't understand,' I said. 'The first person to come here to split?' I nodded my head yes, then I asked: 'What . . . what does that mean?' 'It's something they offer on board,' she said, as the other customer put the sweater back on the shelf. And that's all. I think nearly all the customers come from luxury cruises. They offer to exchange the average number of years that one has left to live in a linear life into multiple lives, two or three or whatever. Like a road that forks . . . all you have to do is pass through the sweater."

Impressed, Onia asked: "And . . . have you ever felt curious to try it yourself?"

"No! If you value yourself in a certain way, it's impossible to want to change your life for another, no matter how horrible it might be," the clerk said sternly.

"How peculiar. I've never valued anything in that way . . . Of course, I can't imagine what it must be like, so I guess I don't really care one way or the other," Onia said.

The clerk folded the sweater, sighed, and said: "I can't sleep at night. What if someone tries the sweater on by mistake? What if the store owner finds out what I'm doing? That's why as soon as I finish paying for the piece of land, I won't let anyone else try it on anymore."

"Don't you have a telephone number or some other way to contact the woman who gave the sweater these strange properties?"

"Angels don't have telephone numbers. Have you never seen one of those movies with angels in them that air at Christmastime? Like the one where James Stewart is going to commit suicide . . . ?"

"I don't like fiction stories. Anyway, I think what your customers do is closer to the devil than the angels."

"You think these millionaires have sold their souls to the devil? I don't see it that way . . . they only change the way they live: less time but in a variety of lives. Choice is no longer a problem for them. Haven't you ever thought: I have to decide whether to do this or that, but if I had more than one life I could do both and I would never have to regret anything? Haven't you ever regretted anything?"

Although she'd never felt anything like regret, Onia remembered that she had once prepared to embark on another life. She could have easily figured out that the clerk had a similar background and age as the children her husband had wanted to adopt. For however small an imagination, it was clear that the boy's terrace could have been the one they never bought. But Onia didn't speculate about any of this, and she didn't ask if the house was in Sitges or if the terrace had art nouveau details. It didn't even occur to her.

So she asked: "And . . . your son . . . you don't think he would be interested in putting his head into the sweater?"

"He doesn't know anything about it," the woman said defensively. She lit a cigarette and shrunk into herself. "Of course he would like to . . . He's like you. And like all the customers who are always right: incapable of glimpsing things his eyes don't see. That's precisely why it's so important to save the view of the sea and the pine forest. Having a building blocking the views wouldn't be such a bad thing for me . . . I can imagine marvelous things from nothing more than a slice of wall. From a crack in the ceiling or a spot of humidity I can imagine roads, caves, and lakes . . . But not him, no. For him, a wall is a wall. Nothing else can be borne from his walls. That's why he can't live walled in, do you understand?"

Onia listened in silence. She wasn't disturbed by not seeing flowers where there weren't any, she didn't consider this tragic.

As she pressed the doorbell for Cristina to let her in, she suddenly thought: *Black market money!* How is she going to be able to buy the land with all that black market money? But then she realized that the girl was very clever and would find a solution. Onia could now forget about this bizarre episode.

The clerk saw her enter her house. She regretted having explained everything. Even though she was convinced the old woman wouldn't say a word. She herself confessed that she was as silent as a grave.

PART III

DAYS OF WINE (WHITE LINES) AND ROSES

EPIPHANY

BY ERIC TAYLOR-ARAGÓN

Barceloneta

There's something that's been troubling me, a gaze that won't go away, and when I close my eyes I see this gaze, and sometimes I think I'll only be able to escape it by moving to a different country or continent or solar system, to some parallel universe where what happened didn't happen. I'm still not sure what I should have done or whether I did the right thing—but I did it and now it's done. And now that it's done, I'm actually glad it's done. Am I making sense?

I'll make this quick. It was right after I broke up with La Princesa, a crazy Spanish girl. I was busted up, in a bad way, moping about, drinking and feeling like life was worthless.

We all know that the end of love is like wartime. It's like being bombarded. People who can't take it throw themselves off bridges, shoot themselves in the mouth. You look for a bunker, you look for shelter, refuge, solace, distraction. And then, just when you think it's safe to come out, you see or hear something—it might be something as innocuous as a bird—or a cell phone ringtone, or a TV show, or a piece of music, and the memories come flooding back and suddenly you hear the whistle blast of bombs, the crack of sniper rifles, the drone of drones. Anyway, there was a TV in the corner of this bar, and when I glanced up at it I saw an ad for dish soap. *Our dish soap*. The dish soap we used to use when we lived together. *Nina, mi Princesa*, I thought . . . My breath got jagged, I felt like I'd been punched in the solar plexus. I held onto the bar to keep from falling down.

I was sitting on an old rickety stool in l'Electricitat, an old-school bodega in Barceloneta, drinking vermouth after vermouth, spending the last of my meager savings. This is a fisherman's bar, mostly locals. The people leave you alone. That's why I like it. Every now and then I looked in the hazy mirror behind the bar. I looked bad. Dark circles under the eyes. Stubble. Disheveled hair. A wild, hunted look. I think I had my little notebook out and maybe every now and then I'd scribble something down, something foolish, something I'd come across in a couple of years and be terribly embarrassed by . . . I was probably writing to La Princesa about how much I loved her and how I'd change if she took me back. I was probably writing to myself, telling myself to get a grip, to ride it out, to try and be normal and content and full of loving kindness (which is the hardest thing of all).

Looking back, I think the final straw was when I threw a typewriter through the café window in Borne. I mean, who the hell walks around with a typewriter these days? So then I spent the night in jail and I called her afterward and she said, "You did what with the typewriter?" and I told her again, "I threw it out the window," and then she started to laugh and replied in English, "You're joking!" and I said, "Who's Joe King?" This is one of our little jokes, but suddenly she wasn't laughing anymore. She said, "I think we need to take a little break . . ." Her name was Nina and I loved her and she'd put up with a lot, even supported me financially for a time, and now she wasn't up for it anymore. I apologized, I groveled and told her I would reform and be a better human being, and she said, "That's what you said last time, and the time before that." Nina is beautiful, with a remarkable bosom and a little birthmark in the shape of an upside-down teardrop just below her right eye, as if she's crying in reverse. Anyway, that night I was thinking about all this and was feeling depressed in l'Electricitat and being devastated by dish soap ads. That was when I met Luca.

He was slight of build, with thick eyebrows perched over big, sensitive eyes, the kind of eyes that a dog flashes at you just after you've kicked it. There was a soccer match on, and a few other people in the bar, but we were the only non-Catalans. He asked me for a cigarette and I told him I didn't smoke and he asked me where I was from and I said, "Peru," and he said, "Ah, Peru," and raised his eyebrows. "I've always felt a deep connection with the Incas," he declared then, looking at me keenly.

The things you have to put up with from Europeans. He told me he was Italian, from Rome, and then later, out of nowhere, he said, "You must like perica," and truth be told, I haven't done much cocaine in my life, just enough to know it would be dangerous for someone of my personality type—and given that I'm having enough problems with this existence thing, I generally stay away. I shrugged and he told me, "Tonight we will do perica together," as if this were a major step forward, as if he were proposing some sort of vision quest.

And then Luca told me that I seemed sad.

"A broken heart?"

I nodded.

"I thought so," he said. "So maybe you can understand my problem."

And then he told me he was in love too, and that it had all exploded in his face. That it was all ruined, a mess. I was a bit surprised to have someone open up to me like this. In fact, I almost felt as if I'd met my analogue, my doppelgänger, my mirror image. I listened attentively, hoping for clues that could help me out of my abyss.

But before I go on, I'd like to describe him a bit more. His laugh was sharp, almost a bark, and his face was intelligent and he had bright white teeth with, if I remember correctly, rather pronounced canines. His eyes were hazel-colored, and this I'm sure of, because when he died, I tried to close them, you know, like in the movies, but they just wouldn't close, they kept popping open. This much I remember, in fact I can't forget it.

He wore a wrinkled dark blue linen jacket (what they call an "Americana" around here) and blue jeans, and while we were drinking, I knocked over his beer by mistake and he caught the bottle in midair, just before it hit the floor, and then he went on talking like nothing had happened. He was the sort of person who didn't move across the street, he darted; he didn't look over at someone, he shot them a glance; he didn't get up from a chair, he sprang to his feet. That was his energy, which I felt immediately—and this is what made what happened later so shocking.

After a while he told me he wasn't from Rome but from Naples. He talked about Naples and his family and he called himself an exile, saying, "I can't go back," with a tone of finality. And when I asked him why, he ordered another round and told me it was a "problema d' amore," very, very complicated, and then he looked down at the bar and seemed to sink a little and then he held his head in his hands like a watermelon and then set his head on the bar and said, "CamillaCamillaCamilla." And then he looked up and laughed. "You see, I fell in love with the wrong woman, like a stronzo, like an idiota. The daughter of a capo, my boss—and what's even worse is that she fell in love with me too."

He'd been a low-level front man for the Camorra's real estate business in Naples. A crooked nobody. A white-collar foot soldier in the di Lauro clan. One day he'd received a call to show a flat to one of the capo's lieutenants. The man showed up with a beautiful young woman. It was Camilla. She was small-boned and had short, curly hair and eyes that were shy and curious at the same time. The man was her bodyguard. In the middle of the tour, the man received a call on his cell phone and rushed away, telling Luca not to let her out of his sight, and to stay in the apartment. The Neapolitan mafia had been in a civil war for the last year and things were tense.

"The bodyguard was only gone for about an hour and a half," he said, "but it was enough for me and Camilla to fall in love. We talked as if we'd known each other our entire lives. I know it sounds like a cliché, but what can I do? It's there. I lived it. She was sublime. Perfect. We arranged to meet a few days later. And then, over the next couple of weeks, we made all sorts of crazy romantic promises, exchanged e-mails and text messages, met quickly and in secret. We said we'd die for each other, that nothing would stop us, that we would find a way, even if we had to leave Naples. It really seemed real. We convinced ourselves that it was going to happen. That it would all turn out alright. We'd have children, make a family, grow old—all the stupid things you promise when you're young and in love and from the south of Italy. And we kissed only once, in a little bar by the port. But someone saw us."

He banged the bar with his fist. My empty vermouth glass gave a little hop. He had big hands, long pianist fingers, and flat broad nails, bitten to the quick.

"What it comes down to is that I'm a coward. When I had my chance I failed. Or maybe it was doomed from the start. A month after we met, I was leaving the office when

I was grabbed by three men and thrown in the back of a car. They took me to an abandoned building, and beat and kicked me until I just lay there bleeding and broken, half dead. And then they said, 'You had better leave Naples, the boss doesn't like you seeing his daughter.' I had over thirty stitches"—here he pointed to some scars on the back of his head, his brow— "and two broken ribs, two black eyes, and a broken jaw. They told me the only reason they didn't kill me was because Camilla had threatened to kill herself if anything happened to me. She told me this later, that she'd threatened her father with suicide, slashed at her wrists. After my beating I stayed in the house of a cousin in the country and then my family bought me a ticket here. Here, I'm like a ghost. I have no friends, no family. We managed to communicate by e-mail for a while, but not anymore. And today I found out why. She's getting married to Giovanni Malatesta, another mafiosi. I am now officially nothing. It's over. And I'm too much of a coward to do anything about it. I'm not a ninja, I'm not Arnold Schwarzenegger—I'm not even Woody Allen. This is not a movie. They would kill me. And I'm a coward and don't want to die."

Suddenly he let loose his barking laugh, "Ha ha ha!" He laughed for a long time, as if he'd just come to a realization, as if something had finally become clear to him, and then he stood up and said, "I must make a phone call." He went outside, teetering a bit. There were a few old grizzled men standing at the bar, one was leaning against a slot machine. He was stout with large forearms and was smoking a stub of a cigar, while his potbelly pressed against the formidable stomach of another man and their heads were at least a meter apart. They were arguing about soccer and spoke in grunts and deep, aquatic bellows, like foghorns or something. It was as if these hard-living ex-fishermen had sprung from the floor of the bar itself, as if they were intrinsic to the place, like barnacles on a whale. A man came in with an empty plastic Coke bottle, handed it without a word to the barman who then went to a huge wood barrel on the left side of the bar, near the back, turned the spigot, and filled it up with a deep red wine. The man dug around in his pocket, stuck two coins on the table with a loud ringing sound, and then he took his Coke bottle and walked away. There was an ad on TV for Burger King. Luca came back in, he smiled. He sat. We continued hanging out. Luca was no longer talking about his girlfriend and I no longer talked about mine. The mood had changed. In fact, he seemed quite cheerful all of a sudden. We got the bartender to fill us up a bottle of wine, paid the bill, and strolled toward his house.

A breeze had picked up and all the clothes hanging in the balconies fluttered and danced in the wind and a dog ran by, almost got hit by a little red Renault which swerved and honked and did not slow.

"Damn," Luca said, "that's one lucky dog," and we continued walking—quickly, with purpose. The façade of his building was covered in old blue tiles and some had fallen off and showed the crumbling tan stucco underneath. We walked up the five flights of stairs. He opened the door and waved his hand toward the tumbledown couch in the living room and then went into the kitchen and started looking for something. I sat down and glanced around. The white paint was peeling off in places and there was a large ocher stain on the ceiling near the window. A single lightbulb hung from the middle of the ceiling, a fading light washed the left side of the room. A clay pot on the windowsill held yellow daffodils, insolent in their brightness. I could hear voices coming off the street, distant cries of children playing on the beach, so faint as to almost be imperceptible.

His phone rang. Two rings before going silent. He walked over to the coffee table, looked at the number, and picked it up.

"He's here," he said, and he stood, went to the bookshelf, took out a book, and opened it. There was a thick sheaf of bills inside. He took out a fifty, put the book back on the shelf, and said, "Give me twenty euros, the cocaine is here."

I gave him my last twenty euros, and I'm not sure why I trusted him and often wish I hadn't because of what happened later, but I gave it to him. The worst-spent twenty euros of my life. And I'm sure that if I hadn't been so busted up I wouldn't have given it to him, I wouldn't have been in that rathole of a flat, but we were brothers, both of us with broken hearts. His story, it's true, was a bit more romantic, but a broken heart is a broken heart, right?

He left the apartment. I walked out onto the balcony, looked down. I could see someone on a moped parked in front. His dark helmet like the head of an ant. Luca exited the building, approached him. A quick transaction ensued. The ant started up the moped and putt-putted away. Luca wheeled around and reentered the building.

I turned around, sat back on the couch. I closed my eyes briefly and felt the moist breeze wending its way, swirling around the room, licking at the cheap dingy white polyester curtains on either side of the window. I looked around the room at the empty cigarette packs, the little inlaid wood box on the table, and the books, lots of books—many books on love, I noticed, many love stories, *Love in the Time of Cholera* by Gabo, *On Love* by Stendhal, even this American book, *Men Are from Mars, Women Are from Venus*, and there, splayed in the corner, César Vallejo, my favorite Peruvian poet, who foretold his own death in a poem and died "of exhaustion" in Paris.

I couldn't help but feel that there was something almost quaint about being so heartbroken and reading love stories and discourses on love and mooning over a capo's daughter named Camilla who you kissed once. As if there was a solution to any of this. As if closure existed. I mean, we all know that the only cure for a broken heart is time, another lover, or death.

I heard his footsteps coming up the stairs two at a time. The balcony door slammed shut, *bang*, and Luca came back in with a rattle, windblown and wild-haired. He brought with him a hard-edged street scent with traces of the damp, almost churchlike smell of the stairwell—but most of all, that languorous funky Mediterranean sea air. A warm breeze was blowing in bursts, capricious little European zephyrs; refined, old world. My new friend spun around the room, quite happy to have scored. But there was something else he brought in with him, though I didn't understand what it was until it was all over.

He sat down, set a little folded piece of tinfoil on the table.

"So did you learn anything?" I asked.

"About what?"

"Did all these books about love teach you anything?"

"Yes, I did, in fact, I did learn something." He was concentrated, bending over the table, carefully unfolding the foil.

"What did you learn?"

"I'll tell you later. Let's have some cocaine."

He opened the tinfoil, revealing a little pile of tan powder. It did not glisten. He shot me a glance.

"That doesn't look like cocaine," I said, and he looked up at me and smiled.

"You don't think?"

"No, I don't. It's brown." I dipped the tip of my pinkie in the powder and tasted it and it tasted strange. "I'm not taking that. You bought heroin, compadre."

"You think?"

He went to the fridge and came back with a lemon. He set it on the table. He carefully poured a bit of powder on the spoon, then a little more, and he asked, "Are you sure you don't want any?"

"Yes." I was a bit put off by the whole thing. I looked around the room, at the pile of books, at the picture taped to the bookshelf of Luca and his girlfriend (I assumed). She was not how I imagined, she had short hair, little rectangular glasses, a dimple in her chin, mischievous, intellectual . . . She looked like what I imagined Marcello Mastroianni's long-suffering wife in 8½ must have looked like when she was younger . . . beautiful but not bodacious.

I suddenly wanted to get out of there, to go mingle with the tourists and stroll down Las Ramblas and watch the street performers, the mimes, jugglers, acrobats, and pickpockets do their silly tricks, to lose myself in the generalized idiocy, to go down to the beach and watch the Nordic women baring their pale, impeccable breasts slowly get sunburned. I didn't want to be here anymore. I wanted to call Nina and beg forgiveness again, just hear her voice . . .

He poured the rest of the powder in the spoon, set it back on the coffee table, picked up a knife, cut the lemon in half, then squeezed juice into the spoon. It flowed down the sides of the little pile of powder, then he started to heat it up with a lighter, and I could see the attraction of it, the ritual of it, the grand tradition, but wanted no part of it, so I just watched him. When the solution started to bubble, he took out a needle from a carved wooden box and set it gently on the coffee table.

"We must let it cool," he said. "I need your help."

"Yeah? What do you need?"

"I need you to hold the mirror." He went to the bathroom and came back with a small round mirror, about as big as my hand, and said, "I'll tell you where to hold it," and then he put a little piece of cotton in the spoon and it quickly turned brown, absorbing all the heroin, and then he stuck his needle in the cotton and put it in the spoon and sucked up all the fluid and gave it a couple of flicks with his middle finger and turned to me and said, "Hold up the mirror."

I did. It was at face level.

"Angle it down a little. There. To the right. No, the right edge toward me. Yes, that's it."

With total concentration, he turned his head and looked upward and left, his eyes trained on the mirror. He brought the syringe to his throat, to his jugular. Carefully, slowly brought the tip to his neck, traced it down, paused, his neck muscles tense, and then sank it in. I winced. And he said, "Hold still!" And I did. Then he pulled back on the plunger of the syringe and said, "Shit. Missed it." He withdrew the needle, grabbed a T-shirt off the couch, dabbed at the blood on his neck.

"Fuck," I said.

"Help me out," he repeated, "I need you to help me out."

I stayed put. He looked up again, held his breath to try and make the vein stick out more, exhaled, said "Higher," and I moved the mirror, tilted it up slightly, and then he sank the needle in and pulled back the plunger and the needle filled with a rich, slow-moving scarlet that swirled around and was beautiful in its way, and then he said, "Ahhhh," and pushed down the plunger and moaned. I set down the mirror and he sat back on the couch and his eyes rolled around in his head, and then he blinked, and opened his eyes, an expression of sweet shock on his face. And then he fell off the couch, the needle still in his neck, and I said, "Luca? Luca?"

Let me be honest here. I let him lay there for a bit.

"Luca?"

Everything started moving in slow-motion. I stood over him and bent down. I put three fingers just beneath the needle. I was afraid to take it out for fear that blood would spurt everywhere. His eyes stared up, far away as if at wheeling falcons, as if he saw a blue Neapolitan sky, a single cloud, a sparkling world, a sea breeze, a woman standing over him saying, *What? What's wrong, Luca? Are you okay?*

It was too much, those hazel eyes. I peered at them closer and saw the curved reflection of the fan's lazy orbit, the curtains twisting gently against the wall, blowing out onto the balcony, the silhouettes of buildings against the dark blue sky. I heard the tinfoil skitter across the table, drop to the floor. I touched the top of his head. I felt beneath his ear, traced down his jaw, and found his vein. I did not feel a pulse. I put my ear next to his mouth. Nothing. Not even a wisp of breath. I placed my ear on his chest. Not even the faintest of heartbeats. I pulled him away from the couch; lay him flat on his back. I went to the bedroom, took the dirty orange sheet off the bed. Standing over his body, a sheet corner in each hand, I raised my arms, flicked my wrists, and the sheet ballooned up, suspended for a second, then billowed a last time, rippling, settling over his body. He was covered now.

"Luca?" I said. "You there?"

I knelt beside him again. I didn't want to see his face, those eyes. I set my ear to his chest. I listened in vain for his heartbeat. I pulled the sheet away from his face, put my ear to his mouth, listened for breathing. Heard nothing. A beatific look on his face, a happy look.

Five minutes. Five minutes had passed. I took the mirror and wiped down the edges with the hem of my T-shirt (I don't know why). I put the César Vallejo book on the shelf. I went to the kitchen, washed my wine glass. Then I went back to the bookshelf, got the Stendhal book (*On Love*), took out the wad of euros, stuck it in my pocket, put the book back on the shelf, walked out the front door, closed it softly, made sure it was locked. My heart was pounding and there was a tingling feeling that went from my chest to my balls. I wound around the spiral staircase, passed through the narrow foyer, and ended up on the street. I started to walk. Children played soccer, shouted, but I heard nothing. A ball rolled by, rolled under a beat-up Citroen. A slender curly haired boy darted in front of me, crouched next to the car, looking beneath it. Then he got on his belly and wriggled under the chassis until all that could be seen were his skinny, kicking brown legs. I paused, turned around, and stared up at Luca's balcony, saw a smear of yellow flowers in the window, the curtains trembling in the wind.

That night I put Luca's money to good use and went to a very high-end restaurant and ate a most excellent dinner. And as the waiter uncorked my second bottle of wine, I had a realization. Nothing, I thought, matters so much to me as love, and yet, right now, as I enjoy this tremendous meal, love suddenly seems almost insignificant. How can this be? Am I that super-ficial? I felt euphoric for some reason, but couldn't understand why. I felt filled with life. Overflowing. There was no doubt about it. So without further ado, I opened my legs, reached down, took out my penis, and pinned my scrotum to the chair with a steak knife. An ecstatic, almost sensual feeling washed over me. That, I thought triumphantly, is love. After all these years of heartbreak, I have finally figured it out.

THE STORY OF A SCAR

BY CRISTINA FALLARÁS

Nou Barris

This isn't something she'll like, you figure. She's never been too motherly, and she gets anxious when work gets tangled up with the other thing. I love this story; but it was a waste of time. And you're right: the scar's absolutely beautiful; she's absolutely beautiful, isn't she? But I'd better tell you the story of the scar and then you can forget it, okay? She doesn't like it.

It all began on a sultry August morning filled with portent. Why not? It was impossible to sleep, one of those nights when you dream you're a goat on a spit and you turn, turn, turn, until your soul is dripping—and then she showed up with rings under her eyes that reached her knees, already swaying slightly in a way typical of her state. She was cute, sour-faced, dressed all in black, decked out with glass beads, and that belly and the same motherfucking moves as always. Damn, one stormy beauty.

"Nothing, right?"

This had been her greeting for more than a month. And my answer, a shrug, my eyes nailed on the damned fan. Yes indeed, nothing was going on in Barcelona, no one came by the office, and recently she'd developed a resistance to air-conditioning; she was totally against air-conditioning. She was slacking and this upset her more than what the lack of clients was doing to her bank account, something that had me worried too. You know, if she doesn't eat, I don't eat either. Well, someone would eventually step up, Victoria already had an established name, and there aren't that many women detectives; hard to deny there's some morbid fascination in that, right? An established name, but some folks step back when they see her belly, of course. And besides, August has never been a good month, it's a shitty month. Oh, but we're also against normal vacations, you know, and air-conditioning, credit cards, checks, and investigating women's infidelities. Add to this gloom a six-month pregnancy, thirty-eight degrees Celsius at dawn, and a humidity that liquefies the air . . . Get the idea? Okay, now add the severed hand of an aging rocker to the mix. Beautiful! Isn't it?

"Look at the paper. At the concert at the Forum the day before yesterday, someone sliced off that old American's hand, the one who used to play with those other two, the hippy and the doped-up guy; now he only plays with his band when he's not too boozed up."

I told her that to entertain her, because the news was rather amusing, and, I don't know, maybe her expression would change a little and her kid wouldn't be born already sour. Who would pay for that, huh? Yours truly. Who else was going to put up with the kid? I had no doubt at all about that. Me. Well, the old gringo was blinder than the black guy who moved his head to get the mic right, and when he saw himself surrounded by a crowd the size of which he couldn't remember seeing in years, the dumbass threw himself into the audience, just like he used to do, to be received by a sea of arms, he would say, that returned him to the stage, as if gliding on air. He could have cracked his head open; I'm not saying that wouldn't have been a good ending, to be squashed like a ripe fig against the floor of the Forum. But no, his audience—and who knows where they had come from, a bunch of haggard dudes of every color like we only see during summer in this city—held him up in the air for a few minutes and then put him back on the stage . . . Up to that point, everything was going just fine, except for a small detail, a gruesome detail, my friend. When the old man stepped on the dais, he noticed that . . . whoa! . . . his right hand was missing, the one of the mythic guitar solos that had earned him the name Magic Hand in the '70s. The motherfucker didn't notice immediately, the paper said, the big motherfucker had to hear the screaming from the first rows, see how they pointed at the bloody disaster, all of them spattered too, and then follow the direction their fingers were pointing to see that, beyond his wrist, there was nothing. Tourniquet, screams, someone fainting, and then off to Bellvitge Hospital.

The story left her silent for quite a while and me up in the air, because when Vicky isn't swearing, she's plotting something or is about to break your heart. They have to go for the kill because of their anger, I say, and who's always there? That's right. She grabbed the newspaper, read it, left it on the table, speechless and self-absorbed for about half an hour, then read it once more and threw it on the floor, as usual. By now you'll have noticed my ability to remain forever in dreamland, not bothering anyone, right? That's how I was brought up, it's from my childhood. This chameleon-like quality saved me from more than fifty spankings. When the storm of insults would erupt, I became a rocking chair, or a living room corner; yeah, I could become a fucking living room corner, limestone, and nobody is stupid enough to smash a wall, right? Well, that's what I did the better part of that morning while sweat began to create blacker black spots on her T-shirt, her forehead shone, and she boiled in her own foul juices.

"Right now that hand is in formaldehyde. Motherfuckers. That hand . . . Magic's divine hand, the hand from my favorite memories; it was mine, ours. We don't matter one fuck now. Motherfuckers. It's not enough to destroy everything, to torture us with stupid music, to ban breathing, eating, fucking, living; no, they had to tear it out by the roots. Motherfuckers. They have it in formaldehyde, wanna bet?"

And thus began the story of the precious scar, I tell you, which is a waste of time.

ᴄᴙ

Back then, it was called the Bronx. But the splendorous mall had now turned the area into something else. Into what? Basically, into the Bronx with a splendorous mall. The junkies from those days, most of them anyway, were dead now, and shovels of cocaine, mall-brand cocaine with slummy neon lights, had replaced heroin. I staked out a place between the few remaining gypsies who hadn't been absorbed by the Cult yet and the large colony of Colombians, Dominicans, Moroccans, and so on.

I was going through a bad time, with no clients, in the red, pregnant, and with good ol' Jesús waiting for me every morning at the office, right on time, so that I would appear and come up with some solution to his life. To his fucking life as a former deadbeat, former drunk, former pusher. Rootless and dirty—the poor wretch was really dirty.

"Looking for something?"

Junkie, I thought. A junkie with money problems and hunting for saps. I looked at her and touched my belly. The gesture didn't mean anything. Not in that place, and we both knew it. I looked the woman straight in the eye, pitiless. Thirty,

I thought, and not looking good for your age at all, girl, with those gloomy rings under your eyes and two teeth fewer than what's needed for a smile to smile.

I waited, I knew silence was a language.

"I've got coke, hashish, and pastis, what do you want? It's all very legal, sister, I'm very legal. Everything's okay, sister, you hear me?"

She still had an Andalusian lilt, probably from her parents, and they got theirs from before, from the grandparents, a lilt that came from hauling bags and long train rides. In her family's case, of course, exodus had not ended in generational success.

"Coke, one gram," I answered without thinking, and handed her a fifty-dollar bill while I changed my tourist-in-Apache-territory look for an obvious murderous warning. It's habit. Your gestures, your habits, they stick to you. I had put one foot in Nou Barris and gone right to the Renfe-Meridiana area, to the junkie blocks from days gone by. Well, to one of the many clusters of dwellings scattered in those neighborhoods, where life went on between sale and consumption, yesterday's heroin, today's coke and pastis. Habit, my habit: Nou Barris, dealers, blow. Precisely because of that habit, I followed her and was treated to the dazzling mall that had not changed the feel of those blocks, though there was a certain something missing that had nothing to do with the surrounding innovations. The throbbing bundles I remembered huddled in the corners had been swept away by death. I thought, *damnitshit*, there's nothing left. I didn't feel sorry for them—they were already cadavers back then—what hurt me was the shadow of the shopping mastodon next to this desert of city blocks, albeit with its big public swimming pool. And Magic Hand's hand was part of my memory, the time gone by, the scooter and the delirium; I had been a stupid and feverish youngster back then, keeping time with that hand that seemed like an essential soundtrack. I felt the silence. I felt old.

Just a second before the woman rang the bell for the eighth floor, I whispered into her neck: "Give me my stuff and take me to the dealer. And shut up!"

That's how it was. Everything was okay, as it always is. There was something left over from the old times. I figured the junkie would get a good beating, because she was gullible and dumb, and the creep who would beat her would know she had it coming, and I wondered why I'd done that. Nostalgia? Probably. Partly, I had a nauseous feeling and the ephemeral happiness that comes from shady deals sewn in the memories of a risky and delicious youth. That's what they called it: risky. And I also had anger.

It was obvious that, with my belly, I wasn't going to put that gram in my body, that poison that was actually less expensive now than twenty years ago, the only consumer item whose price hadn't gone up in that time. It was cheaper now. But who knows what that white powder I had put in my back pocket was actually made of: paracetamol, laxative, amphetamine, lime from the bathroom wall . . . I didn't want poison, I had no real need to meet that fucking dealer, what a face, what pain; I had no intention of getting that poor toothless girl into any more trouble. Let her fuck herself. I only wanted to test the strings, to prove something to myself. There was no soundtrack. Fucking thieves, old-time rats. I'd had a rough time in Nou Barris but I still knew how to get around. It was just that I was checking things out . . . for nostalgia's sake.

"I can't believe it! The queen visiting my humble abode . . ."

It was Santo, still in his flat. Río de Janeiro Avenue, next to the sign reading *Goodbye, Barcelona* right on the outskirts, next to Meridiana Avenue, waving goodbye to the city with the stink of an immigrant buried in poverty and oilcloth. Nou Barris was the sad fringe of the city. It had been the workers' bastion, solidarity with Cuba, oh Nicaragua, Nicaragüita, until victory forever and lunch for the poor, but now nobody remembers any of that. Shovelfuls, millions of bags later, and he was still there, skinny, with his dark hide covered in thick gold chains, stooped like an awning over a passerby, a visitor, the one footing the bill, the solicitor.

"Hi, Go-Getter."

That was him now, the Go-Getter. I noticed my tone of voice. A bit more seductive than required. A bit nicer. I could admit to being nice, but not seductive, damnit, not with that belly.

"Come on in, my queen. Enter my humble abode. You will find something to your liking . . . I'm sure."

But I didn't go in. It took me a few minutes to recognize the smell, the same smell from those other times, of disinfectant and rancid smoke. The smell of a closed bar seems rather sinister in a house. I remembered the nights, so many visits at such a wrong time, without clocks, Santo's bed—he was still Santo—and Magic Hand's solo marking the beat of everything that was going on in that house, with fifty-hour days full of insomnia and crappy poker. He was looking at me from the arch his head formed at the top of the marquise, at the end of his too-long neck; a bird's neck. He smiled, because he knew, and he looked at my belly. His fingernails were yellowed by cigars. His eyes were yellowed by vice. His brown skin was smooth and brilliant on his bones. Short straight hair, brown, soft, a girl's hair.

I went in. "I'm not staying long." I touched my belly: *It's just a moment, little one, a couple of minutes.*

"My queen, even the day you show up here legless, dragging yourself, dry like an empty wineskin, I'll still want you. You know that."

But the Go-Getter didn't want anything. He had it. He had started back in the day, in Santo's day, buying and selling what drugs he could find and even those he couldn't. He was the only opium dealer in Barcelona. He was flexible, and that worked in his favor. When the girls didn't have money, he accepted payment in long, complicated fucks. They were anxious. Barely wet, just sex machines. Then he started to make tapes. Later he set up the mirrored room. Only the dirtiest couples and the men knew about that. They could stay behind the glass in the next room and watch feats with hi-tech dildos and latex costumes in which young girls, who were new to the needle, faked contortions while getting fucked, and generally let anything be done to them. He managed to get quite a clientele. The rest came later, and by then he was already the Go-Getter. Everything, everything you couldn't find through legal channels, everything you could imagine—unmentionable whims were sold in that flat in the slums.

"I want a hand. The hand of an aging rocker who's dying."

He laughed. He always knew.

"I don't have any hands, my queen. I don't deal in them . . . I don't know anything about that business."

"How can you cut a hand so cleanly, so quickly, in the middle of a crowd?"

"You've always been a romantic—"

"How?"

"Look for a reap hook. And above all, a really fucking first-class specialist."

"Where?"

"At the aviary, the old civic center in the Cañellas area . . . And come back."

CR

A reap hook, no less. Do you know what a reap hook is? One of those fucking knives shaped like a sickle, like Arabs have, the blade on the outside, painful just to look at, infallible, *zaz*! She came into the office out of breath, swinging twenty necklaces over those two juglike tits; yum, I swear, yum, yum! She told me we were going to Cañellas to look for a reap hook. Cañellas, no less. That's how it is with her. And why? Don't ask.

Located on the fucking outskirts of town, it's well known that the only outskirts that are any good are the ones with swimming pools. But people in Cañellas hadn't seen any pools other than the puddles made by their own piss walking back from dives in the middle of the night. It was next to the woods, close to the foot of the Collserola range, where Barcelona ends, but on top, on the upper part. Cañellas was so far out on the fringe that they hadn't even been able to put up a shitty mall, if that gives you an idea. And the worst of the worst were the small barracks—that's what they called them, barracks—that the socialist city council had set up when there were still placard-carrying neighbors around. She loved that, the placard-carrying neighbors, but now there were no more neighbors and no more placards, there were only unemployed fuckers, and the children of the bitterly unemployed with their stupid graffiti.

We went to what had been a youth center and was now . . . how can I explain it to you? It was at the foot of a hill that, if I took a picture and showed it to you, telling you it was Barcelona, you'd burst out laughing. There appeared to be a hen coming out of it . . . it was full of bums. Shit, Moorish bums, you know, in case you wanted a rug or some couscous.

They were waiting for us.

"Everything's fine here. You don't want anything here."

They were talking to me, of course, because you can imagine that a woman like Vicky, and with that belly to top it off, would surely make the hair on their asses stand on end. She wouldn't say a word to them. And so, well, I had to talk.

"Go-Getter sent us. He says perhaps you might be able to help us with what happened with the rocker's hand . . ."

The fucking rocker's rotten hand, what the hell did we care about the stupid hand, it was only going to cause us problems and not make us a cent. You can't understand women and, besides, when they're pregnant, they're fit to be tied, fit to be tied . . . Of course, I was the one who had to talk, she couldn't; the last thing we needed was to piss off the Moors . . . But she talked, of course she did. I think that as soon as she saw it was going to happen, she couldn't *not* talk. She started, and that's when things got bad for us—because as soon as Vicky opened her mouth, another five Moors came out, all very serious, bearded, barefoot. And I said to her, *Victoria, you're fucking us up. Vicky, cut it out, these guys aren't kidding around, what the fuck?*

"I'm here to find out who contacted you to cut the poor old man's hand off. I'm not interested in anything else. You know who I am. I couldn't care less about the old man. I couldn't care less about the guy who did it either. And I don't care about you. What I want to know is who has the hand? Who paid for the hand, the collector?"

I still wonder what got into her about the rocker's hand. I swear, I still don't know why, or who the collector was, or what the hell, but the fucking hand almost cost us big time, you understand? You get my meaning? It was just a scar but it could've been a prayer for the dead, right?

There we were, me shitting in my pants and her with a flashiness that already smelled like a run through the woods, surrounded by guys murmuring the way they do, which no god other than their god can understand. Then, in an attempt to warm up to them, she tells them it's okay, and she takes a bag out of her back pocket. Why don't they offer her some tea while she lays out some lines? Tea! Lines! I swear, I couldn't believe it. The chick was out of her mind. She thought she was in our neighborhood, because we all know the Moroccans in the corner shops are Moroccans, but it doesn't matter, because nothing ever does in those places, but everywhere else, with those beards, they're another kind of Moroccan, you understand what I'm saying? They looked at each other and whispered amongst themselves again, and yes, she can go with them, but I have to stay outside.

"The ugly dude can't come in."

It was the spokesman who said this, and you had to see him, the guy thought he was Omar Sharif. Do you think my objections had any weight? Oh, it would be better if she paid attention to me sometimes. I've been around the block a few times but she's a know-it-all, she does everything on her own, and whatever she gets, she earns unassisted. Unassisted. I stood there like a jerk, looking at the sign on the door where you could still see *Centre de Joventut de Canyelles*. I had no time to come up with a plan because my lovely eyes were still on the sign when I heard her scream and saw her rush out, her hand covering her bleeding face. God, I ran after her as fast as fear allowed; it didn't even cross my mind to go in and ask who the fuck had hurt my boss. I didn't even consider it. If those Saracens already thought my face was so ugly, I sure didn't need a scar. I wasn't going to be the one to tell them they were wrong, no fucking way.

CR

The Go-Getter had sent me to the slaughterhouse. Why? They could have hurt me even worse, but the cut on my nose would leave a mark. I didn't want to think about it. They almost sliced it off, damn them, eight stitches. And my pride. Nou Barris was built on the backs of Andalusian, Extremaduran, Galician immigrants, with strikes, demonstrations, and civil guards, but now there was only shit left, nothing of that area from the '70s full of small struggles and early drug usage, all to the tune of long-haired guitars. There was nothing worthwhile left of old Magic Hand. There were two zeros left in my checking account, sort of like my possibilities. I cursed the moment in which fucking nostalgia gave way to that fit of passion.

"I saw the reap hook, Go-Getter. Very funny. We could say I even tried it."

Once more at the door. I was back, like he'd asked, and I was furious.

"Touché. You look at me like that one more time and you'll kill me, my queen."

"Why?"

"Do you expect me to talk in the doorway? If you say yes, I will bring a couple of chairs to the landing—"

"Why did you have me cut?"

"Oh my Queen, my queen, I would never do anything to alter your tremendous beauty."

I went in. I got to the living room, grabbed a beer bottle on top of the TV, and threw it against the glass shelves. A storm of raining, cascading glass. A glass jar remained untouched and I threw it against that horrific stained-glass door to the kitchen. I had always found it threatening. Only the lead molding was left.

"Don't stop now, darling."

The Go-Getter opened a small built-in compartment in the bar. Cups, tall glasses, short glasses, fat glasses, and miniatures. I looked at him with a raving hunger to hurt. My blood pressure made the patch on my nose burn. I bit down.

"Why?"

"My angry queen, you are the only one to blame for that cut, though I have no doubt it has a delicate and glorious future on your face. You alone are to blame."

"Who has the hand?"

"Are all your cravings like this?"

"I want the hand."

"My nostalgic empress . . . What do you think you're looking for, Victoria? A queen doesn't rummage about in the garbage. I fear your treasure is now in some dump outside of town, rotten, devoured by rats."

"Don't fuck with me, Santo."

But he was no longer Santo, just the Go-Getter. There was no reason for him to fuck with me. I was being ridiculous. I felt ridiculous, my legs, my belly, the boobs about to blow up. I had to sit down. Stupid. The memory of the night when Magic Hand played for us, for Santo and me—or only for me, because that was how I remembered it—that magic summer night in which I decided to be who I was during the course of a concert aglow with bonfires and the smell of Sant Joan gunpowder; to be who I used to be—that memory played a dirty trick on me. You can't have your soundtrack ripped off like that, you can't be thrown off like that, all the time, by things as strange as a mall. That hand had worked my patience so hard; I had turned it into a symbol, a personal aggression that had now become pure, hard shame in front of this guy, the Go-Getter, no longer Santo.

It was getting dark and the multicolored lights from the expansive mall surprised us through the large window like a balm. The inside of that dirty cave wasn't the same either. Pink, lilac, blue, yellow neon lights. I let enough time pass so that my Santo's explanation, the old Santo, wouldn't embarrass me too much.

"Give me some of that whiskey, dude." I touched my belly. *It's all good, little one. Just a drink.*

"Have you heard of Dubai?"

I'd heard of Dubai, of course. Who hadn't? "Do you have clients on that fake palm-tree island, Go-Getter?"

"No, but if I did, I'd try to comply with my commitments. If you stick your nose in other people's business, they'll chop it off. Look at yourself. That's a warning, you owe me for that. If you make a commitment to do a concert, you play your fucking music, whether your name is Magic Hand or Manolo, and if Magic had a hangover, or if he was lazy or had a prima donna attack, it would have been better for him to swallow it, because these guys don't put up with nonsense, my queen, these guys pay, and if they don't get what they want, they get it back the only way they know. So if you say you'll give a concert for them, you play. At least I would. The punishment for stealing from them is rather gruesome, isn't it?"

It was a good thing he didn't turn the light on. The tower from the mall was surrounded by blinking neon lights: pink, lilac, blue, yellow.

Pink, lilac, blue, yellow.

BRINGING DOWN THE MOON

BY VALERIE MILES

Gràcia

> *"Let the black flower blossom as it may."*
> —*Nathaniel Hawthorne*, The Scarlet Letter

He split her open like a pomegranate, and I knew then I had made a big mistake.

That late-June day had been airless and hot and caused tears of sweat to trickle down the valley of muscle that cupped my spine. I was hiding, crouched in a tiny space behind an unsteady dressing screen in her boudoir. Heel bones dug hard into my rump to keep balance, wary to make the slightest move lest I upset the wicker screen safeguarding my intrusion.

The bell tower of the Rius i Taulet plaza tolled three p.m. I knew she would be coming. My body tensed at the sound of the third chime and sent a hard cramp through my thigh. It felt as though someone were pulling a ribbon of red muscle straight out of my leg. I grunted through the pain. Even the slightest move echoed in wicker-speak and wobbled the delicate screen. I had been compelled to the dirty enterprise, but it would soon be over, I told myself, trying to relieve my conscience.

I heard Lydia open and close the door of the workshop where she spent her mornings with the hermanas Furest. They were expert weavers, the three of them, and she oversaw their work on fabric designs, sewing splendid patterns. Her light staccato steps tapped over the old stones of the courtyard as she crossed the open-air garden, which was encircled by a gallery of arches and intricately carved stone columns. The *tic, tic, tic* . . . punctuated the soporific murmurs of the plants growing there. This was all that remained of an edifice that at one time must have belonged to an opulent family. The rest of the palace, now located in Vila de Gràcia, was built around this ancient spot over a hundred years ago, before the city of Barcelona swallowed the village in its thirst for expansion. Now, one could hardly imagine such a lush and centuried interior—always still, so very still—existing among the boom and bangle of daily life in this rough and tumble part of the city.

Lydia spent most of her time here, caring tenderly for her breathing things: the ivy serpents and tendrils of morning glory that had grown over and bearded the statue of a dancing faun, the purple blossoms hanging like jewels from his marble flute. Sometimes a slight wind would rustle the buds, making it seem as though the creature were dancing or playing a melody. She also grew savage herbs such as belladonna, monkshood, cinquefoil, foxglove, and herb-of-grace, or rue. A row of Japanese blood grass encircled the fertile foliage, guarding the place at the center reserved for the dusky flowers. There, only black blossoms did Lydia grow.

Lydia would have stopped at the marble fountain on her way across the courtyard; its pool of cool water was what sustained these extraordinary botanicals. It was something she did every day, a ritual ablution of sorts: wet her hands in the gurgling water, anoint her brow, brush her throat with long, delicate fingers.

I admit it, yes. I used to watch her obsessively, this exquisite creature perusing her private garden. My office overlooked the courtyard from the second floor and I would observe her as she indulged in unusual displays of affection, being otherwise so guarded. Every once in a while, I could almost feel the moment her finger would break the water's skin at the fountain. I imagined myself as one of the succulents in her charge, receiving these tender affairs. Sometimes she wore delicate, homespun fabrics and I could glimpse the outline of her taut figure against the light. But I knew all too well to keep my distance.

As I squatted in wait, I conjured a perfect picture of her in my mind's eye: kissing the amulet she wore around her neck, a piece of black onyx carved hollow to hold a sprig of herb-of-grace. *Gràcia*. Whispering under her breath in tender communion with her vegetable children, she would coddle and sniff the raven blossoms: mourning bride, queen of night tulips, black pearl lilies. She caught me watching her a few times. Once, already inside the dark space of the boudoir, she leaned back again over the threshold and looked straight up at me; her face half in darkness and half in light, one blue eye holding both of mine hostage. I saw the slightest wrinkle cross her white brow, as if it bore a weight of generations. Then she went back in and closed the door behind her.

Now I was on the inside of her threshold. She brushed by the wicker screen on her way in and I caught the whiff of a delicate perfume. Almost like a divining rod, she held a black calla lily before her, plucked from the garden; a robust blossom with a long black stamen. She set it on the bed, pulled back the curtains that hung from the canopy, and opened the domed skylight in the ceiling above. A flood of light spilled over a white Indian bedspread embroidered with small pieces of mirror and lit the room up with a burst of fiery reflections.

She removed the lion brooch that held her chestnut mane in place and a rush of heavy curls tumbled freely down her back. She stood very still for a moment, her blue eyes sparkling and jaw set high, defiant. She seemed to be focusing on some spot deep inside herself; a beautiful automata.

She began to undress. First her blouse and brassiere, then she stepped out of her shoes and sat up on the edge of the high white bed. Her delicate feet dangled over the side like a child's. Could she not hear the pounding in my chest? It seemed impossible to me and I began to sweat profusely. Her hair glowed in the afternoon sun, the locks teasing the dimpled triangle of her lower back. She moved gracefully across the bed, rousing a flotilla of tiny incandescent motes. I could feel my own self budding in reaction despite the sweat and the heat and the cramps.

Then she lifted her hips and pulled off her skirt, the elastic band cutting into her flesh as it rode down her thighs. She picked up the calla lily and laid her naked body back on the pillows, holding the swarthy blossom and its stamen nestled like an ink stain between her breasts. I felt a strong desire to jump out of my hiding place and stop her right then. Though I had no reason, no claim, I felt protective of her. I wanted to save her from this daily torture of having to lay with an old man.

The clock struck the quarter hour and there was the telltale warning knock at the door. Old Señor Candau walked in right on schedule, three-fifteen, to pleasure himself with his beautiful young wife.

Lydia had saved her father, one of the last direct descendents of an ancient Catalan family, from the embarrassment of bankruptcy by marrying a man his own age. Sr. Candau came from the deep inland countryside and had built a veritable empire in the most astonishing way: traveling from village to village gathering scrap metal on the back of a mule. A resourceful man and very ambitious, he eventually moved into textiles and shipping. But soon money was not enough.

When he showed up in Barcelona word spread quickly. More than one paterfamilias begged him to take over their failing businesses. Times were changing and privilege was not enough to keep a family rich anymore, as it had during the Franco years. And so Sr. Candau paid Lydia's father twice the value of his textile factory as a sort of dowry. He also bought this crumbling old palace in Gràcia to house his executive offices and keep his young wife close by at all times. It was the noise and grit of Gràcia that had attracted him, the cocktail of bohemians, anarchists, and gypsies. "Better than sharing the sidewalks with all those penniless, inbred old snots in Pedralbes," he had said once with characteristic candor. So Lydia refurbished the interior quarters for their residence and her workshop, and the courtyard for repose.

I have never known how willingly Lydia went along with the arrangement, but nevertheless she held herself with the dignity of her breeding. She was ostensibly compliant, distant without being entirely cold, and certainly too proud to play the part of sacrificial lamb. After all, she was now a very rich woman and he doted on her as long as she remained quiet and submissive. As time went by, though, Sr. Candau became more and more obsessed with her icy beauty, her graceful detachment. There was something in her carriage, in the way her blue eyes sparkled under that mat of chestnut lashes; it hinted of a rich inner world that could never be conquered by a peasant king.

As for me, Sr. Candau had been a part of my life since birth, but only as a character in my father's stories. They had been inseparable during their childhood years of penury after the civil war, and Father used to tell tall stories of their trips into the woods together, hunting and fishing. How Sr. Candau had strangled a hungry dog with his bare hands when it attacked one of their sheep, how tough he had been, full of spit and vinegar; a bully to most, but always very protective of him. How he would remember him whenever he smelled mushrooms and wet leaves. But I never found out what had happened between them, what had estranged them for the rest of their lives. Why one day my father ran away from the village and never went back.

So when Sr. Candau called one day, I found it strange to be confronted with the fact that he was for real. He told my father that he was now a wealthy man, but could trust no one and so he wanted his childhood friend at his side. Yet my father was in fragile health by then, and suggested that I go to Barcelona instead. I was reluctant, since I had studied to become a teacher, not a businessman, but my father urged me in no uncertain terms to drop my romantic ideas and take advantage of the opportunity. He had always known that Sr. Candau would call one day, and that day had come.

I arrived in Barcelona a few years ago and Sr. Candau treated me well in his own gruff way. Like the son he didn't have, the son whose absence was by now a source of growing tension. His wife was his reward, but she was also expected to give him an heir; the more besotted he became with her, the more impatient he grew. Hence the daily *ars amatoria* in her afternoon boudoir; Sr. Candau was a man accustomed to getting what he wanted. What good could possibly come from a man so obsessed with his own wife?

One afternoon Sr. Candau walked into my office just as I happened to make an offhand comment about one of the secretaries. He asked to speak with me privately and I followed him to his rooms thinking he would berate my indiscretion, or reprimand me for being so chummy with colleagues below my rank. No, that was not the case at all. He obliged me to admit that his Lydia was more beautiful than the secretary. He wanted to hear me say it. Out loud.

"Lydia is the fairest of them all, sir. " I smiled, at first thinking it was some sort of a joke.

"Yes, she is, Guillem. But how do you really *know* that? You haven't seen her finest qualities, son. You haven't seen her, you know, naked."

He sat behind his desk rubbing his forehead, sizing me up from beneath bushy white eyebrows, studying me to see how I would respond. I wasn't really sure how to respond. The conversation didn't only seem outrageous. It seemed dangerous.

"I don't need to see her naked to imagine . . ."

His eyebrows arched menacingly and I shut my mouth with a nervous cough. What would happen to any man who dared lay a finger on Lydia Tudó de Candau? I thought. Rue the day, sir. Sr. Candau, the dog-strangler, had the temper of a man who built an empire from scrap metal and mules.

"Honestly, Sr. Candau, you are a very lucky man."

"What does luck have to do with anything, goddamnit?" Sr. Candau spit his words out as if they were embers burning his tongue. "She's mine because I bought her from her sniveling good-for-nothing father. The rat sold her like a piece of prime real estate. But she's my property now and I stick my flag into it every chance I get," he said. "Now I want you, son, to learn the lay of the land."

"I-I-I'm not sure I understand. Um. Sir."

"I want to find a way for you to see her, shall we say, in all her glory."

"With all due respect, sir, I think it's better if I don't. You know, *thou shalt not covet thy neighbor's wife* and all that. These things always go wrong."

"For the love of God, shut up and stop sniveling, you sound like a parish priest. We can get away with it just fine. Go into her boudoir before she arrives and hide behind the screen there. Then when I come in, I'll send her into the bathroom for something and you can sneak back out. She'll never be the wiser."

It was the vulgar idea of a man no longer in control of himself. I knew it would lead to no good and I stated it as many times as he would hear me. But Sr. Candau would not hear me. And how could I say no? After all, he owned me too.

That's how I found myself crouched like an animal behind a wicker screen in a beautiful woman's bedroom on a sweltering day in June. Lydia was holding the black lily between her perfectly truculent, pointed little breasts. And when Sr. Candau walked into the room, and saw her like that, lying in the bed like a dead woman, everything went horribly awry.

"So you think you're funny? Eh, puta?" He grabbed her by the ankle and pulled her toward him at the edge of the bed. She yelped at the sudden violence of his gesture.

"Stop it! You're hurting me. The mirrors are cutting my skin."

He was breathing hard through flared, taurine nostrils, his mouth a corrugated scowl. He brought his arm back as though he was going to hit her.

"After everything I've given you, this is how you repay me? Would you prefer to be dead, then? Because it can be arranged, you know."

"Please, Marcelo. It blossomed just last night under the new moon. I undressed before I thought to look for a vase, and fell asleep. Here, take off your shirt and relax, let me rub your shoulders."

He let her leg go, turned around, and sat on the edge of the bed, removing his shirt and pants. A grin replaced the grimace, but then it grew into a smirk, and finally a full sneer the moment his eyes found mine behind the wicker screen. He nodded at me in furtive recognition and his eyes went black as coal.

Lydia kneeled behind him and began massaging his hairy white shoulders, letting her nipples brush lightly against his neck and arms, trying to appease his anger. Sr. Candau reached up and fondled one of her breasts, turned his head, and sucked at it. Then he pinched it hard enough that she let out a whimper.

Everything hurt. I had been crouching for so long my feet had gone numb. My wrists ached from holding myself up and I desperately needed to move. Only a primitive old goat like Sr. Candau could come up with something as shabby as this. He kept staring at me, as if this was some act of collusion between us. My throat was dry and stung with bile, which I tried to swallow away to no avail.

Suddenly he turned and grabbed Lydia by the hair and pulled her down to the floor in front of the screen.

"Stand up."

"Marcelo, what has gotten into you today? What are you doing? You're hurting me."

"Look at me and bend over."

"Marcelo, please. Stop it."

"I said, bend over, Lydia, or I will bend you over myself and I promise you, it will be a lot worse."

So she stood up in front of him, her back to the wicker screen, and bent over. He pulled off his underwear and grabbed the offending flower from where it lay on the bed. He began to caress his lifeless penis, hitting her lightly in the face with the lily, poking at her lips with the long black stamen.

"We're going to change the menu today."

"That's not part of our understanding," she growled.

"There's a new understanding now."

He grabbed her chin and brushed her hair to one side. Then he placed his palm at the back of her head and forced her face into his crotch, the whole time keeping his eyes locked on me through the slit in the screen. When she finally gave in and closed her mouth around him, he let his head fall back with a gasp, his eyes fluttering half-shut. His cracked tongue lolled over yellow teeth, poking out from time to time to suck the edges of his wrinkled lips, covering them in flecks of dry white spittle. His breath came in short gasps. He grabbed the lily again and slid the black stamen down her back. He smacked her with it a few times, moving it in and out of her thighs, which were scratched in various places and speckled with drops of blood where the mirrors had broken the surface of her white skin.

And then it happened. He threw the black flower hard at the screen, nearly toppling it, and stood up. He bent over her slowly, following the contour of her back and hips with his hands. Then he reached down and placed a hand on either side of her buttocks and pried them apart, his fingers squeezing and kneading her flesh like worms trying to burrow into the meat of a ripe peach. He let out a wild, guttural sound and spread her buttocks wider and wider still; he stretched and he patted and he slapped and he squeezed the velvety folds, opened her up like a pomegranate with great force as he picked her up off the floor, his face contorted into a frenzy of madness and idiot glee.

A thousand tiny spiders of panic crawled over my skin. His beautiful wife opened up in front of me like a pig. I was shocked and sickened at the violence of the scene, but I was also mesmerized by the sight of it; the primordial oceanscape of pinks and browns, the puckered maelstrom, the scalloped anemone unfolding from around a tiny coral button. I couldn't *not* watch. I couldn't tear my eyes away. I watched as he split her open wider. And all I wanted to do was touch. And I grew harder despite my loathing him, despite the violence, and I ached somewhere so deep I couldn't begin to tell you where, some place, some hole inside of me opened just a little bit wider and I throbbed, my own groin set afire, my whole body in a fever-frenzy of titillation and lament. And I touched it, myself, while I watched. I touched it because it pinched and throbbed, I touched it because it hurt, because it wanted me to touch it, because I had to, because I couldn't *not* do anything else. I distinguished a tiny crimson birthmark at the point where her whitest skin turned pink; it bore the shape of a crescent moon. I glimpsed the ghostly mark only for a few seconds before the clouds of his fingers covered it again, yet the vision seared itself into my mind as if I had opened my eyes to the midday sun.

When he finally put her down, he spun her around and mounted her from behind to finish himself off like a wheezing, rickety dog. I was spent, but he was still grunting and jerking, and by now her face was no more than a few inches from the wicker screen. The pendant with herb-of-grace dangled between her breasts and marked the rhythm of his charges. His beady black eyes were open again, staring straight at me. But I turned mine exclusively to her. She kept her jaw raised high, but her eyes brimmed with tears and there were signs of distress cracking her once defiant expression. Not a single sound, not a single movement did she make on her own. She just looked straight ahead, eyes staring, fixed upon nothing I could see. *Toc, toc, toc* . . . the amulet played out the rhythm of an ancient lullaby against her chest, hypnotizing the universe into slow-motion.

I was struggling to hold myself still, but it escaped me. Something issued from that dark place that had opened when I was touching: barely audible, just a slight groan under my breath. Her pupil caught it immediately, honed in on that tiniest sound. I saw her enter into the recognition of my presence and our eyes met through the laced wicker. A single tear fell from the pool of her bluest eye. Not a tear of sorrow, don't be fooled: it was a tear of rage.

Just then Sr. Candau sounded, his face all purple and distorted into a grotesque expression. He finished himself off in a paroxysm of conquest emitting a feeble, ridiculous, amphibian croak and fell back onto the bed. Gasping for breath, he dropped back and patted the bed beside him.

"Now come and lie down with me for a while. But first, get yourself cleaned up a little. There's a good girl."

She walked into the bathroom on unsteady legs and closed the door behind her. He motioned at me with a wink and a tic of his head to leave the room.

That night my dreams were haunted by dark creatures and contagion: dwarves dressed as courtesans, nymphs and imps dancing and drinking in an enchanted grotto. They led me into a cave, at the end of which was a door with a little lunar rune, an exact replica of her tiny birthmark, set aglow and pulsing. I ran my fingers along the engraved edges of the phantom mark: the door opened and the company spilled back into the courtyard garden. It was the witching hour of night and the hermanas Furest were there, standing with their backs to me, holding Lydia's dog at bay. But their faces were those of old hags and each one dropped a gold coin into my hand, screeching and cackling and spitting spiders. The dog was digging furiously at a spot near the old fountain. They let it go and it ran a few yards to devour a piece of meat on a stick. The rope around its neck yanked a mandrake root from the ground and a shrill scream pierced the blackness of the night. A tiny bearded man ran across the courtyard and into the boudoir.

Something had shifted in me that day and an incipient darkness infected my dreams. I went at my colleagues in fits of rage and the only way I could calm my nerves was by drinking myself to oblivion. I was tortured by the vision of his putrid flesh hammering into her, the *toc, toc, toc,* of her talisman; that unnatural rhythm followed me like the hallucinatory pounding of a telltale heart. The scene had bored itself into my psyche and laid its devil eggs, spawning all manner of sinister reveries. I gave in to fits of hot need like spells of thirst that had no earthly quenching.

I avoided Sr. Candau, couldn't bear when he looked at me with his lecherous wink, poking out the purple raisin of his tongue and oozing complicity. I did what business I could in the confines of my office, avoiding contact with anyone else, and continued to watch her in the garden. I ached to have her, to help her, to protect her. But not once did she ever look up or acknowledge me. Never the slightest show of curiosity to know if I was still there.

On the fourth day, early on the eve of Saint John's holiday, which pagans call midsummer, one of the hermanas Furest appeared in my office. "From the señora," she said, handing me a black calla lily. I was expected to join the Candaus for the Verbena de Sant Joan that evening in the courtyard. "La Señora has asked that you come early to help her prepare the garden for the festivities. Sr. Candau had to step out."

My throat constricted at the thought of being alone with her and my head throbbed from the previous night's binge. I sniffed at the black flower and tried to get ahold of myself, but the musty perfume only intensified my state and revived the sordid images in my head. I went to the bathroom and threw cold water on my face before going downstairs. When I arrived she was smoothing some loose soil near the fountain. Without turning around she motioned for me to follow her into the boudoir. She closed the door and motioned me to sit down on the bed. She was more beautiful now in this subtle, dusky light than I had ever seen her before.

"I know my husband put you up to it, and he made it impossible for you to say no. He can be a very persuasive man. But you have witnessed something that was not yours to see and you will have to pay for it."

She parted my legs and moved in close. I reacted immediately to her smell but didn't dare move to hide it. She came in a little closer and brushed her hip against my thigh and touched me. She smiled at the strength of my response. "I like tall men," she said, blue eyes twinkling. She brought her fingers to my mouth and kissed me, nibbling my lip till I could taste blood.

"Alright then, I have a proposition to make. I will give you a choice."

Dusk was diffusing the shadows and the moon appeared ghostly at the courtyard's horizon. We hung lighted dragonfly garlands and set candles around the gallery and built a tower of twigs and branches for the bonfire inside the circle of blood grass. We dressed the marble fountain with bowls of herbs and incense, coca de forner pastries and cava for toasting. The leaves in the garden seemed to sway in communion, following some sort of organic rhythm, and the garden looked richer and more lush than usual. Every so often a black blossom would set off into a shiver like a cat's tail, and the ferns rattled their deep green, spider lace leaves. A slight breeze flickered the candle light and jostled the blossoms that covered the garden's faun. I was sure I saw his merry flute closer to his mouth than ever.

Sr. Candau came up behind me and slapped me so hard on the back that it sent me into a coughing fit. The shadows seemed to suddenly deepen and panic burned the pit of my stomach.

"Lighten up, son. Let's have a drink. Look like you could use one."

"Here, Marcelo," Lydia said. "It's an infusion I made especially for the verbena. And here's a little something for you too, Guillem. I know you are going to like it."

"Lydia, dear, you know I don't like those concoctions you are always making me drink. I want some real spirits. It's been a very long day."

"And spirits you shall have, darling. But first, humor me. Let's celebrate this midsummer moon. It's when the beekeepers harvest, you know. Poor bees, they work so hard then the keepers just come in and take it all away."

I was nervous to drink her brew, but I knew I had no other choice. My fate had been sealed when I agreed to witness things I wasn't supposed to see. So I drank it down in one long draught, resignedly. It started as a mere suggestion of something tickling the base of my spine. It felt good. I was content and relaxed. Something warm had entered my blood-stream and was spreading slowly through my veins and capillaries. My ears began to hum and everything took on a kind of dreamscape quality. I was so light, as if my skull could no longer hold me inside, and I was going up and up and floating over the moon. I watched myself from above, quite at peace with being freed of this mortal coil; my body a shell, an automata way down there in the garden below.

I saw in Sr. Candau's eyes the shock of realizing that something was terribly wrong. He was losing control over his body, becoming paralyzed little by little. He fell to his knees, then to the ground, writhing, fighting. But eventually he lay still, looking upward at the glittering freckles of the nocturnal sky. In a last act of sheer will, he raised his hand as if to grab at the crescent moon above, to gain purchase. But then his face froze into an expression of terror like some theatrical death mask and his hand dropped to his side, useless.

Lydia and the hermanas Furest waited for the shadows to swallow the rest of the courtyard. The snaps of children's fire-crackers outside gave way to an orgy of pyrotechnics—Roman candles and cracking girandoles—announcing the adult veneration had begun. The night air burst with whips and whistles and thunderous explosions, sending clouds of acrid smoke into the atmosphere. Lydia called her dog into the courtyard so it wouldn't be spooked by the tumult and it ran straight to Sr. Candau, lying inert upon the garden floor. It sniffed at his fingers and nipped at his crotch.

"It's time. First the left hand, like I told you," Lydia said as she handed me a silver stiletto.

From above, I watched myself slice his wrist open in one clean stroke as I had been shown by the hermanas. It was so very easy. They bled him and poured the liquid into the fountain, which gurgled and tinted the water with a deep ruby cloud. I sliced the other wrist and repeated the ritual as instructed.

The night was hot and my scalp tingled with the agitation of our deeds. And yet I was deeply at peace, as if my life had always been leading me right here. I cleaned my hands in the fountain and didn't recognize my own reflection; it seemed as if some other man was looking back at me. I smiled at this shade of me and took a deep breath to prepare myself. Then I turned right around, picked up the axe, and chopped Marcelo's left hand off in a single blow.

I have yet in my life to see a bonfire like the one we set ablaze that night. Its lips snapped hungrily all the way to the second floor of the palace. The five of us kept to our task throughout the evening, cutting Marcelo up and feeding the pieces to the flames, perfuming the night air with sprigs of herbs, until there was nothing left of him but ashes. A little past midnight I began to feel the weight of myself once again, the blood rushing into every extremity, engorging my fingers, my toes, my lips. My groin tingled and came to life. Lydia had been watching me and waiting. When she saw my expression she sent the hermanas away and initiated me into the ways of her garden.

Now, when I am called by the treble chimes of Rius i Taulet to lie with my wife, I make it a point to stop and linger for a moment near the fountain. I stand in contemplation of the black lily that grows ever stronger, nourished by the ashes of that midsummer's fire. I water it with excessive care and remove any weeds that threaten the health of the dusky token. And bow my head in a moment of silence to thank him for all that he has given me.

THE SLENDER CHARM OF CHINESE WOMEN

BY RAÚL ARGEMÍ

Montjuic

The secret of any great city—let's say, Barcelona—is that it comprises many cities juxtaposed one over the other, breathing side by side but with few actual points of contact.

You can be yourself in any of those parallel worlds and then cross the street and become someone else, completely different and free of your previous identity.

But there are people who are born distinct and so the residents of each of these worlds recognize them with the same name, alias, or nickname, without realizing that at other times, with other people, they're the same, but different.

That's what happened with Delgado. He had an inadvertent talent, almost animal-like, to transform himself so that in each city he was perceived as one of the locals.

Delgado's story only took up about a week's worth of police bulletins, each time more brief, until it got lost in the whirl of those humid and suffocating summer days. But I wasn't the only one who thought that the Barcelona of brothels, of Japanese tourists, South American waiters, and junkies from all over the place—to name a few Barcelonas—could be stalking grounds in which hunter and prey would kill each other without impediment.

Naturally, there are three professions that facilitate jumping from city to city: cop, musician, and journalist. My excuse is that I'm a reporter. "Freelance"—in other words, like a pirate searching for the treasure that will save me; most of the time I just have to be satisfied with leftovers from the lions.

I first found out about Delgado, or El Delgado, on a Monday.

It was early, or late, a relativity that's typical of juxtaposed realities, and I'd arrived alone at Clavié, because Paty, my longtime girlfriend, had left me at some point, perhaps tempted by a better offer. She also has the excuse of being a journalist.

I had to wait awhile. Like everywhere else, Clavié, an afterhours joint, pretends to be closed, so they took their time in responding to my rapping on the door. Patience. When all the bars are closed, your last resort to get away from a bed filled with failed dreams is an afterhours place, and this piano bar didn't smell bad and wasn't full of drunks.

Inside, time seemed to stand still. The fresh air from the AC, the low lights, and the sound of the piano accompanying the movement of the waiters made the world seem far away. The customers were the same as always, or looked the same as always. They were the appropriate mix for an afterhours spot, dressed uniformly, with drinks in hand, chatting or singing along with popular classics, anything to avoid going home.

And, well, because fate can be this way, that Monday was the first time I ever saw Delgado. It was impossible not to see him, since he was almost as big as the piano on which he rested an elbow; he was wearing a yellow shirt. He smiled and bopped along to the music.

Cavalcanti, who's there every night with the religiosity of a sinner, was singing a schmaltzy tango in the company of two older, and perhaps temporary, gal pals. Cavalcanti saw me as

I came in and, just as he was letting his throat warble to produce a sheep-like "vibrato," he winked my way and nodded
toward the tables that were a couple of steps down from the
piano and the singers.

He'd taken a liking to me since he'd found out I'm a reporter and had begun to gather material, characters from Barcelona nights, for a future book. To be honest, he didn't have
a job and mostly got by on his utopian disposition.

The old tango singer landed at the table and ordered
whiskey. With a wave, he brought Delgado over and let his
two gal pals join us as well. They looked me over, we looked
each other over, and then we all ruled each other out.

The man extended his hand, as big as an oar, but didn't
break my fingers, and then sat down in a crimson armchair,
muttering a greeting I didn't quite understand.

As usual, Cavalcanti was high on coke. That was his biggest charm with women: he always had a lot of coke, and he
was generous with it. But his gal pals had decided to switch
gears, now that they were at a table, and to light up a hashish
joint.

Cavalcanti gave me a lopsided smile, like Gardel. "We
have to forgive them," he said. "They still allow themselves
childish things, hippie things."

I had enough time to nod and sip the whiskey before Cavalcanti spoke up again in his Argentine and Iberian–fused
Spanish: "This guy here, just look at him—he has quite the
past, my friend."

I glanced at Delgado and couldn't imagine anything but
Wrestlemania. Of course, I understood that Delgado was his
surname.

Later, when I saw him pop up in the papers, one of the
messier points was, in fact, his name. What's important now,

what matters, is that everyone called him Delgado, and when he wasn't around, El Delgado, the Slender Man.

As so often happens, his nickname had nothing to do with his physical presence. He was a huge mound of a man, tall and wide, with as much muscle as fat. A mound with slow, deliberate movements that framed his constant smile, no matter what was going on, and dry hair like hay that stuck up and crowned his head. Between the smile and hair there were two tiny eyes, blue pinpoints that looked like they belonged to someone else—someone who was spying from inside his body, waiting to figure out who knew what.

That was Delgado. At first sight, he was laughable. A clumsy giant, a guy who could stand there all night, not drinking or smoking, just laughing at everybody else's stories, even when everybody else was pretty sure he didn't understand a thing.

He was inoffensive.

Inoffensive until silence fell, and then he'd say something to save himself, in a chewed-up Spanish filled with weird echoes that some thought were Bosnian or Moldavian or Danish or Bulgarian gypsy, or maybe some mixed argot from a shipless sailor.

He widened his smile a little more, looked at the ceiling with the blue pinpoints, and said, "Ah, the slender charm of Chinese women."

That's why they called him Delgado. Because then he'd lower his eyes and the psycho crouched inside him would look at us from under his fleshy lids until the silence thickened and someone would try, clumsily, to start a conversation or suggest we sing.

That's what happened the first time I met him. For a few minutes, we passed the joint around and laughed haplessly, as if we were in a hurry.

Over the next hour, Cavalcanti tried to convince me the man was a Vietnam vet, one of the gal pals tried to get close to Delgado, and the other downed four whiskeys without showing it. The women who end their night at that bar are real women. They can be drunk off their asses but you'd never know it. They're such ladies that if they have to puke, they do it in private.

"This guy you see here is a war hero, my friend."

Cavalcanti called everybody "my friend," or used the Argentine *pibe*, because he couldn't remember anyone's name.

"Cavalcanti, that's impossible. This man wasn't even born during the Vietnam War, or if he was, he was in diapers."

"Are you nuts, pibe? That was practically yesterday! I'd left the orchestra; I was hanging out with some Colombians. Miami, Las Vegas, Cali, Medellín . . . We partied our asses off!"

"Were you dealing drugs?"

"No, pibe, no! What are you thinking? Music! We imported tropical stars, we opened for them. I want to die whenever I remember all the women. Drugs weren't part of the deal, they were just for pleasure. Here, take a drag . . ." He casually slipped a diamond-fold of coke in front of me.

"Cavalcanti," I said before heading to the restroom, "it's been more than thirty years since Vietnam. If you weren't so out of your mind, you'd realize that."

When I came back, pissed at anybody who cuts coke with plaster because it burns your nose, the old singer was looking at three of his fingers as if they belonged to someone else; the drunken gal pal continued in her elegant catatonia, and the other was whispering who-knows-what into Delgado's ear while he just smiled.

When I tried to give the coke back to Cavalcanti, he showed me his fingers and his generosity. "You can keep it," he said. "I have more. I'm getting old, my friend. Three decades. Do you realize what that means? It makes me want to die . . ."

"Not tonight, Cavalcanti. I'm not in the mood for a wake."

Cavalcanti's laugh was purely operatic. He dried a tear and, with the effects of his last whiskey in plain view, made his way to the restroom.

It was late. I know this because after a while I started to see everything as if it were underwater, through a submarine porthole. At that hour, exhausted and sleepy, I knew—and that's why I would never try it—that if I stretched my hand to touch somebody, my fingers would just bump up against the porthole.

Cavalcanti returned rejuvenated, his nostrils smudged with white powder.

"You're right," he said emphatically. "It was the Gulf War."

"What?"

"Delgado was decorated in the Gulf War."

"I don't believe you, it doesn't make sense. El Delgado isn't even American. What the fuck was he doing in the Gulf?"

He didn't respond, just drank his shot of whiskey and raised various fingers to order another round for everyone.

"Hey, buddy . . . big guy . . . I'm talking to you, deaf dude . . . show your arms to this piece-of-shit Uruguayan who doesn't believe me."

El Delgado hesitated before grasping what he was being asked, then finally rolled up his sleeve and stretched his arms out, both hands on the table. They were full of scars too small to be smallpox.

"They used needles, wooden splinters, and who knows what other shit," Cavalcanti explained. "The Turks tortured him."

Delgado stayed in the same position for a long minute, raising his little blue eyes at me as if he was waiting for something—maybe congratulations, or a word of support—until he eventually rolled down his sleeves and took cover again behind his smile.

I didn't say anything because at that moment I saw Cavalcanti making faces like he was at death's door and I thought perhaps this was the big one and that it had all come to pass thanks to his dedication to cocaine. But I was wrong. Delgado then widened his smile and took bites at the air as if he were a shark in a Disney cartoon. He had false teeth, and the upper dentures hit the bottom ones like castanets, revealing bright blue gums smeared with spit.

"They kicked his teeth out. What do you think of that?"

I couldn't tell him what I thought because, just then, the night's drinks and tobacco turned my stomach and a cold nausea indicated I had to leave unless I wanted to roll around on the ground like a poisoned dog.

I left Clavié with the shakes. The sun was shining outside, promising to cook us all.

A few days later, Paty, my sporadic lover when she's got nothing better going on, asked me to accompany her somewhere. One of those sources who can't be revealed had told her they had some ugly info for her, and the place to confirm it was ugly too. Knowing Paty's nature, I prepared for the worst.

The meeting was set at a "piso patera," one of those spaces shared by workers on rotating schedules, in Poble Nou, a longtime manufacturing neighborhood whose factories were now only empty shells. As illegal immigrants from all over the world arrived, the old buildings were recycled into housing for eight or ten people per room. It was good business for a few.

Most pisos pateras aren't mixed, and this one housed black people. It smelled just like Chester Himes would have wanted for one of his Harlem novels: a hot and swampy mix of rotting food, dirty laundry, and life at its most primal. The windows, overlooking an interior courtyard, were covered with cardboard.

It's tasteless to say it's hard to see a black person in the dark, but that was the problem. When we arrived, a man greeted us with a nod and a slight gesture, which provoked an African parade to file out the door; he spoke in a low, expressionless voice. It was nearly impossible to tell if he was lying.

"Ma'am," he said, "they tried to kill one of our sisters. They raped her, they tortured her, and they choked her. They wanted to kill her but she survived. It's a hate crime and you have to help us."

"Can I speak with the girl?" asked Paty.

The man took his time to consider this. I lit a cigarette so I could get a look at his face in the light of the flame. He was over thirty and he stared at us with cold, disdainful eyes. Sweat made his skin shiny.

"Maybe you'll get her to talk. She hasn't talked to anyone."

He opened another door inside the apartment. I managed to see a small shadow on one of the mattresses on the floor before my friend went in and closed the door behind her.

"Where did they attack her?" I asked, just to say something.

"Near Parallel, in the plaza with the three chimneys."

"Those streets are always packed with people."

He moved away, irritated, as if talking to me was a waste of his time, but I trudged on. My relationship with Paty had cooled recently and I needed to score a few points.

"I don't know why but I think you know who attacked her."

"Maybe."

"Did you report it to the police?"

Silence followed that idiotic question. An illegal immigrant never goes to the cops.

"Why don't you give me a clue? I promise I'll leave you out of whatever investigation follows."

"There's a guy who sleeps in the back of the electric company, next to the plaza with the three chimneys. Do you know the place?"

"There are a few guys who sleep back there."

"White trash," he said venomously, and he was right: there were no blacks among the homeless who hung out there. "It was one of them. The one who seems German. The big one. The one who sleeps in a camouflage sleeping bag."

"His name?"

"Ask for El Delgado. I'm not saying any more."

He kept his word, and I shut my trap. I lit another cigarette because in that darkness the red tip was something to hold on to, and I drowned myself in the stink of crocodiles and resentment. I kept to myself the fact that I might know the Delgado he was talking about. I kept it to myself because Cavalcanti's friend, the decorated hero from whatever war, might have simply provoked this black man's paranoia. He had all the key elements to do that: he was an animal with a crazy look, and white too. I would see what I could find out.

Then Paty stepped out of the room and, after a very brief exchange of promises and phone numbers, we went back out to the street.

She was walking like she wanted to break a speed record.

"The black guy says they attacked her near the three chimneys, around Parallel. That's still Montjuic, isn't it?" I asked.

"Shit! Shit! Shit!"

"What? What did you find out?"

"That guy's a fucking liar!"

"Why would he lie?"

"Because he's covering his own ass! Because he's a pimp!"

"Ah . . . the girl's a prostitute."

"Oh, you Argentines are so kitschy, of course you had to say *prostitute*."

"First, I'm Uruguayan, and second, don't start with me. I actually got him talking and I think I might have something."

She looked at me like she wanted to kill me, and then told me the story as if speaking to someone mentally challenged.

The girl had been attacked by two men because she'd gone into Russian territory, just outside the Fútbol Club Barcelona Stadium; they'd grabbed her and thrown her in a car. It had been easy because the girl didn't weigh more than a hundred and ten pounds and couldn't put up much of a fight.

"Do you know how old she is? Fourteen! That fucking asshole, or his buddies, brought her over from Guinea with fake papers and put her out on the streets!"

"So why did he tell me it happened at the plaza with three chimneys?"

"Why do I give a fuck what he said? Why don't you go back and ask him why he's lying? Fucker! They raped her, they choked her, and they left her for dead . . . and you're asking why that piece of shit is lying? Mother of God!"

"But—"

"She's just a girl! Do you get that? A little girl!"

I wanted to argue with her but Paty raised her hand, opened the door of a taxi, and left me gazing at it as it disappeared up the street. I have no idea how she does it; I never have any luck with taxis.

* * *

Later that week, there was an anonymous call. A body had been found in the trash at a building in Poble Nou. It was a girl.

She was Chinese, very young. They'd tortured her before strangling her. Her torn vagina and anus indicated a vicious sex crime but the police actually thought it might be worse, and they'd shut down the block. They didn't even want to think about the possibility that it was gangland revenge.

The ghosts of Eastern European immigration nourished the fears. Russians, Chechens, Serbians, and Bosnians all arrived marked by war, and their methods were especially brutal. They weren't afraid of anything and only the Chinese competed with them, except when it came to exploiting the homeless, which was dominated by the Romanians. It's possible that in Europe no one would have taken a Chinese beggar seriously.

But I'd already added two plus two and I'd come up with El Delgado's massive figure.

The dead girl had been found not too far from where the black pimp had told me the suspect was. That the girl was Asian also reminded me of the night at Clavié when, with that crazy expression, he'd muttered the cryptic phrase about the slender charm of Chinese women.

There was something to what that black guy had told me. It would turn into an article I could sell for a good price, or information with which I could barter.

As the morning wore on, I neared the plaza with the three chimneys, which is situated in a neighborhood that extends from the edge of Montjuic and blurs into Parallel, with its porno theaters and its ancient memories of sin.

Not even fascist bombers who used to aim at the three

chimneys during the civil war could have recognized this place now. Each day, it got more and more crowded with skateboarders from all over Europe. If one were to go missing, nobody would even notice.

As if to compensate for all the skating noise and hot speed, the plaza was also packed with Pakistanis with their cricket sticks.

But the ones I was interested in were the homeless, the guys who slept up against the electric company building.

There were only two still around. A toothless drunken woman who laughed a lot and a tiny man, almost a dwarf, as dirty as she was, who was trying to win her favor with beer.

There wasn't a trace of the so-called German. He could have been the nighttime tenant of any one of the folded cardboard sructures between buildings that served as precarious beds. Those two were the only ones around to question.

As I approached, the man puffed out a tubercular chest, just in case I wanted to challenge him for Julieta's fleas. They lowered their guard a bit when I gave them some money. She grabbed the bills with a fierce look directed at her suitor and shoved them in her bra.

I couldn't get much out of them while they tried lie after lie to see which one could loosen more euros. The description of the so-called German coincided quite a bit with Delgado, but they hadn't seen him in a while.

I didn't have to be anywhere and the spectacle of the Pakistanis playing so British a game was a good enough excuse to sit in the shade for a bit.

I'd been there for some time, getting bored watching the formerly colonized swinging their bats, when a thin Moor with several bottles of beer in a sweaty bag approached me. I bought one and he immediately offered me hashish and coke.

I said no, because I never buy on the street, but he didn't leave, he stuck around, smiling with just his lips.

"What's up?" I asked.

"If you tell me what you're looking for, I might have it."

I was about to tell him to go to hell when it occurred to me this skinny guy might have seen me talking to the couple and might have a certain take on the neighborhood.

"El Delgado. What do you know about El Delgado?"

"A beer?"

I understood and passed him a few bucks, enough for five beers.

He made a vague head movement. "They say he went up," he said, then turned his back and left, happily searching out other customers.

At that moment, I was certain he was pulling my leg. He was telling me Delgado was up in heaven with the angels. It took me awhile to realize I was wrong.

For a couple of weeks I did some media outreach for an ethnic music festival and I forgot about Delgado. I didn't even think of him when the news hit about the Russian girl.

She wasn't young but very small, with a body like a little girl, and they'd found her on the beach at Barceloneta. Her corpse had been left out in the open. Like a message for somebody. Raped and strangled. It was impossible to identify her, but her features suggested she was from the former Soviet Union, where they're as much Slav as Mongolian: blond hair, high cheekbones, gray eyes that seemed vaguely Asian.

I didn't think about Delgado again until early one morning when inertia took me to Clavié.

There were a couple of people at the piano, straining themselves singing ". . . estranyer indenai!" and Paty, who I hadn't expected to find there, was tearfully killing her fourth gin and tonic.

"You men are all sons of bitches," she said, warmly gesturing for me to sit with her.

She was in a stormy mood. That afternoon she'd interviewed the father and brothers of a girl who'd recently disappeared. Muslim Algerians with strict traditions, they struggled without news of the girl and became angrier and angrier with every passing hour.

"You must have seen the photos, the fliers. They're on the lampposts," she said.

"Maybe she ran off with somebody."

"Or at this very moment, she's being raped by twenty shit-ass machos," she replied, pronouncing each syllable so as to pound it into my head. "Do you know what will happen if they find out who did it?"

"They're going to cut him into little pieces?"

"Sweetheart . . ." she said, her eyes blurry from liquor, tears, and disdain, "he's gonna hate his mother for ever having given birth to him."

I was ordering a rum and Coke, which helps recharge the batteries at that hour, when I felt a hug and heard Cavalcanti's voice.

"You're exactly who I want to see," he said. "I'll buy you whatever you want; let's talk business."

"C'mon, man, I'm with my girlfriend. Why don't we leave it for another day?"

The tango singer wrinkled his nose and, with a smile from golden times, bowed toward Paty.

"My dear lady, darling of Cupid and all gods with good taste, may I steal your intended for just a few minutes?"

Paty grinned from ear to ear because, curiously enough, she and Cavalcanti always got along quite well.

"Oh, noble gentleman," she answered, "if you take him

and lose him in some battle, this lady will be forever grateful."

Since I had no choice, I followed him to a corner and drank his whiskey while acting like I wasn't really listening.

"What a woman, pibe, what a woman! You know what I'm saying? You don't deserve her."

"Cavalcanti, don't mess with me. What do you want now?"

"Remember Delgado?"

"The Vietnam War hero who was tortured in the Gulf War?"

For a moment, the nocturnal tango clown disappeared and I felt I was caught in the gaze of a man who perhaps had a couple of corpses to his credit.

"Pibe, you're never going to learn. You mustn't believe everything you hear at night. The ones trying to figure things out are cops, or worse. Don't be fooled by appearances. I come off like a fool because wise guys always lose. But don't tell me you're the fool and you haven't heard yet."

"If you're going to make me listen to your philosophy lessons, then at least buy me another whiskey."

"Fair enough," he said, and with a wave of the hand he conjured a couple of double shots. "I don't know if you've bumped into El Delgado lately . . ."

"Why would I?"

"Why would— No, you wouldn't. But, since your girlfriend told me you'd been to an African 'holding cell,' I thought you might have run into him. Delgado is like God, he can show up anywhere, whether among junkies or barefoot Carmelites."

"I've noticed. A black guy told me he sleeps up by the three chimneys and a Moor told me he's gone to heaven . . . Why are you interested in Delgado?"

"If you come with me, I'll tell you." He took off, with his canine gait, toward the bathroom.

He carved three lines on the sink and after he sucked up two, he was more explicit.

"The Russians have it in for him, and I have to get along with the Russians. You follow me?"

I shrugged as I leaned on the sink.

"It seems he worked as a heavy in some whorehouse. Sometimes the customers . . . you know, they get out of line and have to be set straight."

"I figured he worked with his hands somewhere."

"Something like that. The problem is, he fell in love with the Russians' little star. Some girl who had been an Olympic champion on the parallel bars. You know, one of those girls who spins in the air as if she doesn't give a shit about the laws of gravity."

"So?"

"Nothing. Except the girl was older, though she was so small she looked like a schoolgirl. So what can I tell you, some guys will pay a fortune to get into bed with a schoolgirl."

"Right, and that animal surrendered to her slender charm—"

"It's worse than that. The Russians are fuming, they say the idiot stole her from them."

I don't know if it was the coke or instinct, but I had a sudden illumination. "Cavalcanti, you're talking in circles. It's clear from your description that it's the little Russian girl who was found on the beach, raped and strangled."

He stared at me hard. "And what if it is? The Russians are looking for Delgado, and I'm going to hand him over."

"The big guy killed her?"

"The big guy is obsessed with skinny women with Asian eyes."

"That doesn't mean much."

"Since when are you judge and jury?"

"What am I getting out of this?"

"Now you're talking," he said, and mentioned a sum that, for my drooping pockets, was simply exorbitant.

"I'm going to be honest with you, Cavalcanti: I'll look for him, but I don't want anything to do with the Russians."

"That's reasonable."

"I'll look for him, but once I find him, what do you want me to do?"

He must have known how our conversation was going to go because he stuck his hand in his pocket and pulled out a card with a phone number.

"I'll be there anytime you need me. You tell me where he is and then forget about it. We never had this conversation."

"And they're gonna pay just for that?"

"I swear on my blessed little mother. Moreover, and so you won't think I'm messing with you, I'll put up the money myself. I have business with the Russians and I don't want to fuck up the relationship. You have to be generous with investments in order to make the little coins multiply."

"Cavalcanti . . ." I said sincerely, "you've never seemed as suspicious to me as you do now."

"Young man," he said sympathetically, "anybody who lives to be old is suspicious. I thought you already knew that."

We had to interrupt the conversation because Paty came in all of a sudden and, before heading back out to the streets, handed me a napkin with a phone number scribbled on it and a flier surely taken down from a wall somewhere.

"The Algerians with the missing girl have offered a reward. I wouldn't turn anybody in but you guys are cut from a different cloth. They're looking for a big guy with a stupid face who sounds like a friend of yours. If you know where he is . . . I don't want to know."

The girl on the flier also had almond-shaped eyes.

I took the napkin, only to see Cavalcanti wink my way and shake his head with his index finger pointed at his own chest. "You call me first," he said.

That's when I remembered the skinny vendor with beer, hashish, and coke at the three chimneys. And that's why, the next morning, I went back to the plaza where half of Europe's skaters could be found; the skinny guy didn't take long to make his appearance.

I repeated my question, doubled my bribe, and got the same answer and a gesture toward Montjuic. That's when I understood he didn't mean heaven when he said Delgado "went up," and I gazed over at the rolling green that, indeed, went up behind the buildings.

The Montjuic has a military fort at the top where tourists have their pictures taken; its paths are crowded with trees and bushes. Those paths have always been the refuge of drug addicts and immigrants who are poorer than dirt. Every now and again, the cops raid and disperse them, but they come back like mushrooms after a rainfall.

I left civilization behind and climbed up to test my luck. I'd never been there before, and a part of me warned that I was headed toward anger's nesting ground.

I was breathing hard and my knees were buckling when I ran into a tent made of plastic bags, garments rescued from the trash, and clumsily crossed branches.

I don't know how many people were housed under that roof, but the smell of old dirt and bodies in need of washing was overwhelming.

They barely spoke Spanish and, after their initial surprise, offered me, for very little money, the favors of a girl who was, at most, twelve years old. When I said no they pulled down the pants of an eight-year-old boy, but as soon as they saw my disgust they simply asked me for cigarettes.

As lost as I was, I continued up. How would I ever find Delgado if I couldn't even figure out how many of these settlements there might be? Trees and all sorts of surprises in the landscape hid them from me, and I ran into them without warning. I soon realized that if I didn't stop, somebody would probably knife me.

And I wouldn't have made it at all if it hadn't been for the calm man.

I named him that because, from the moment he appeared in the midst of the weeds, he gave me the impression that he was beyond good and evil.

"Can I help you?" he asked. "This place can be very inhospitable to unexpected guests."

I looked him over, which he allowed. He didn't smile but his eyes permitted my inspection and sought trust. So I went along; I decided to trust him.

"I'm looking for a man in a lot of trouble. If I find him in time, it might do him some good."

The calm man had thin lips, like a monk, and a slightly foreign accent, which I couldn't quite place.

"Do you know his name?"

"They call him Delgado, or El Delgado."

The man nodded. "I know who he is. I know pretty much everybody here . . . and I make sure that nobody's problems take us all down. But you still haven't told me anything that would make me help you."

"There's a little girl, an Algerian, who ran away from home and may have been seen with him. The family is Algerian, Muslim, you know what I mean."

"Yes, I know what you mean . . . Our buddy has gotten

into a lot of trouble."

"And you are . . . ?"

"Let's say I'm from somewhere in the Balkans, one of those places that changes names from time to time. Follow me," he said as he started up the path. He moved quickly, with the economy of a tiger, or a soldier.

I tried asking him a few questions but both his silence and the panting of my lungs made me shut up right away.

Delgado's refuge was a green tent, a military leftover.

The calm man approached as if it wasn't necessary for him to knock, and we entered lowering our heads.

The girl—the little Moor—was preparing tea on a burner and looked scared to death when she saw us enter.

Delgado didn't make a move; he was sitting on a camouflage sleeping bag. It was clear he trusted the calm man, and that he could only fit in the tent if he was sitting or lying down.

Then the calm man squatted and began to talk in a language that was unintelligible to me, in the sleep-inducing cadence of an animal trainer.

He talked for a long time, and I could see Delgado's face registering shame. As his tiny eyes filled with tears, he made an attempt to explain himself by wearily gesturing toward the girl. He uttered only two or three phrases but they were enough for the calm man to lower his head as if he needed a minute to think things through.

Then the calm man spoke again, but this time it was with a different tone. It was an order. The kind of order that can't be disobeyed. "Get your things and go. Your family is waiting for you," he said to the girl.

"They don't want me," she responded, on the verge of tears.

She made a move toward Delgado for protection, but the big guy pushed her away and whispered something that must have been definitive, because she simply lowered her head and left, without taking anything, and without looking back.

"We're finished here," said the calm man. "I'll go back with you, so you don't get lost."

When we were almost at the end of the path, I twisted my foot and he let me rest for a moment. I decided to take advantage of the stop to ask him a question: "Can you tell me what the fuck that little girl was doing with Delgado?"

"She's pregnant, and she's afraid of her family."

"Right. Delgado likes skinny little Asian girls."

"You're wrong. Delgado, as you call him, is medically incapable of having sex."

"What are you saying?"

"The truth," he said. And as if it were the most natural thing in the world, he unveiled the story of the big scary guy who, out of the blue, liked to say, "Ah, the slender charm of Chinese women."

He'd been a soldier—though now I'm not sure if he was Serb, Croatian, or something else—when the people in that part of the world all turned on each other. He was a combatant in one of the many battles in that senseless war, in which the enemy had been a good neighbor until the day before.

In one skirmish, they'd massacred some Muslim families and, as was the custom at the time, they'd raped a young woman—practically a girl, really—until she died. To fight and drink were the only rules in that killing game.

And soon those who fought and drank died in an ambush of which the only survivor was El Delgado. And then a woman—perhaps the dead girl's sister or mother, a woman thin as a reed, with slanted eyes—took her revenge on Delgado.

Two days later they left him for dead. They had used needles and wooden splinters to make a porcupine of his body. Pincers and boots did away with his teeth. And with a pair of pliers, or a nutcracker, the woman tore off his genitals. Never again would the guy known as Delgado be a whole man.

"You see . . . he survived so he could carry his cross in this world," said the calm man. "You can go the rest of the way by yourself." Then he turned his back on me and disappeared into the thicket.

I only really believed half of what he told me. He didn't quite convince me and I wasn't going to let him screw up my little business deal. That's why I made both calls, to Cavalcanti and to the Algerians. With my information, it wouldn't be hard for them to find the tent.

A few minutes later I got scared, and I began running down the hillside, out to the streets, to that other city, with a couple of tears in my clothes and some scratches on my hands.

It was like arriving in a foreign country. I had a moment of disorientation when I saw three blondes—English or German— showing off their young flesh with short skirts. And I confirmed my border crossing when I saw a group of Chinese or Japanese stopped at a corner with their bird steps and avid tourist eyes.

The Russians arrived first. It was in all the papers. A photo of the Russian gymnast was found in the battered giant's pockets, making it easy for the police to close the case. The guy was crazy, so they attributed the rape and murder of the Chinese girl to him; he carried this blame to his grave.

Everyone was pleased, myself included, although I still had some doubts.

Had El Delgado been connected to the Russian girl? Maybe. He was crazy, he'd had his balls cut off, and he'd given refuge to a pregnant little Moor—this all made him seem like a delirious savior of whores and injured women.

Had he been the victim of a crossfire, a settling of scores which would have been best avoided at any cost? I don't know, I don't want to know. What probably happened was that he was killed because of his gift for ubiquity: he had been in the wrong place at the wrong time. Or maybe what killed him was his obsession and his disturbing mantra about the slender charm of Chinese women. In any case, he'd been dead a long time, he just didn't know it.

Everyone was pleased, myself included. Sometimes a lack of ambition can save your ass. It's best to be content with the leftovers from the lions.

THE POLICE INSPECTOR WHO LOVED BOOKS

BY FRANCISCO GONZÁLEZ LEDESMA

El Raval

E verybody knows that Méndez is an old cop who lives (badly) on the streets of Barcelona. Just like everybody knows Méndez eats cheaply in the city's worst restaurants; every now and then, the owners invite him for a free meal so he'll recommend them to the *Michelin Guide*. One time, to support his friends, he took a TV crew to one of those places so they'd give it some publicity, but after they ate, the cameraman couldn't make it to the door.

As everybody suspects (although they don't know for sure), Méndez will never get anywhere because he doesn't believe in a single law except the law of the streets. Plus, he feels sorry for petty delinquents and rarely arrests them. Nonetheless, they say he once detained a fellow with a limp. As everybody suspects, Méndez was watching from the balcony at the station on Nou de la Rambla Street, which was the most sordid in all of Barcelona; it was so bad that sometimes not even the cops would go in at night for fear that they'd be assaulted in the doorway. From that balcony, Méndez could see all the neighborhood's thefts, assaults, fights, and philandering.

There are other things the whole world knows about Méndez, the old cop: for instance, that his apartment is full of books and that he always carries one in his pocket, which is why the lapels on his uniform are always out of shape. There's a great antiquarian book fair in Barcelona each year and Méndez is a loyal customer because he loves stories by dead novelists. In fact, he has more books than he can possibly read in what's left of his life.

That's not so uncommon. There was a great writer from Barcelona, Néstor Luján, who kept books even in the bathroom, and there's a true story about a bourgeois man who had so many books that his wife got fed up and told him, "Me or the books." And the bourgeois man said, "The books."

Well, I've already mentioned that Méndez had more books than he could possibly read in what he has left of life, and that it's not so unusual—in spite of the fact that Barcelona's climate is usually better for taking a stroll than staying at home with a book. One time, Méndez met another man, a senior, who suffered the same problem.

"I'm obsessed with books, I love them," Méndez's friend told him one day. "I've spent my life collecting them and taking care of them. But I'm desperate, because I now have more books than I can possibly read in a lifetime. To make matters worse, I'm going blind."

"What are you going to do?" asked Méndez.

"The day I realize I can no longer read, I'll kill myself, because then my life will be useless."

Méndez understood all too well.

And this is where we arrive on terrain that nobody's too sure about, but that we suspect. We suspect two things: first, that Méndez owns more than one illegal gun—well, the man's spent half his life in the company of thieves; second, that he's bitter, but keeps it secret. Though others will say he's never lost faith in humanity.

So Méndez replied to the old man, but it's unclear whether he did so with ill intentions, or because he thought nothing would come of it: "Here, I'm going to give you this antique pistol, which is worth quite a bit. I'm giving it to you so you can kill yourself whenever you want."

The bibliophile must have been pretty determined because he took it without hestitation. "Thank you," he said.

Six months went by and Méndez didn't see the old man again, although he imagined he probably couldn't even pick up a book anymore.

So Méndez went looking for him in Las Ramblas, in the old bookstores, in the city libraries, in the few parks left in Barcelona, trapped between blocks of apartments.

He came across many book lovers, but not his friend. Until one day he finally found him. He was wearing very thick glasses.

"Did you make it through your whole collection?" Méndez gasped.

"Absolutely not!" said the man. "You should see what I still have left!"

"Then what did you do with the gun? You didn't kill yourself . . ."

"No way! I sold the gun to buy another book."

ABOUT THE CONTRIBUTORS

ERIC TAYLOR-ARAGÓN is half-Peruvian and half-British, and graduated with a degree in literature from UC Berkeley. He's currently at work on his second novel, *Pocketman*. He lived in Barcelona (Barri Gòtic and El Raval) for three happy, wine-drenched years, and currently lives a nomadic existence between the United States and Spain.

Ronald Michael Stallard

RAÚL ARGEMÍ is the author of seven novels that have been translated into various languages: *El Gordo, el Francés y el Ratón Pérez, Los muertos siempre pierden los zapatos, Penúltimo nombre de guerra, Patagonia Chú Chú, Siempre la misma música, Retrato de familia con muerta,* and *La última caravana.* His work has been awarded several prizes, such as the Dashiell Hammett 2005 as well as the Luis Berenguer, Brigada 21, and Novelpol awards. He was born in Argentina and lives in Barcelona.

DAVID BARBA, born in Barcelona in 1973, is a writer, cultural journalist, and professor of journalism and humanities at the Universidad Autónoma de Barcelona, where he also teaches meditation. He published the official biography of Spanish porn star Nacho Vidal and is an expert in pornography. He lives in Barcelona.

Regina Saura

LOLITA BOSCH was born in Barcelona in 1970, but has lived in Albons, Spain, India, the United States, and, for ten years, Mexico City. She writes in both Spanish and Catalan, directs a literary collective, and lives in Barcelona with her dog. For more information, visit www.lolitabosch.com.

Loïda Farelo

ANTONIA CORTIJOS was born in Barcelona in 1948. She graduated from the Escuela Massana de Barcelona, where she studied design and painting, two passions she still dedicates time to when she isn't writing. Cortijos is the author of the highly acclaimed thriller *El diario de tapas rojas*, as well as *Ruido de agua* and the story collection *Isla Plana*. Her fouth novel, *Atlántidas*, will be published in 2011 and she is at work on a fifth book.

JORDI SIERRA I FABRA was born in Barcelona in 1947. He has published hundreds of books and received dozens of literary awards from both sides of the Atlantic, among them Spain's National Literature Prize, and is that country's most widely read children's and young adult author—his books have sold more than ten million copies. He is the founder of the Fundaciò Jordi Sierra i Fabra in Barcelona and the Fundación Taller de Letras Jordi Sierra i Fabra for Latin America.

CRISTINA FALLARÁS is a writer and journalist whose work has appeared in *El Mundo* newspaper and several Spanish television and radio programs. She is the author of the novels *La otra Enciclopedia Catalana, Rupturas, No acaba la noche,* and *Así murió el poeta Guadalupe,* which was a finalist for the Dashiell Hammett prize in literary crime fiction in 2010. She was born in Zaragoza and has lived in Barcelona since 1986.

ISABEL FRANC was born in Barcelona and is the author of the celebrated Lola Van Guardia trilogy featuring Emma García, the first lesbian female detective in Spanish literature. She is the editor for the new Spanish version of *Ladies Almanack* by Djuna Barnes and was awarded Spain's Premio Shangay for *No me llames cariño.* In 2010 Franc published a graphic novel about breast cancer, *Alicia en un mundo real,* with the illustrator Susan Martín.

FRANCISCO GONZÁLEZ LEDESMA was born in Barcelona in 1927. He won the Premio Internacional de Novela for *Tiempo de venganza,* a novel originally banned by Franco, when he was twenty-one. In 1984, he received the Premio Planeta for *Crónica sentimental en rojo,* which featured his most well-known protagonist, Detective Méndez. The Detective Méndez series soon became an international success. He was awarded the Premio Pepe Carvalho in 2005.

AESA

ADRIANA V. LÓPEZ is the founding editor of *Críticas* magazine and edited the story collection *Fifteen Candles.* López's journalism has appeared in *The New York Times* and the *Washington Post,* and her essays and fiction have been published in anthologies such as *Border-Line Personalities, Colonize This!* and *Juicy Mangoes.* Currently, she is translating Susana Fortes's novel *Waiting for Robert Capa,* and she divides her time between New York and Madrid.

ANDREU MARTÍN is the author of various novels, including *Prótesis* (made into a film directed by Vicente Aranda) and *El hombre de la navaja*, which have both won numerous prizes including the Premio Círculo del Crimen and the Premio Hammet. He also creates screenplays, television scripts, plays, and children's literature. A regular contributor to *El Periódico* and *La Vanguardia*, his most recent novel, *Bellísimas personas*, won the Premio Ateneo de Sevilla in 2000. He lives in Barcelona.

Nina Subin

VALERIE MILES is an American writer, translator, and publisher who has been living in Spain for over twenty years. Her work has appeared in the *Paris Review, La Vanguardia,* and *Granta en español.* After directing the imprint Emecé for some years and then the Madrid-based Alfaguara, she has recently launched a new publishing house, Duomo Ediciones, for the Italian group Mauri Spagnol. She lives in Barcelona.

Círculo de Lectores

IMMA MONSÓ was born in the western Catalonian city of Lleida. Her novels and stories, originally written in Catalan, have been translated into various languages and awarded prizes such as Premi Ciutat de Barcelona, Premi de l'Associació d'Escriptors en Llengua Catalana, and the Premi Prudenci Bertrana, among others. She lives in Barcelona.

Kaloian

ACHY OBEJAS is the translator (into Spanish) for Junot Díaz's Pulitzer Prize–winning novel *The Brief Wondrous Life of Oscar Wao.* She is also the author of several books, including the highly acclaimed novels *Ruins* and *Days of Awe;* and editor of *Havana Noir.* Obejas is currently the Sor Juana Writer in Residence at DePaul University in Chicago. She was born in Havana.

CARMEN OSPINA directs the digital program at Random House Mondadori in Barcelona. Born and raised in Colombia, she lived in New York for eight years where she co-edited *Críticas* magazine and worked as an editor at Umbrage Editions and a freelance journalist for *World Press Review* and *NY1 Noticias.* She has lived in Barcelona since 2006 and rides her bike every day.

SANTIAGO RONCAGLIOLO, born in Lima, Peru, in 1975, is the author of the political thriller *Abril rojo*, which won Spain's prestigious Alfaguara Prize in 2006. His first novel, *Pudor*, was adapted to the big screen in 2007. His most recent offering is the sci-fi novel *Tan cerca de la vida*. His books have sold more than 150,000 copies in the Spanish-speaking world and have been translated into more than thirteen languages. He lives in Barcelona.

TERESA SOLANA was born in Barcelona in 1962 and published her first novel, *Un crim imperfecte*, winner of the Brigada 21 award, in 2006. She subsequently published the novel *Drecera al paradís* and the story collection *Set casos de sang i fetge i una història d'amor*. Her work has been translated into English, French, German, Spanish, and Italian. Her latest novel, *Negres tempestes*, recently received the Crims de Tinta prize for the best noir novel in Catalan.

Also available from the Akashic Noir Series

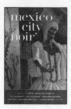

MEXICO CITY NOIR
edited by Paco Ignacio Taibo II
176 pages, trade paperback original, $15.95

Brand-new stories by: Paco Ignacio Taibo II, Eugenio Aguirre, Eduardo
Antonia Parra, Bernardo Fernández Bef, Óscar de la Borbolla, Rolo
Diez, Víctor Luiz González, F.G. Haghenbeck, Juan Hernández Luna,
Myriam Laurini, Eduardo Monteverde, and Julia Rodriguez.

"Set across Mexico City in a variety of neighborhoods, the stories
feature a cast of characters as diverse as the city, from homeless people
to young children to innocent passersby. This is a strong collection,
both for the way it showcases outstanding short fiction in the noir
style and for the way it demonstrates how a strong sense of place can
drive a narrative." —*Booklist*

HAVANA NOIR
edited by Achy Obejas
360 pages, trade paperback original, $15.95

Brand-new stories by: Leonardo Padura, Pablo Medina, Carolina
García-Aguilera, Ena Lucía Portela, Miguel Mejides, Arnaldo
Correa, Alex Abella, Moisés Asís, Lea Aschkenas, and others.

"A remarkable collection . . . Throughout these eighteen stories,
current and former residents of Havana—some well-known, some
previously undiscovered—deliver gritty tales of depravation, depravity,
heroic perseverance, revolution, and longing in a city mythical and
widely misunderstood." —*Miami Herald*

PARIS NOIR
edited by Aurélien Masson
300 pages, trade paperback original, $15.95

Brand-new stories by: Didier Daeninckx, Jean-Bernard Pouy, Marc
Villard, Chantal Pelletier, Patrick Pécherot, DOA, Hervé Prudon,
Dominique Mainard, Salim Bachi, Jérôme Leroy, and others.

"Rarely has the City of Light seemed grittier than in this hard-boiled
short story anthology, part of Akashic's Noir Series . . . The twelve
freshly penned pulp fictions by some of France's most prominent
practitioners play out in a kind of darker, parallel universe to the tourist
mecca; visitors cross these pages at their peril . . ."
—*Publishers Weekly*

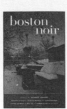

BOSTON NOIR
edited by Dennis Lehane
240 pages, trade paperback original, $15.95

Brand-new stories by: Dennis Lehane, Stewart O'Nan, Patricia Powell, John Dufresne, Lynne Heitman, Don Lee, Russ Aborn, J. Itabari Njeri, Jim Fusilli, Brendan DuBois, and Dana Cameron.

"In the best of the eleven stories in this outstanding entry in Akashic's noir series, characters, plot, and setting feed off each other like flames and an arsonist's accelerant . . . [T]his anthology shows that noir can thrive where Raymond Chandler has never set foot." —*Publishers Weekly* (starred review)

HAITI NOIR
edited by Edwidge Danticat
318 pages, limited edition hardcover, $24.95; trade paperback, $15.95

Brand-new stories by: Edwidge Danticat, Madison Smartt Bell, Gary Victor, Yanick Lahens, Kettly Mars, Mark Kurlansky, Evelyne Trouillot, Katia D. Ulysse, Ibi Aanu Zoboi, Patrick Sylvain, and others.

"A wide-ranging collection from the beloved but besieged Caribbean island . . . The 36th entry in Akashic's Noir series (which ranges from Bronx to Delhi to Twin Cities) is beautifully edited, with a spectrum of voices." —*Kirkus Reviews*

ROME NOIR
edited by Chiara Stangalino & Maxim Jakubowski
280 pages, trade paperback original, $15.95

Brand-new stories by: Antonio Scurati, Carlo Lucarelli, Gianrico Carofiglio, Diego De Silva, Giuseppe Genna, Marcello Fois, Cristiana Danila Formetta, Enrico Franceschini, Boosta, and others.

From Stazione Termini, immortalized by Roberto Rossellini's films, to Pier Paolo Pasolini's desolate beach of Ostia, and encompassing famous landmarks and streets, this is the sinister side of the Dolce Vita come to life, a stunning gallery of dark characters, grotesques, and lost souls seeking revenge or redemption in the shadow of the Colosseum, the Spanish Steps, the Vatican, Trastevere, the quiet waters of the Tiber, and Piazza Navona. Rome will never be the same.